DEATH & THE BREWMASTER'S WIDOW

This Large Print Book carries the
Seal of Approval of N.A.V.H.

AN AUCTION BLOCK MYSTERY

DEATH & THE BREWMASTER'S WIDOW

LORETTA ROSS

THORNDIKE PRESS
A part of Gale, Cengage Learning

GALE
CENGAGE Learning·

Farmington Hills, Mich • San Francisco • New York • Waterville, Maine
Meriden, Conn • Mason, Ohio • Chicago

GALE
CENGAGE Learning®

LIBRARY OF CONGRESS CATALOGING-IN-PUBLICATION DATA

Names: Ross, Loretta, 1966- author.
Title: Death & the Brewmaster's Widow : an auction block mystery / by Loretta Ross.
Other titles: Death and the Brewmaster's Widow
Description: Large print edition. | Waterville, Maine : Thorndike Press, 2016. | © 2016 | Series: Thorndike Press large print mystery
Identifiers: LCCN 2016000755| ISBN 9781410489067 (hardcover) | ISBN 141048906X (hardcover)
Subjects: LCSH: Auctioneers—Fiction. | Private investigators—Fiction. | Arson investigation—Fiction. | Murder—Investigation—Fiction. | Large type books. | GSAFD: Mystery fiction.
Classification: LCC PS3618.O8466 D425 2016b | DDC 813/.6—dc23
LC record available at http://lccn.loc.gov/2016000755

Published in 2016 by arrangement with Midnight Ink, an imprint of Llewelyn Publications, Woodbury, MN USA

Printed in Mexico
1 2 3 4 5 6 7 20 19 18 17 16

DEDICATION

*This book is lovingly dedicated
to the memory of
Beth Ann "Trinka" Hodges,
a bright soul gone too soon.*

"Friend, I will remember you."

ACKNOWLEDGMENTS

I'd like to thank the following for their help in my research for this book:

Captain Tom Gillman, St. Louis Fire Department, Ret., for his generosity in sharing his knowledge of the workings of that august institution.

Firefighter/EMT Sean Grigsby, for answering my random, oddball questions about firefighting.

Jordan Woerndle, for sharing information on the fascinating Lemp/Cherokee caves. As I'm writing fiction, I should note that I took liberties with that information. I should also note that this cave system is closed for safety reasons and I do NOT encourage anyone to go exploring there.

And Deputy Jeramiah Sullivan of the Henry County, Missouri, Sheriff's Department, for his insight into police procedure. (Any errors that remain in this area are my responsibility alone.)

Finally, I'd like to thank my friends and family and the members of my community for being so kind and supportive of my writing career.

ONE

Death and the fire captain came in through the front door.

Wren Morgan came out of the kitchen with a coffee pot and three cups on a tray. The lean black man in the St. Louis Fire Department dress uniform was a stranger to her, but she'd been watching through the blinds as the two men talked on the sidewalk and she knew who he was now. She'd seen pictures of him in happier times, posing with Death's younger brother, Randy.

"Honey, this is Captain Cairn. He was my brother's commanding officer. Captain —"

"Call me Cap. Everyone does."

Death shot him a faint grin. "Cap, this is my girlfriend, Wren Morgan."

"Miss Morgan, a pleasure to meet you."

"And you. Would you like some coffee?"

"Yes, please."

They settled around the coffee table and Cap set his briefcase on the table and

9

opened it. "One reason I needed to see you is because we still have to settle your brother's estate."

Death was surprised. "It's not already settled?"

"No. You didn't know?"

"By the time I woke up in Germany, it seemed like everything was already done. I just figured my ex-wife got any money and spent it while I was overseas."

"I see." Cap rustled some papers. "Actually there was a complication. The day before Bogie — Randy —"

"It's okay," Death said with a wry grin. "I was Bogie in the Marine Corps, too."

"Right." Cap spared him a brief smile. "The day before Bogie died he got word that you'd been killed in action. Glad that turned out not to be true, by the way."

"Thanks," Death nodded.

Wren, sitting beside him on the sofa, ran a hand lightly down his arm in silent agreement. In contrast to Captain Cairn, Death wore old blue jeans and a tattered T-shirt. There was a smudge of grease across his forehead and a light sheen of sweat coated his muscular arms. The last thing he looked was fragile, but she knew that in many ways, he was.

Death had been through hell in the last

year. He had been wounded in action in Afghanistan and spent three days hiding in an area controlled by insurgents before being found by allied forces. When he finally woke up, after spending weeks in a coma, he learned that his younger brother had died in a fire and his wife had cleaned out their bank account and left him.

"Anyway, that morning he got a call from, ah, your ex-wife?"

"Madeline."

"Madeline. Right. They had a bit of an altercation and the upshot was that he rewrote his will at the last minute. He left everything to the fire station — I don't think he could think of anyone else right then and he was determined that, if anything happened to him, Madeline wasn't going to profit by it. After he died and you were found alive, Madeline filed to contest the will, arguing that he wouldn't have written you out of it if he knew you were still alive. Frankly, we agree, and there shouldn't be any problem with having that will thrown out and his previous will reinstated. However, we can't just do it on our own."

Death sighed and looked down at the floor between his feet. Cap's voice softened. "Are you alright talking about this, son?"

"Yeah, I guess. It just . . . feels kinda like

blood money, you know?"

"I know, but your brother would have wanted you to have it. I tried contacting you through Madeline, but after you divorced I wasn't able to get in touch with her. I just happened to see your name in the news and the police chief here knew where to find you. Anyway, I've got some papers here for you, so we can finally get this taken care of. Also," he reached into his briefcase, "I thought that maybe you'd like to have this."

He pulled out a silver shield, set against red velvet in a burnished silver frame. He offered it to Death, who took it with a puzzled frown. "It's your brother's badge," Cap said.

"Yeah, I know but . . . did he have two? Because I already have one the coroner sent us."

He got up and went to a curio cabinet. Though he slept at his own apartment, Wren's place was quickly becoming home. His pictures and few mementos sat on the shelves and hung on the walls beside hers now. He came back with a small box containing a copy of the badge in Cap's hand. Cap took it with a frown. "Did the coroner say where he got this?"

"He said he took it off the body."

"That's impossible. The morning he died, Bogie snapped the back off his badge. We got called out before he had time to fix it. When he went into that fire, his shield was lying on my desk."

"I didn't even want Bogie working that day," Cap said.

They had moved into the kitchen, where the light was better. Cap sat with his hands locked together on the surface of the table. Death was out on the front porch talking on his cell phone.

"I thought he needed some time off to deal with everything. He looked so lost when I tried to make him leave, though, I didn't have the heart to send him away. I wish now that I had, of course."

"It wasn't the fire that killed him, though. Right?" Wren posed the question gently. "It was an aortic aneurysm. Nothing anyone did caused it, and there's no way anyone could have foreseen that it would happen."

"Still . . ." Cap's voice trailed off.

Wren refreshed his coffee and her own, then sat down across from him and pulled the two badges over to look at them. "How do you think this happened?" she asked. "Where did the extra badge come from?"

"At this point, I don't really know."

"Could someone have thought his badge was lost in the fire and replaced it so his family would have one?"

He thought about it. "Maybe." He sighed. "Probably, I suppose. The fire department doesn't just give out badges. Someone has to buy it and fill out the paperwork. When I tried to do that with Bogie's badge, our battalion chief already had. He was a friend of the boys' grandfather and I figured he just wanted to clear a way for Death to have his brother's badge. He could have gotten a replacement badge if he thought Bogie's had been lost. I don't understand why he wouldn't have come to me about it, though."

Wren looked up. "These badges aren't identical, you know? The numbers are different."

"What? Let me see."

She moved her chair over closer to him and slid the badges across the table so they could look at them together. "See, the one you brought says '4103' but the one Death already had says '4183'."

"That's Bogie's badge number. 4103. The other one is wrong."

Death came back in. "I couldn't get hold of Madeline. I did talk to her mother, Evelyn. The coroner's office shipped Madeline

14

a carton full of Randy's personal effects. Evelyn was there when it arrived. The badge was on top, in the box, and there was a note with it, but Evelyn doesn't remember who it was from or what it said. They put the carton in the basement. Chances are it's still there. If I can get hold of Madeline and get that carton, maybe there'll be some explanation."

"Bogie had a friend at the coroner's office," Cap said suddenly. "An assistant M.E., Sophie something. We'd see her sometimes at fatality incidents. I think your brother was sweet on her, to be honest. She always made a point to talk to him."

Death stood in the middle of the floor, hands in his pockets, studying the worn linoleum. His stance was uneven, like a sailor standing on the rocking deck of a ship or a man standing on an Earth that was no longer reliably solid beneath him. His face was closed, guarded, and when he spoke his voice was tight. "Cap," he said, "I gotta ask —"

"No," Cap said immediately. He rose and crossed to the younger man, put a hand on his shoulder, and guided him to a chair. "I know what you're going to ask, son. The answer is no."

"But, if it wasn't his badge —"

"You were a commanding officer," Cap said. "In the Marines. You had guys you were responsible for, so I know you're going to understand when I tell you this. That kid was *mine*. I would give anything if there were some way he could still be alive. But I was there. I saw his body. I identified him. The coroner's office double-checked against his dental records. I'm sorry, Death. I'm so sorry. But your brother is dead."

Ten months earlier. St. Louis, Missouri.
They called it the Brewmaster's Widow.

The Einstadt Brewery had closed with the onset of Prohibition in 1920 and never reopened. Some of the company's buildings had been torn down and some had been reclaimed for other uses, but the malt house, with its massive brick grain silos along one end, sat untouched.

To the trained eye of a firefighter, a single glance was enough to recognize an arson fire. Everything was burning, even things that were not flammable. Blue flames danced across brick walls, the accelerant leaving behind telltale swirls. Where the fire met real fuel, ancient wood and rubber and fabric, it burned a deep, angry red. Billows of smoke filled the room, obscuring the remains of brewing tanks and decaying equipment. Visibility was almost nonexistent. Even moving was treacherous. Along the north side of the building was a two-story warren of offices and storage rooms. The doorway into it glowed like the gates of Hell.

The whole place would have to be searched for victims, and the grain silos were a dust explosion waiting to happen.

Captain Cairn was pulling a line with his engine crew, helping 27's fight the fire while his truckies searched the building and his Advanced Life Support unit stood by hoping not to be needed. The heat was intense, the heat from the fire adding to the heat from the day. Twenty-five pounds of turnout gear, not counting the breathing apparatus, did nothing to help that situation.

He tightened his hands around the 2-inch hose and blinked sweat out of his eyes, leaning forward to see through thick, black smoke. The fire was loud — so loud that it drowned out all other sounds, becoming more a pervasive silence than a noise in its own right. And then another noise broke through, a noise that was designed to be heard even over the roar of flames. A sound that sent a chill of fear through every firefighter who heard it.

It was a personal alarm. Somewhere in

the building, one of their own was down.

One of *his* men. The alarm came from the offices and storerooms where Tanner and Bogie had gone to search.

Every firefighter in the building had heard the alarm and was responding. Cap called in Talia and Yering even as he and his engine crew made for the doorway, using their line to knock down the flames around them and snaking their way through the debris. Behind them, 27's set up to clear and maintain an easy exit. Cap and his men reached the doorway just as Tanner rushed out of a room down the hall and to the left. Rowdy caught sight of them and gestured without pausing, indicating a door to their right and shouting over the flames.

"Cap! Bogie!"

The wooden floor trembled beneath their boots as they rushed down the corridor. Blue flames from the accelerant danced across the brick walls and they soaked the floor as they passed so that it wouldn't catch fire beneath them. The scene inside the room where the alarm sounded was one that would live in Cap's nightmares for the rest of his life.

A heavy wooden bookcase, a floor-to-ceiling bookcase that had taken up one whole wall of the room, had collapsed and

18

was burning with all the heat that well-dried oak could produce. Randy Bogart's left boot was just visible at the bottom of the fire.

They knocked down the flames and dug him out, but he was unresponsive. The falling bookcase had broken his face mask and his face was badly burned. His brother firefighters got him outside and the paramedics with the ALS unit did their damnedest, but it was to no avail.

It wasn't until later they learned he'd died of an aortic aneurysm, a weak spot in his aorta. It must have been something he'd always had, a silent killer lying in wait. When the bookcase fell on him, the spike in his blood pressure would have been enough to pop it open. In all probability, he was dead in less than two minutes.

"So where do you think the extra badge came from?"

Wren shrugged.

Outside in the bright morning sunlight an auction was just underway. Sixty-three-year-old Sam Keystone had the gavel and had started selling off a long table of knickknacks and mismatched dishes while his twin, Roy, heckled him from the edge of the crowd. Inside the cash tent, set up on the lawn of the house they were going to sell

19

that afternoon, it was shady and cool, with a light breeze tossing the tent flaps and rustling the edges of the receipt book.

"The extra badge is totally authentic. If it didn't have the one number wrong it would be identical to Randy's real badge. Captain Cairn says that actual badges aren't that easy to come by. There've been too many cases of people getting into homes by claiming to be firefighters checking on fire codes and things like that. There was a serial rapist that operated that way on the East Coast a few years ago." Wren snagged a soda, then sat on the ice chest. "There are only a few companies that are licensed to make badges and you have to have all the right paperwork and authorizations to order one. And impersonating a firefighter is a crime, just like impersonating a police officer is." Leona Keystone shuffled her stacks of one-dollar bills into order and closed the lid of the cash box with a snap. "Well, somebody managed it. What about the guy who really has that number?"

"A boot over at Station 17."

"A boot?"

"A new guy. They call them boots. He wasn't on duty that day and his badge is accounted for."

"Where's Death now?"

"He's trying to finish up a case he's working on. Industrial espionage. He's figured out who's behind it, he's just gotta catch them in the act. He's trying to clear up everything he's got going on now so he can go to St. Louis and settle Randy's estate."

"Are you going to go with him?"

Wren hesitated.

"You know, if you need the time off, that's not a problem."

"Thanks. I appreciate it. I really do. But . . . should I go? I mean, I want to be there to support him if he wants me, but I don't want him to feel I'm smothering him either." She chewed on her lower lip.

"When he first married Madeline, she wouldn't let him go anywhere or do anything alone. She was always so jealous. And he said at first he was flattered, but when he was sent overseas she cheated on him almost immediately. He figured then that she was suspicious of him because she was inclined to cheat herself. So I don't want him to think that I don't trust him because I don't want him to think that he can't trust me, though I don't think that he thinks that and I don't want him to think that I don't want to be there if he needs me either." She sighed. "Am I overthinking this?"

"I think you might be," Leona said,

amused, "but when you figure it out you just let me know."

Two

"Fire at will!"

Death had shot a man at near point-blank range.

The man was a deranged killer and he was coming at Death with a knife, but still. He focused on the black and white target fixed at the end of his lane as gunfire echoed through the concrete block shooting range, muffled by his ear protectors, but not silenced. Sometimes it seemed the gunfire was never silent.

He could still feel the slick warmth of another man's blood on his hands and face. The rattle of small arms fire conjured older ghosts, shadowy insurgents who hovered at the edges of his vision with promises of terror and death. Death forced himself to breathe normally. His heart pounded but his hands were steady as he took aim and fired off six shots, all grouped inside the bull's-eye.

He had been a soldier once and there was a part of him that would always be a soldier. When he had a job to do, he did it. His job was to hit the target.

The shooting range was filled with cops this afternoon. The East Bledsoe Ferry Police Department was preparing to face the Rives County Sheriff's Department in a shooting competition on the Fourth of July. Chief Reynolds, a friend of Death's, had asked the Marine marksman to coach his officers. "What's the prize in this contest?" Death had asked.

"Winner gets to shoot Farrington," one of the cops had joked.

Eric Farrington, small but cocky and much disliked, held his job as a jailer only because his uncle was the mayor. He was present today, too, trying (again) to pass the concealed carry exam.

The echoes of gunfire died away as the shooters expended their ammunition. Death pulled the magazine and double-checked his gun to make sure it was empty before laying it on the counter and stepping back. Around him, the cops were all pulling their targets and comparing their scores.

"You morons better practice," Farrington said. "I'm gonna get so good at this, I'm gonna leave you all in the dust."

"Did you actually hit the target this time?" one of the cops asked. "Did you hit the paper that the target is on?" another goaded. "Did you even hit the wall?"

"Ha ha. Very funny. Let me tell you jack-asses something —"

As he was speaking, Farrington walked over to the group of officers. He hadn't bothered to lay down his gun first and now he swung it around, gesturing with it as if it were an extension of his arm. The barrel came up, pointed at Death's face and . . .

He was back in Afghanistan. The sun blazed, hot and blinding, the red sand and mud-brick buildings glowing with the light. Shadows were pitch-black, the lines between light and dark as sharp as razors. The gunman came out of the shadow, screaming in an unintelligible mix of Arabic and English. With no time or room to bring his rifle to bear, Death reacted on instinct, slapping the gun away. He body blocked his adversary, twisting the gun away from him with his left hand while his right came up across the man's throat. He pinned him to the wall, brought the gun to bear. A sandstorm arose from nowhere, sucking all the sound away. The world hovered in a shocked silence. Light and shadow spun around him and . . .

Death stood in the cool expanse of the shooting range at East Bledsoe Ferry. He had Eric Farrington pinned to the concrete block wall with an arm across his throat. Farrington's own gun was in Death's left hand, pointing down at the terrified young man, the barrel an inch from his left eye.

With a shuddering breath, Death stepped back. All activity in the building had ceased. The gathered cops stared at him. They'd frozen, all of them, as if afraid to provoke him. Chief Reynolds moved forward cautiously, one hand raised in a placating gesture, approaching Death the way one might approach a skittish horse.

Death released Farrington and the kid slid limply to sit on the floor, his smart mouth silenced for a change. Death fell back himself, raising his own empty hand as if to fend off his friend's advance. He was shaking all over. He felt the hot flush of blood rising to his face. He was breathing hard, his damaged lungs exacerbating the situation. Spots danced before his eyes. "I —"

He looked at the older man's face and the pity he saw there shamed him. Trying to force his breathing to slow, he flipped the gun in his left hand so that he held it by the barrel and extended it butt first. Reynolds took it from him. Death felt like the strings holding him up were being cut, one by one.

"I'm sorry. I . . . excuse me."

Shouldering past the officers, he stumbled his way to the door and out. The rifle range sat at the edge of a park. Children played on the swings a hundred yards away. There was a game going on in the baseball diamond. The Missouri sun was softer and gentler than the blazing orb that haunted his memories and he sank down on the nearest bench. Chills wracked his body and he was violently trembling.

Reynolds came out and sat on the other end of the bench but didn't interrupt the silence. Death fought to get his breathing under control. Slowly the black spots before his eyes receded. "So what happens now?" he asked finally, when he was sure he could control his voice.

"What do you mean?"

"Do you need to arrest me? Am I going to lose my license?" He laughed without humor.

"I probably should, shouldn't I?"

"Why in God's name would I arrest you? Or should you lose your license?"

"In there." Death waved one hand in the

27

general direction of the shooting range. "I just assaulted Farrington. I could have shot him."

The Chief of Police snorted. "You didn't assault anyone. You disarmed a moron who was waving a gun in your face. There's a reason Farrington keeps failing his gun safety courses." He waited a moment, letting the silence draw out. "Are you having problems, Death? Talk to me, son."

Death felt the tension drain away. It left a cold, empty spot in his chest. "Nothing like that's ever happened before."

"What did happen?"

"I don't know, I was just . . . it was like I was back in a war zone. I saw someone coming at me with a gun and I just snapped."

"Flashback?"

"That sounds so melodramatic."

Reynolds casually reached over and smacked the back of Death's head. It was a gesture his father used to use on him and Randy and it brought with it a wave of homesickness so powerful it was almost his undoing.

"It's not melodramatic. And it's nothing to be ashamed of. If you need some help, don't you hesitate to ask for it. Going it on your own isn't being macho. It's being a moron."

"I did," he had to stop and clear his throat. His face was burning with embarrassment now, but he pressed on. "I called the VA and asked about counseling. I can't sleep with Wren," he admitted, surprising himself with the revelation. He glanced over at Reynolds. The chief was looking at him with concern, his face carefully void of expression. "I mean," he felt stupid, "I'm not saying we don't fool around. I mean, I can't *sleep* with her. I was having a nightmare and she tried to wake me up." He shuddered and scrubbed his hands against his jeans. "I almost snapped her neck. It was so close."

"And what did they say? The VA, I mean?"

"They put me on a waiting list."

"Hmph. Yeah, that figures. Listen." He cupped his hand around the back of Death's neck. "I know you haven't been around here that long, but you've got a lot of friends in this town. God knows, none of us are professionals, but any time you need somebody to talk to, someone's gonna be there. And I'm one of those someones, so if you need something, you just ask." The cold spot in Death's chest warmed. The knots in his stomach loosened. "Then, could you do me a favor?" he asked.

"Name it."

"I went off and left my gun in there."

"You want me to go in and get it for you?"

"I'd like for you to hang on to it for me. For a little while, at least."

Reynolds studied his face. "Are you sure? You don't think you're going to need it, Mr. Big-Shot Private Eye-slash-Bounty Hunter?"

Death felt a tiny smile tug at one corner of his mouth. "Not that dangerous. Most of my cases are infidelity or missing persons. And you know as well as I do, bounties are few and far between. Anyway, I'm fixing to take some time off. I need to go home to St. Louis and settle my little brother's estate." His mind's eye put Randy in the middle of the baseball game. He could hear the echoes of his laughter among the voices of the children on the swings. "A gun is one thing I'm not going to need."

The Keystone family, of Keystone and Sons Auctioneers, was huge. Sam and Roy, originally the sons in the equation, now had sons and grandsons of their own. When their whole clan had an event, it required the Community Building to accommodate everyone. With three Keystones in the senior class at East Bledsoe Ferry High, the graduation supper was such an event. Death pulled his ten-year-old Jeep into the parking lot and sat for a moment after he turned off the motor. He was wearing a suit for the first time since his parents' funeral. Wren, beside him in the passenger seat, was dressed in a sleeveless green shift. Her red hair was still short after the loss of her trademark braid and it stood out around her head in a wild halo. Death called her his feral pixie.

She turned to him now, her face a mask of gentle concern.

"Are you okay? We don't have to go in if you don't feel like it."

He dropped his head. "You heard about what happened at the rifle range." It wasn't a question.

"It's a small town." She didn't insult him by trying to deny it. "Cops are the world's worst gossips."

"Great. I'm the local freak now."

Wren smacked his arm. "Freak nothing. You publicly humiliated the most disliked person in a three-county area. Today, Batman wears Death Bogart pajamas."

He laughed in spite of himself and before the conversation could continue a sharp rap on his window made them both jump. Death opened his door and Roy Keystone pulled it out of his hand and peered in at

31

them. "No necking in the parking lot! Come on. Hurry! We've gotta get inside."

"What's the rush?"

"Are you kidding me? There's food in there. And there's teenage boys coming. Have you ever seen what a bunch of teenage boys can do to a table full of food?"

Death climbed out of the Jeep, reaching back for the casserole Wren had prepared. She gathered the pile of gifts they'd brought and came around to join him. Holding hands, they strolled with Roy to the big, white stone building. "He did used to be a teenage boy," Wren reminded her boss.

"And a Marine," Death added. He laughed, remembering. "My first time overseas I spent Thanksgiving at Pearl Harbor. Our sergeant's wife cooked dinner for our squad. Three big turkeys, all the trimmings. She was planning on sending us back to quarters with leftovers."

"No leftovers?" Wren guessed.

"We barely left bones."

Later, when they were all seated at long tables, feasting, Roy's wife Leona singled Death out. He tensed when she called his name, expecting some comment on his encounter with Farrington, but Leona's mind was elsewhere.

"Wren tells me you're working on a case

of industrial espionage! That sounds fascinating. Can you talk about it?" He shrugged, taking a second to chew and swallow.

"Not that much to tell really. High-tech firm up in the city. I can't tell you what they do. I don't mean I'm not allowed to tell you," he clarified. "I can't. I have no idea. Whatever it is, it involves proprietary information stored on flash drives kept in safes in the offices of the engineers responsible for them. A handful of those drives disappeared. The drives were tagged with security devices so they couldn't be taken out of the building without setting off an alarm. Their internal security was getting nowhere, so they called me in as a fresh pair of eyes."

"How long did it take you to solve it?"

"Are you sure I solved it?" he teased.

Leona smiled at him. "Wren's sure. So spill. What happened?"

"Well, when I first started looking into it, I really wanted the guy who was responsible for the information to be the one who had stolen it. Guy was a jackass. Rude, condescending. Called people insulting nicknames. Naturally, he was the prime suspect, so he'd already been thoroughly investigated. He came out clean, even though he was the only one who had the combination to the safe and his fingerprints were the only ones on it.

"There were no security cameras in the office where the safe was, on the grounds that cameras could be hacked, but the hall outside was covered by a camera and there were cameras on the bank of elevators and on the fire stairs. In the course of their investigation, they'd scoured the tapes for any sign that someone might have put in a video loop. They were even debating the possibility that one of their rivals could have designed a high-tech suit that would interact with their cameras to make the person wearing it invisible on film."

"That sounds like science fiction," Sam observed.

"To me, too," Death agreed.

"So, what did you do, smart guy?" Wren asked.

"First thing, I went back over their own investigation. I noticed right away there was one person coming and going from that office at will who they had never even questioned." He looked around the table, enjoying having a rapt audience. "It was a janitor, guy named Hector Boyd. Actually, they refer to him as a maintenance engineer. The reason they never considered him was because he has Down syndrome. He works there as part of a program to employ the mentally disadvantaged. He can handle a broom and push a dust mop, but how would he get a safe open or know what to take? And even if he did, how would he ever smuggle it out and sell it to their competitors? The only thing he takes out of the offices he cleans is trash and he just takes the bags directly to an incinerator and drops them in."

"He doesn't really have Down syndrome," Sam's wife Doris guessed. "It was just a cover for him to break in and steal all their data."

Death grinned at her. "Nope. He's just exactly what he seems to be. A fifty-four-year-old man with Down syndrome living in a group home and working as a janitor."

"So . . . ?"

"So remember how I said the guy responsible for the information was a jackass? Just imagine how someone like that treats someone with a physical or mental impairment. Boyd didn't steal the information in order to sell it. He took it to get back at the engineer for being hateful to him. They couldn't figure out how he got the flash drives out of the building because he didn't. He just threw them away."

"But how did he get them out of the safe?" Sam asked. "Did the engineer go off and leave the safe open?"

"No. But he opened it in front of Boyd. It never occurred to him that Boyd would be able to remember the combination. And when he opened the safe, Boyd just used a dust cloth to keep from leaving fingerprints. He's handicapped. He's not stupid."

"Is he going to be in a lot of trouble?" Wren asked, concerned. "Boyd, I mean?"

Death smiled at her and reached out to trace one fingertip down her cheek. "Nah, not so much. They're mostly relieved the information didn't wind up with their competitors and they figure he didn't understand what he was doing. I'm not so sure of that bit, myself, but the engineer really isn't a pleasant person so I'm not sorry he's the one who's going to suffer. He got taken down a peg for being careless with his safe combination, plus he's got to redo all the work that was destroyed."

"People always underestimate the handicapped," Leona said.

"The invisible demographic," Death agreed. "Also, with a lot of people, there's a broad tendency to overlook service personnel. The janitor, the waitress, the kid mowing the grass."

"Tell me about it!" Rory Keystone, gangly and awkward, leaned over from a table full of teenagers to join in the conversation. "You know, I got a job at the market doing carryouts. Yesterday I was taking out a cart of groceries for these two ladies and they were having this conversation you would *not* believe. It was like I wasn't even standing there. I just wanted to run away screaming."

"Really?" Death asked innocently. "What were they talking about?"

Rory's ears turned red and he stammered. "Stuff," he managed finally.

"Stuff?"

"You know. Woman-ey stuff. Really graphic woman-ey stuff." His blush deepened as his peers and elders merely watched him expectantly. "One of them was having problems. You *know.*"

"Woman-ey problems?"

"With her stuff," Leona nodded. "Her woman-ey stuff."

"Her lady parts," Roy clarified. Rory was aghast. "Grandpa!"

"What? You're shocked that I know about lady parts? Let me tell you something, son. If I didn't know about lady parts, half the people in this building wouldn't exist."

"Can we have a moment of silence," Sam

37

said, "so that I can pray for salvation for my brother? Or possibly from my brother?"

"You can act like an old maid all you want," Roy said, "but you've had the occasional brush with lady parts yourself, and I can point out a dozen or more pieces of evidence without even turning my head."

"Perhaps. But I don't talk about it at the dinner table."

"Maybe I just know more to talk about."

"You do know about lady parts," Leona agreed placidly. She reached over and patted her husband's hand. "Just don't go imagining that you're an expert."

THREE

The town square surrounding the Rives County courthouse in downtown East Bledsoe Ferry consisted mostly of tall, old stone buildings. The late eighteenth-century architecture was so predominant here that the handful of newer structures stood out like scars against their older counterparts. Death's office and the connected studio apartment where he slept were located in one of the oldest buildings, above the Renbeau Bros. Department Store.

Wren was alone in the apartment. She was packing clothes into a duffel for Death to take with him to St. Louis when the bell rang, announcing that someone had opened the door from the street. "Oh, Death!" a woman's light, melodic voice called. "Sweetie? Are you up there?"

Wren took a deep breath. *I will not kill the ex-wife,* she told herself. *I will not kill the ex-wife. Unless she's thinking she's going to get him back, in which case I might very well kill the ex-wife.*

She went to the top of the steep, narrow staircase that led from the sidewalk up to the office. "He's not here, Madeline."

Madeline was waiting at the foot of the steps. She wore a light summer frock and sandals, her hair was perfectly styled and her makeup flawless. She was a tiny, elegant, exquisitely beautiful woman and Wren never failed to feel like an ox next to her. She carried her infant son in his carrier, her pose such that the first thing a person's eyes were drawn to, if they were standing at the top of the steps, was the baby's innocent face.

Benji had been conceived while Death was fighting overseas. Death adored him, even though he was not his, and Madeline was not above wielding him as a weapon. Madeline's pretty face puckered into a bitter grimace. "Where is he?"

"He had some errands to run. Is there something I can help you with?"

Madeline huffed an impatient little sigh. "I brought over the carton with his brother's things. It's in the back of my car, but I can't lift it. Do you know when he's coming back?"

"No, I don't. Let me see if I can get it." Wren clattered down the stairs, ignoring the

40

sour look Madeline was giving her.

Madeline raked her stare up and down Wren's body, face a picture of disapproval, and Wren involuntarily glanced down at herself. She was wearing sneakers, ragged blue jean cut-offs and — oh, yeah! — one of Death's old USMC T-shirts.

Ha! she thought. *Suck on that, Hooker Barbie!*

A large, white shipping carton sat on the back seat of Madeline's car. Madeline opened the door and Wren pulled it out carefully. It weighed no more than five or ten pounds and she canted an eyebrow at Madeline.

"It must be nice to be so strong and manly," Madeline said snidely.

"Strength is not gender-specific," she replied pointedly and led the way upstairs. Madeline followed, lugging Benjamin. Wren thought it ironic that the baby in his carrier surely weighed more than the carton she was carrying.

Death's desk was a sturdy old wooden affair that had probably come out of a classroom. Every time Wren looked at it, she expected to see a chalkboard on the wall behind it. She set the carton on it now and hopped up to sit beside it. Madeline dropped into one of the two visitor's chairs

41

and looked around with interest. The connecting door to Death's apartment stood open, the clothes Wren had been sorting for him spread across the bed. A pair of Wren's own underwear was mixed in with them. It was only there because it had been static-electricitied to one of his shirts in the dryer, but Madeline didn't need to know that.

She drummed her fingers on the top of the carton. "What's in here, do you know?"

"Just Randy's uniform and his helmet. All that heavy outer stuff —"

"His turnout gear?"

"I guess. All that was issued by the department. My mother sorted through it and sent it back to them. She also washed his uniform before we packed it up and put it away. Mother adores Death, you know."

"Well, Death's an adorable guy."

Madeline fidgeted. "Where does he think the extra badge came from?"

"Best guess is that someone at the coroner's office realized it was missing and thought they'd lost it. Rather than admit to misplacing it, they somehow got another one to replace it with."

"Cover your ass," Madeline observed.

The bell rang again and Wren heard the distinctive sound of Death's heavy breathing as he struggled his way up the stairs.

Madeline made as if to jump up and go help him, but Wren stayed her with a fierce look. "Don't!"

"But . . ."

"No. Don't."

He reached the top and stood for a moment braced against the doorframe, catching his breath. Wren beamed at him. "You only had to stop twice! You're getting better!"

He shrugged and came over to lean against the desk beside her. "Well, I saw both your cars out front. I thought there might be a girl fight going on."

"And you didn't bring popcorn?" she asked tartly.

"I've got cheese curls in the cupboard." He made faces at the baby, then glanced at the white carton and his face sobered. "Randy's things?"

Wren rubbed his upper arm. "Are you sure you're up for this?"

Instead of answering, he took out his pocket knife and slit the tape holding the carton closed. He opened the flaps and the air that rose out carried the scents of dust and fabric softener and the ghost of burning things.

"I can still smell a hint of smoke. Am I just imagining it?"

"No." Death shook his head. "Gramp's things were the same way, years after he retired."

"But Mom washed his uniform," Madeline objected.

"It'd be in his helmet lining." Death lifted a typewritten letter from the box and glanced over it before passing it along to Wren. It was an official letter from the coroner's office, expressing condolences and listing the original contents of the carton. The letter noted that Randy's turnouts were the property of the St. Louis Fire Department and that Death would need to contact them about their disposition. In the contents list someone had placed a neat check mark in blue ink next to each item of turnout gear.

Randy's badge was on the list, between his station pants and a flashlight. Death had taken a second letter from the box, this one handwritten.

Dear Sergeant Bogart, We've never met, but I've heard so many stories about you that I feel as if I know you well. My job includes responding to fatality incidents such as fires and traffic accidents. It was in this capacity that I met your brother. Though I never told him so, and I'm sorry now that I did not, I was always impressed with Randy, with his charm and his sense of humor and with his integrity. Though I saw him at the worst of times and under the most difficult circumstances, I never knew him to act without courage and compassion. I know I don't need to tell you that he was a credit to his department and to this city. To me, he was a dear friend and I shall miss him greatly. Please accept my deepest condolences and, if ever there is anything I can do for you, do not hesitate to contact me.

Sincerely, Sophie Depardieu
Assistant Medical Examiner,
City of St. Louis

"She was sweet on him," Wren said.

"Do you think so?"

Madeline nodded; for once the two women were in agreement.

"She'd be the one who polished the badge and put it in the jewelry box," Wren added. "She probably thought his original badge was lost in the fire and she wanted you to have one."

"She's put her phone number on the letter. I'll call her when I get there tomorrow. I expect you're probably right."

Randy's helmet lay on top of the items still in the carton. Death lifted it out reverently and set it aside. Beneath it was a uniform, a dark blue-gray polo shirt and matching cargo pants. A heavy metal flashlight lay across the neatly folded shirt. Wren leaned over and frowned into the box. "What's the matter?"

"Shouldn't there be boots in there?"

"Boots are part of turnout gear. They'd have gone back to the department. Somebody else is wearing them now. His helmet's theirs, too. I probably need to return it as soon as possible."

"Oh, no," Madeline said. "The helmet's yours. The department told Mom that you could have it. They said they'd normally present it to you at the funeral, but —" she broke off and looked away. Death was focused on a point on the opposite wall and Wren, sitting next to him and between the two, felt but did not understand the sudden tension between them.

"Okay, look," Madeline clicked perfect nails against the chair arm. "I handled everything really crappy. I know that. And I'm sorry, Death. I am so sorry. But you have to understand that none of it meant that I didn't love you."

"I know," he said softly, and Wren felt suddenly as if she had been set adrift. Death put his hand over hers on the desk, anchoring them together, and continued. "But everything that happened . . . happened. There's no point now in regrets or recriminations." He turned his attention to Wren. "Madeline claimed Randy's body. She had him cremated and asked the fire department to do something with his ashes."

"But surely they would have waited for you."

"I asked them not to," Madeline said. "I thought he was going to have enough to deal with when he woke up. If he woke up. Some of the doctors didn't think he would, you know."

"His station had a nice ceremony," Death said. "There were pictures in with the papers Captain Cairn brought me. They took him out on a fire boat and sprinkled his ashes on the Mississippi, just below the confluence where the Missouri comes in." With her free hand, Wren picked up the helmet, cradled it in her lap, and looked down at it, wondering about this man who had meant so much to the man she loved. As she focused on what she was seeing, she frowned.

"Death? Honey?"

"Mmm?"

"There's a sort of a little badge-thingie on here, made out of leather, with a number on it."

He laughed a little. "The badge-thingie on his hat would be his hat badge. It's a matched set with his regular badge."

"And the numbers on them, they would match too, right?"

"Yeah. Why?"

She turned the helmet so he could see the front. The number on it was 4183. "It matches the wrong badge."

Belle Fontaine Cemetery, under a cloudless summer sky, looked more like a painting than like something that should really exist. Death guided his Jeep through the main entrance and followed well-known lanes that led to the Bogart family plot.

It had been raining the last time he was here, he remembered. He and Randy, riding in the back of a funeral home limousine, followed the hearse that carried their parents' coffins. It had been a closed casket funeral — the car accident that killed them quick and brutal. Madeline had ridden with her mother, several cars back. He'd come home on bereavement leave and she'd stayed apart from him almost the entire time. Even then she'd been distancing herself, though he didn't realize it at the time.

At the time, he'd been too caught up in his grief and in taking care of his brother. Randy's experience with car accidents had served him poorly. He was too able to imagine the crash and its after effects and he'd had nightmares nearly every night. They'd also had their parents' estate to deal with. Only in their late forties, the elder Bogarts hadn't been prepared for sudden death. In the end it was necessary to sell their house to settle their debts.

Randy had felt particularly bad about that. He'd inherited their grandparents' place and their parents' house was supposed to eventually go to Death. He'd offered to sell his house and split the profit with Death, but Death had declined. The Corps had promised him a permanent assignment at Whiteman after his tour was over and he and Madeline were buying a house just off base.

That was Madeline's house now. Death had let her keep it on the understanding that she would be responsible for the payments. They'd had a pre-nup — his grandmother had convinced them to do that — and he hadn't been required to give her anything. He had done it, though, even though it left him homeless, so that Benjamin would have a safe place to grow up.

Death pulled over when he was as close to the plot as the road would take him. Wishing he'd thought to pick up some flowers, he jumped down and paced across the green grass, skirted a larger monument, and stopped beside a stone that read BOGART. His grandparents were buried to the left, his parents to the right, each couple sharing a stone. Nonna (Terhaar) Rogers, his maternal great-grandmother, was buried next to her husband down in Ste. Genevieve. All five of them had died within the last three years.

There was no stone for Randy, of course, and it occurred to Death that he should set one. His brother deserved a memorial, even if there was no body to go under it.

Death didn't know why he had come here. A sense of responsibility, maybe? The idea that it was his filial duty, and a duty that he left too long undone? He opened his mouth to apologize, for not coming for so long, for not bringing flowers, for not taking good enough care of Randy or, at the very least, seeing that he was properly laid to rest.

The words wouldn't come. He didn't feel his family's presence here. There was nothing in this tranquil green and growing place but sorrow and loss. In the not quite two years since their funeral, the soil of his parents' grave had subsided. The outline of the grave was sunken, with a deep crack running around one corner. He thought, with a frisson of horror, that if he stepped closer he would be able to look down into the earth and see the concrete vault in which their broken bodies were interred.

The cemetery darkened as a cloud drifted across the sun. A chill breeze sent a shiver through him. He sighed and closed his eyes. Bowed his head. Then he returned to his Jeep and drove away.

"Bogart," he said. "D. D. Bogart." The St. Louis County Medical Examiner's office was in a big, brick block of a building. Given the nature of the place, he couldn't bring himself to present himself as Death, even with the different pronunciation.

"And who was it you wanted to see again?"

"Ms. Depardieu. We spoke on the phone. She should be expecting me."

The young man at the reception desk checked his computer and leaned back, looking perplexed and horrified. "It says, um, it says she has an appointment this afternoon."

Death sighed. "With death?"

"Yeah."

He fished out his driver's license. "That would be me. It's the first D."

"Your parents named you Death?"

"It's pronounced Deeth. I was named after a fictional detective. Lord Peter Wimsey, maybe you've heard of him. Some of the books have been done on Mystery on PBS." He read a lack of comprehension in the other man's face. "Nevermind."

"But . . ." the guy frowned. "But, if you were named after a Lord Peter, shouldn't your name be Peter?"

"It was his second name. He had four. He pronounced it to rhyme with breath, but my kindergarten teacher hyperventilated so my mother said we could pronounce mine, as Lord Peter said most who have the name do, to rhyme with teeth."

"So when you were a toddler your name was Death? As in death Death?"

"What can I say? I was a badass toddler."

The heavy metal door that closed off the entryway from the rest of the building opened and a young woman in a lab coat stuck her head through. "George, has anyone —" she broke off and caught Death with a piercing look. "You have got to be Sergeant Bogart. You look just like your brother."

"I always told him I was the handsome one. You must be Ms. Depardieu."

"Please, call me Sophie."

"Only if you'll call me Death."

She held the door open and motioned him through. "If you'd like to come through here, my office is this way."

Her office was not small, but it felt crowded with a large, cluttered desk and overflowing book shelves. Death took the seat she offered him and accepted a cup of coffee. She filled his cup from a coffee maker that sat next to a sink at the side of the room, then topped off her own cup. "Sometimes I swear I live on this stuff," she said, pausing to take a long drink.

A picture of Randy, a framed snapshot on the wall behind her desk, had caught Death's eye the moment he walked in. He motioned to it now. "You didn't take that at a fatality accident," he observed.

Randy, in uniform, was leaning against the door of his brush truck, his body hiding part of the station logo. He was just a shade shorter than Death, his hair was darker, and he didn't have the bulky Marine Corps muscles that Death had, but the resemblance was striking. He was grinning at the camera with an easy charm that lit his whole face. It was the smile he saved for pretty girls and Death reflected that Captain Cairn had been right. If Sophie was the one who'd taken this picture, then Randy had been sweet on her.

"I took that one day when I had a flat tire on my way to work. Randy and Rowdy passed me, going on a grocery run, and stopped and changed it for me. He was always kind that way. Never too busy to lend someone a hand." She stopped speaking and held up one hand, asking for a moment. Overcome with emotion.

Wren and Madeline were right, Death thought. She had been attracted to Randy too. He took the opportunity to study her. Under other circumstances, she might have been potential sister-in-law material. She was taller than average, big-boned and slightly heavyset. Her face was more interesting than traditionally pretty, but it showed character. Randy would have been attracted to that.

"I'm sorry," she said. "You didn't come all the way out here to watch me cry. You said on the phone you had some questions. I've got a copy of Randy's death certificate and, if you think you want it, I can get you a copy of the autopsy report. I know this must have been a shock to you. I talked to his doctor during the course of the investigation and he had no idea that Randy had had heart problems."

"It's not so much Randy's death that I need to ask about," Death said. He took the jewelry box and the hat badge from his pocket and laid them on the desk. "I need to know about these badges. I need to know where they came from."

FOUR

Sophie Depardieu frowned, puzzled. "They came off your brother's uniform," she said. She indicated the larger, metal shield. "This was his main badge and this," pointing to the leather emblem, "was his hat badge. It was fixed to his helmet."

"Yes, but they're not Randy's."

"I'm sorry, but I don't think I understand."

"The morning he died, Randy snapped the back off his badge. When he went into that fire his badge was on his captain's desk waiting to be repaired. We discovered that I'd gotten the wrong badge when Captain Cairn brought me the right one." He reached into his shirt pocket and came up, this time, with Randy's real badge in its silver frame.

"The number on the badge your office sent is wrong. Randy's badge number was 4103. You probably have that on your paperwork somewhere. The badge I got from you is number 4183. It's a counterfeit. The real badge 4183 is accounted for. I'd thought that maybe someone thought his badge was lost and took it upon themselves to replace it, but then I looked through the carton you sent and found his hat badge. It also has the wrong number on it.

"I'm not out to get anyone in trouble," he said. "I just need to know what happened."

Sophie looked completely bewildered. Death was a good judge of people — in combat situations you had to be — and in his own mind he was certain that she was not just pretending.

"That badge," she said, "was on Randy's shirt. I helped get his body out of the turnout gear. I opened his bunker coat and took the badge off his chest myself. There wasn't any funny business. I swear to you."

Death tapped the edge of her desk, thinking hard. "You undressed his body?" He couldn't say why exactly, but he was a little weirded out by the concept.

"I only helped with the bunker gear." She looked down at her lap, gathering her thoughts before speaking. "I'm a medical examiner. We see pain and grief and sorrow every day. Sometimes that pain and grief and sorrow is our own. And that sucks. But what we do is important, to the living and the dead, and if I had been assigned to Randy's autopsy, I would have performed it because I am a professional."

"I'm not doubting you," Death said. "I'm just trying to figure out how this happened."

Sophie sighed and sat back. "His helmet didn't come in with him."

"What?"

"No. It would have been left behind at the scene. The paramedics pulled it off when they tried to revive him. They also opened his turnout coat and slit his shirt up the front so they could put EKG leads on his chest. You probably saw that his shirt was cut."

"Yeah, I saw that. I was surprised my mother-in-law didn't throw it out. His T-shirt's gone. I'm really hoping she didn't turn it into a dust cloth."

Sophie frowned. "He wasn't wearing a T-shirt."

"What? That's nuts. Randy always wore a T-shirt."

"Well, he wasn't that day. Unless the paramedics stripped him in the field and then re-dressed him without it. I can't see any reason for that, though."

"You said you opened his turnout coat?"

"Someone had closed it up again, just a

few of the clasps."

"But why would he not be wearing a T-shirt?"

She leaned forward. "Death," she said gently, "your brother had just been told that you were dead. When he got dressed, he probably wasn't thinking too clearly."

"Yeah, okay, I can see that. But that doesn't explain where the other badge came from."

"No. And there," she sighed, "I don't know what to tell you."

Nathan Broome was a coin collector, but not in the traditional sense. At some point he had decided to collect his life in coins. His collection included a penny minted in every year from the time he was born until the day he died. At five-year intervals he added a nickel to the collection, a dime every ten years, a quarter every twenty-five, and a half-dollar at the fifty-year mark. The most valuable pieces in his collection were eighteen wheat pennies valued at a whopping six cents each. The entire collection, in its oversized, custom-built frame, was shiny and impressive and worth $3.97.

And nobody wanted it.

The sun beat down on Wren's bare head, making her scalp itch and sending trickles of sweat down her back. Not a breeze stirred, bees droned in the clover along the edge of the yard, and the nails in the wooden stepladder she was sitting on were hot enough to burn bare skin if it accidentally came in contact with them. She was hot, tired, cranky, her phone was buzzing against her hip, and her throat was dry and scratchy. She swallowed hard and made one last, valiant attempt to persuade the crowd that this was a Neat Thing and something they absolutely Had To Have.

"Okay, let me ask you something. How many people here are carrying plastic? Hmm? Just about everyone, I'm gonna bet. And you know why? Because hard, cold cash is becoming obsolete. Someday there won't be any coins anymore, and when that happens, this collection is going to wind up being a heck of a great investment for whoever's smart enough to snatch it up. Why, if these were ancient Roman coins —"

"We'd be bidding on them," someone in the crowd heckled.

Wren growled under her breath and resisted the urge to start pulling pennies out of the frame and throwing them at people.

Off to her right Sam Keystone nudged Felix Knotty, the irascible Vietnam vet who did odd jobs for the business. Oh, thank

God! They were going to take pity on her. Felix raised one hand languidly. "One dolla!"

Wren pounced on him. "One dollar! I have one dollar! Anybody else? No? Good! Going once! Going twice! And SOLD to the gentleman in the snazzy ball cap!" Felix doffed his battered ball cap to her and she set the coin collection aside. Sam had come up beside her now and motioned her off the ladder.

"My turn."

She handed over the microphone, limp with relief, and went to the cash tent for a soda and some shade.

As she cleared the edges of the crowd, she pulled out her phone. There was a text message from Death: *Call me when you get a chance.*

Leona and Doris were busy cashing people out so Wren helped herself to a soda and stepped back outside to make her call in the shade of a majestic weeping willow. Death answered on the first ring. "Hey. How's the auction going?"

"Well, I haven't strangled anyone yet."

"That good, huh?"

"I've seen better. How are you doing? Where are you?"

"Burger joint. Stopped for a late lunch. I

61

went by 41's but they were out on a call."

"Have you been to Randy's yet? Is everything turned on?" Death was planning on staying at his brother's house and he'd called to arrange to have the utilities turned on again.

"Ah, no. I haven't been there yet. I should probably do that next."

Wren could hear the reluctance in his voice. *Maybe you should just get a hotel room,* she wanted to say. *Maybe you could wait and deal with this later.* She wanted to say, but did not. He was going to have to face all of this someday. It wouldn't help anything to put it off.

"I talked to Sophie at the coroner's office today."

"Oh?"

"I think you were right. She had a thing for Randy. She didn't have a clue about where those badges came from, though. And she made a good point. Randy's helmet never passed through their office. The badges had to have been switched at the scene."

"But it was in the carton . . . ?"

"Because Evelyn put it there. You know? My mother-in-law? I called her just now. She took Randy's turnouts to HQ and turned them in. The battalion chief came out and talked to her. They had Randy's helmet there and he gave it to her then." He sounded discouraged. "None of this is making a damn bit of sense."

They talked for several more minutes before saying goodbye. Wren touched the end call button and stood, pensive, staring down at her phone. She heard the sound of someone clearing their throat and looked up to find Roy Keystone standing a few feet away watching her.

"Wren Morgan," he said. He gestured toward the auction going on beyond the thin, green curtain of willow fronds. "Is this *really* where you need to be right now?"

The neighborhood had declined since Death's grandparents bought their retirement cottage a few blocks north of Forest Park. Driving there, he passed countless "for sale" signs. Many of the houses — single family dwellings from the early twentieth century — showed signs of neglect. Here and there a derelict property had been boarded up and vandalized and a few of the homes sported burglar bars on the windows.

On Randy's block, things were a little better. The old building just to the south of his house was crumbling into ruin, but that was nothing new. In their childhood, that had been high on the list of Places You Better Not Let Grandma Catch You. The other houses were bright and well-maintained, and it did not escape Death's notice that Randy's porch was swept and his lawn as neatly mowed as the others.

Randy's house sat back from the street with a slanted and uneven concrete walk leading up to the door. It was built of red brick, small and quaint, with a single dormer window. The full front porch featured filigreed iron railings and posts to hold the roof up. During his grandparents' day the front and side yards had been a riot of color, but Death's grandmother's roses had proven no match for Randy's brown thumb.

Death went around the block and drove down the alley to reach the backyard and the detached garage. It wasn't equipped with a garage door opener, so he had to get out, unlock it with the spare key Randy had given him, and raise it manually. Here, too, there were signs that someone had been by to tidy up. Randy had never in his life left a room this neat. All the tools were put away above the workbench and there was room for Death's Jeep beside Randy's classic Mustang.

You should get a Mustang. A gray Mustang. So help me, God, Randy, if you make that lame joke again . . .

You'll what? Say "Bite me"? Again?

You do and I'll knock another tooth out.

Yeah, yeah. I'm quaking in my boots. Any-way, you're not cool enough for a Mustang. You should get a Pinto. A gray Pinto.

Well, then, you should get a white one.

A white one? Why a white one?

Because Pestilence rides a white horse.

In the end, Randy was the one who had gotten the Mustang. He was the one who wanted one all along. He'd gone with a classy, non-symbolic dark blue. In other circumstances he might have chosen red, like a fire engine, but War rode a red horse and war wasn't something to joke about when your only living relative was getting shot at in Afghanistan.

Death pulled his Jeep next to the Mustang, relocked the garage, and entered the house through the back door. The kitchen was spotless, counters bare and cupboards closed. The refrigerator was unplugged and the door propped open with a chair. The shelves were empty and clean. Death plugged it in. The light came on and it started humming so he knew the electricity was on. He closed the door so it could get cold, wandered into the living room, and dropped onto the sofa.

The weight of his memories was overwhelming. The sight and the scent and the *feel* of the place conjured the dead.

Randy had the walls covered with pictures, some hung properly in frames and some tucked into the corners of other pictures or stuck up with tape. Death studied them from the sofa for a few seconds, then dragged himself up to get a closer look. There was no order to them. Family pictures mingled with pictures of his friends on the fire department and on the softball team he played for. There were comics cut or torn from the newspaper, things printed off the Internet, and pictures of women. Some of the women Death recognized and some he didn't.

There were no pictures of Death.

He frowned, puzzled and hurt and unsure what to make of it.

There were blank spots — lots of them — where his picture might have been. But the pictures themselves were gone.

"He took them down. He couldn't bear to look at them."

Death spun so quickly he made himself dizzy.

A short, chubby brunette stood in the kitchen door. She saw the effect she'd had on Death and held out a hand as if to steady him, instantly contrite. "I'm sorry. So sorry! You left the back door open and I'm afraid I've gotten used to coming in."

"And you are . . . ?"

"Annie. Sorry! Annie Tanner." She waited a few seconds for recognition. "Rowdy's wife?"

"Annie? Yes! Annie, of course. Randy spoke of you." He glanced around, adding things in his head. "You're the one who . . ." he waved one hand in the air, indicating the house in general.

"Rowdy and I. And the other guys too, sometimes. We've just been keeping an eye on the place. I hope you don't mind?"

"Mind? No. No, of course not. I appreciate it."

"We came over that day, after," she shrugged and looked away, not wanting to say it. Death nodded that he understood. "We came over, cleaned out the refrigerator, tidied up the place."

"I could sure tell somebody had. Randy was a lot of things, but neat was never one of them."

"No," she smiled, warm and sad. "No, neat he was not. You know, we thought the world of your brother, Death."

"I know." He looked around. "He pulled down my pictures, huh?"

"Took them all down. Destroyed a few of them, I'm afraid. Ones of you in uniform, mostly. And then he felt bad about it. He was so *mad* at you. He said you knew better than to get killed. He told you. It wasn't rational, but —"

"I understand."

"He spent the night before he died at our house. I didn't see anything — *anything* — to suggest that he was sick! I mean, he was upset, yes. Terribly upset. But —"

"He spent the night with you?"

"Captain Stone, from C shift, called Rowdy. Randy was at the firehouse when the Marine Corps tracked him down. It was his day off, but he was pulling OT so one of the guys from C shift could take his son to a ball game. The Marines called and talked to Captain Stone first and he called Rowdy to be there when Randy got the news. He called Cap, too. They came here first but eventually Rowdy brought Randy home."

"I appreciate you looking out for him. He meant," Death had to stop and clear his throat. "The kid meant a lot to me."

"You meant a lot to him, too. You know that, right?"

Death nodded awkwardly and for a moment they just stood in an uncomfortable silence. It was Annie who broke it. "So, what are you going to do? Will you live here now?"

He looked around, tried to picture himself occupying this space and could not. There were so many memories here, but not a one that wasn't tinged with loss and sorrow. This was his past and his future was across the state with his feral pixie. In that moment, he missed her so much his heart hurt. "I think . . . I think I'll probably sell it. Keep a few mementos, let the rest go to auction. I really do appreciate the work you've all put into keeping it up."

"It's no problem. We did it for you, because Randy would have wanted us to. An auction is going to be a lot of work. I hope you know you can count on us to help all we can."

"Thank you, so much. I might take you up on that. First, I need to consult an auctioneer."

After some consideration, Death dialed the business number for Keystone and Sons. If he was going to use an auction as a pretext for getting Wren to St. Louis, he felt he should do so through proper channels. It was getting late in the afternoon, now, and the day's auctions would probably be over, but he knew that Leona kept an eye on the business phone around the clock. He was expecting her voice and a polite, business-like greeting.

Instead, the phone clicked to life and an old man whispered at him to shush.

"What?"

"Shh! Dammit, boy! Don't you understand shh?"

Death lowered his voice. "Why am I shhing?"

"This damn phone's stuck on speaker and I can't figure out how to turn it off. Leona's coming. You don't shh, she's gonna find where I'm hiding."

Death put his own phone on speaker, balanced it on his knee and sat back on the couch to wait. Odd knocks and rattles came over the line. Footsteps approached and a door squealed.

"Roy?" Leona's voice was distant, but not too distant. "Roy Keystone, I know you're in here somewhere. Eventually I *am* going to find you and when I do, you are going to be one sorry little man. You hear me?" The footsteps receded. The door shrieked again and then closed with a bang and Roy Keystone giggled like a naughty schoolboy.

"Do I want to know what you did to her, Roy?"

"What makes you think I did anything?" A series of scrapes and groans came from the phone. Some of them sounded like wood or metal, some of them sounded like tendons and bones. "Good Lord, this is ridiculous. I don't know how Matthew fits into these places."

"Matthew is seven. That probably helps."

"Blah blah blah. Did you call me up just to criticize me?"

"No, I —"

"Why did you call me up, then?"

"Well, I heard this was the business number for Keystone and Sons Auctioneers. I wanted to talk business, so I gave it a call. You still haven't told me what you did to Leona."

"No, I haven't. What do you think you want to talk business about?"

"I'm, well, you know I'm over here in St. Louis to settle my brother's estate. I'm thinking I need to have an estate sale and I was wondering if you guys might be willing to handle that. I mean, I don't know if there's enough here to make the commission worth your while, but I thought maybe you could send somebody over to have a look at it and . . . ?"

"We could do that," Roy agreed. "Say, Felix Knotty or one of the grandsons?"

"Oh. Um, well, I was thinking —"

"No, you weren't. What's your middle

71

name?" the old man demanded suddenly. "I know you've got one. It starts with a D."

"How do you know that?"

"Leona told me. She made you show her your driver's license to get an auction number one time, remember?"

"Yeah, but I thought that was just teasing me."

"It wasn't teasing, it was being nosy. She plays it off real cool, but my wife is about the nosiest old biddy in the county."

"Roy! That's no way to talk about your wife."

"No? But it's true. And I say it with love. Anyway, Leona's seen your driver's license. She knows your height, your official eye color and hair color, your birthday, and how old you'll be. You were still using your ex-wife's address, you've dropped at least forty pounds of muscle since you got the license, when they took your picture you were just about to sneeze, and your middle initial is D. Only she can't find out what the D stands for, and it's driving her crazy."

"So you're thinking you can use my middle name to buy your way out of whatever trouble you're in?"

"It wouldn't hurt."

"Not you, maybe."

"Besides, I need to know it so I can yell at

you proper."

"What?"

"I gotta have your middle name to yell at you. That's how kids know they're really in trouble. If I just holler Death Bogart, then you might think I was being friendly. But I yell Death Dwight Bogart, *then* you sit up and pay attention."

"It's not Dwight."

"Dwayne."

"No."

"Delancey?"

"What do you want to yell at me about?"

"It is Delancey!"

"It's not Delancey! Answer the question!"

"I want to yell at you for thinking you need to hire your girlfriend. Girlfriends that you hire aren't girlfriends. They're hookers. I tell Wren you confused her with a hooker and you're going to be the one who needs a cupboard to hide in. Doug."

"It's not Doug. And I didn't . . . I just, I know you're trying to run a business. And Wren has a job to do. And I really do need help with this auction."

"Just with the auction?" Roy's voice had taken on a gentle, serious undertone.

Death sighed, defeated. "No."

"You're across the state, all alone, trying to settle your brother's estate. If you need

Wren there, all you have to do is ask her. You know the only reason she didn't go with you is because she was afraid you'd think she was crowding you."

"I wouldn't think that."

"Of course not. That's why both of you need to learn to use your *words,* as we tell our toddlers. Dirk."

Death just laughed. "I guess I'd better call her then."

"Good plan. She's probably halfway to New Orleans by now."

"New Orleans!" he bit down on a spike of bitter disappointment. "Why's she going to New Orleans?"

"Well, she isn't going there on purpose. But she left here three hours ago headed for St. Louis, and you and I both know how that woman navigates. I'd look for her in the foothills east of Jeff City."

"She's coming here?" The room warmed and brightened around him.

"She's certainly trying. Damien."

"It's not Dirk and it's not Damien. So what *did* you do to Leona?"

Roy giggled as if he were six instead of sixty-three. "She was complaining about the heat, so I cut off the hot water while she was taking a shower."

Death chuckled and shook his head, even

though there was no one there to see.

"Man, you know she's going to get even with you."

"Oh, I know it. That's half the fun, son."

FIVE

Maria Vasquez stood, as she did twice a day, in front of the sink in the master bathroom. The window was open, a light morning breeze tossing the curtain and tugging at the ruffle around her apron. Mister Grey would have done that, she thought, reaching out to close it and keep the conditioned air inside. He had an odd tendency to open windows now, just one of the personality quirks he'd picked up after the stroke, just over a year ago, that had nearly killed him.

Maria set the row of pill bottles out on the counter and began carefully counting pills into little paper cups. She could do this in her sleep by now, and after a moment her mind wandered and her eyes strayed back to the view out the high window.

The stroke had changed her employer. The paralysis that made the left side of his face droop was all but gone now, and he'd regained the ability to dress himself (with help) and move around. But his memory was shot full of holes. From one day to the next he would forget people's names. He never knew where he was and had to be constantly monitored so that he didn't hurt himself. And his personality had changed. The crude, brash playboy had been replaced by a man who was polite, even diffident. Even to the servants, which annoyed his wife to no end.

Maria took a clean glass from the cupboard below the sink and filled it with water, then arranged the medicines and the glass on a silver tray. Outside the morning sun glared off the roofs of neighboring houses. Beyond and just above them, the old grain silos of the Einstadt Brewery rose into a blue and cloudless sky.

"So one of the guys over at 16's got hold of these peppers. Bought them at a farmer's market somewhere and the guy selling them told him they were Thai Red Dragons, which are supposed to be some of the hottest peppers in the world. So he made up a batch of chili with them. He was being crazy careful — wouldn't handle them without rubber gloves on, wore his SCBA when he cut 'em up. Cooks up this chili, and he dares Bogie to try it. So Bogie says —"

"What's in it for me?" Death interjected.

"That's our boy! Well, the guy had a sister who was really hot, but kind of stuck up and he offers to get Bogie a date with her if he can eat a whole bowl of chili. Only Bogie, he says he's not interested in a woman who's not interested in him and he wants . . ." Rowdy Tanner paused and looked at Death expectantly.

Death grinned. "Cold, hard cash."

"Well, the guy at 16's didn't want to part with the lucre. They dickered back and forth a bit and finally agreed that, if Randy could eat a whole bowl of the chili, the guy at 16's'd eat a box of chocolate-covered ants."

"Ugh!" Wren turned aside to address Annie Tanner. She and Death were sitting at a picnic table in the Tanners' backyard. Randy's whole crew had turned up, and they were grilling burgers and swapping stories about Randy while a small crowd of children had a water gun fight around them. "Is this a fire department thing?" she asked Annie. "The gross foods, I mean? Because the firefighters back home do that sort of thing, too."

"The single ones, mostly," Annie said. "I think the married ones pretty much realize that there are limits to what they can come home having eaten."

"Lips that touch slime will never touch mine," Rowdy recited dutifully.

"So what happened?" Death prodded. "Did Randy eat the chili? 'Cause the kid had a cast-iron stomach, I know that."

"Oh, he ate the chili all right. Turned out the farmer's market guy was lying. They weren't Thai Red Dragons, weren't even hot. They were just ordinary sweet peppers. Dude at 16's was stuck. You should have seen his face. To this day he can't look at an ant without turning green."

A couple kids ventured a little too close to the grill. Cap chased them away, then turned back to the conversation. "So, have you found out anything about where that badge came from?"

Death and Wren exchanged a glance. Death reached in his shirt pocket.

"When my mother-in-law returned Randy's turnouts to HQ they gave her his helmet, or they said it was his helmet, to pass along to me. This was on it." He tossed the hat badge down on the picnic table. Cap picked it up and frowned at it.

"That's the wrong number. This is nuts!"

"I called and talked to a secretary at HQ this morning. She said that the Captain of 27's brought the helmet in the morning of the fire. So then I called and talked to him.

He remembered picking it up off the ground beside where they were working on Randy. When he got word that Randy didn't make it, he took it over and turned it in to HQ."

"What —" Wren paused and tapped the table, looking around at the men and women gathered there. "I know that nobody wants to relive this, but, what exactly happened at that fire? After you brought him out of the building?"

"We did what we'd do any time an unconscious firefighter is brought out of a building." The speaker was a woman in her mid-thirties, with fine blonde hair and blue eyes and a light sunburn on her nose. "We stripped off his helmet and breathing gear and checked his vitals. He wasn't breathing and we couldn't find a pulse. His nose was broken and his face badly burned, so we performed a tracheotomy — that is, we inserted an airway through his neck — and put him on forced oxygen. We opened his coat, cut open his shirt, and Yering started chest compressions while I set up for an EKG. The EKG showed flatline, so we pushed epinephrine directly into the heart and continued CPR. I set up an IV port, we put him in the rig, and got him to the hospital. We worked on him all the way and they continued for awhile at the ER, but by then it was pretty clear that nothing was going to work. It was the ER physician who called TOD."

"What happened then? Do you remember?"

"The whole crew was there by then. We just sat in the waiting room and cried like babies. He was one of ours, you know?"

There was nothing to say to that and for a few minutes they all sat there in a pensive silence. Wren slipped her hand into Death's. The Tanners' backyard was lovely with lush grass; flowers growing on the fence line; and a big, fancy wooden swing set for the kids. The Gateway Arch rose against blue sky and wispy clouds on the eastern horizon. She turned to the southeast and picked out, among the alien landscape of factories and high-rise buildings, an old brick monster with silos on the end.

"Is that the Einstadt building?" she asked, pointing. The others turned to look.

"No," Rowdy said. "That's the Lemp Brewery. It's also abandoned. They look a lot alike, but you can't see the Widow from here. It's not far from there, though. The old breweries are all grouped pretty close together down there. They built them on top of a series of caverns, the Cherokee Caves. In the nineteenth century, before they had refrigeration, they used the caves to keep the beer cold."

Death heaved a frustrated sigh, raked a hand through his hair, and tapped one finger on the hat badge. "I gotta figure this out. This is making me nuts. Did *any* of you notice *anything* odd that day? Anything at all?" All of the firefighters shook their heads except for Rowdy, who hesitated. Death looked to him expectantly.

"It's nothing," he said. "Really, it's nothing. I didn't even give it a second thought at the time. It's been bugging me since, but I can't imagine that it could mean anything. Only, like you said, it's odd."

"What, Rowdy? What was odd? What did you notice?"

"Randy was lying on his back when we dug him out." He glanced around at his audience. Death and the other firefighters looked like they understood the significance. Rowdy must have read the confusion on Wren's face, because he spoke directly to her. "When someone passes out, they usually fall forward. He should have been lying on his stomach, probably with his legs bent. But he was lying on his back, kind of half on his side because of his air tanks, and his legs were straight. It was almost like someone positioned his body."

■ ■ ■ ■

"You'll need some albums," Wren said. "Some albums and some picture frames. Some of these you'll want to put up on the wall and some you'll want to put away and just take out from time to time."

They were back in Randy's living room, looking at the wall full of pictures and mementos. The prospect of dealing with all this, of sorting out his little brother's house and car and all his possessions and somehow tidying them away so he could move on with his life, was daunting. The fact that much of this had also belonged to their grandparents didn't help. Everything was connected to a memory and even the best memories were bittersweet, tainted with loss. In the midst of it all, Wren was a calm and practical presence. She was an anchor for his spirit; the eye of the hurricane that was his life.

"Start simply," she advised him. "Pick out the things you know you want to keep. But don't feel like you have to keep everything. It's not a betrayal if you donate his clothes to the Salvation Army or sell his living room furniture. You're just doing what you have to do. We both know Randy would understand."

"For now, I guess we'd ought to just take them down and put them in boxes."

Wren had arrived with the back of her truck loaded with empty boxes and crates. "This is what I do for a living," she'd reminded him. "I know what to expect. I'll help you. Everything will be okay."

Now she opened a sturdy carton, took out a pair of plastic boxes with snap-closed lids, and set them on the coffee table. "We can put anything small or fragile in this one, and the other can hold pins and thumbtacks." Nails, pins, tacks, putty, and even duct tape held up the eclectic assortment of things on display. As they set to work, pulling them down and sorting them into boxes, Death shook his head in bemusement.

"I'd never have dared to put needles and tacks and duct tape on Grandma's walls. I'd have expected her to come back and haunt me. Randy, though, he always could get away with anything. He'd get this wide-eyed, baby deer look and Mom and the grandmas would just melt."

"What's the funniest thing you remember ever happening in this room?" Wren asked, pulling down dozens of cartoons that were plastered around the door into the kitchen.

"This room?" Death thought about it. "There was the time Uncle Biggers set his butt on fire."

"Uncle Biggers? He set his butt on fire?"

"Yeah. He wasn't really our uncle. He was my grandad's best friend. They served together on the department for nearly thirty years. It was almost Christmas the year I was . . . I dunno . . . nine. He and Grandpa had been out shoveling snow. He and his wife lived just down the street and every time it snowed, he and Grandpa made a point of clearing the sidewalk and shoveling out the walkways for everyone on the block. Dad and Randy and I were helping, of course, but by the time we got done we were all about half frozen. We were getting warm around the fire and Uncle Biggers turned his back to the fireplace and bent over, 'cause he said his 'other cheeks were cold too.' Well, just about that time he, uh," Death glanced at Wren and blushed, but plowed ahead. "Well, he broke wind. The fire lit it and set the seat of his pants on fire. He had to run out and sit in the snow to put them out."

"Oh, dear." Wren's face was red, too, but she was smiling at him.

"Crass, I know. And I don't think the ladies appreciated it. But to a nine-year-old boy, that was comic gold, let me tell ya."

Wren put the stack of comic strips in one

of the boxes and moved back to the wall. "Oh, look," she said, her voice gentle. "This looks familiar."

Death shuffled the photos he was holding into as neat a pile as was possible and came over to see what she'd found. "It's the picture from the school fire safety day. The same one that Cameron gave me."

Cameron Michaels was a friend of Wren's — they'd even been engaged once before he'd come to terms with the fact he was gay. They were still close and, when she and Death had met, Cameron used his resources as a newspaper reporter to check up on Death. One of the things he'd found was a newspaper story about Randy, dated the week before he died. He'd printed it and given it to Death before Wren framed it to hang on her wall.

It was a human interest story that had run on the front page of the paper, about Fire Station 41 hosting a fire safety day at one of the local elementary schools. Among the pictures on the front page was a shot of Randy, in uniform, explaining something to a small group of children. Studying it now, Wren frowned.

"That's odd."

"What?" Death asked, trepidation churning his stomach. The last thing he needed in his life right now was more oddity.

She pointed. "Honey, look at Randy's badge."

He lifted the picture out of her hand and held it up to the light. "What the — ? No. That does not make sense." In the photo, Randy's badge was clearly visible. The number on it, as plain as day, was 4183.

Six

Death turned his Jeep into the drive on the side of Station 41 and followed it back to the lot where the firefighters parked their personal vehicles. "Have you been here before?" Wren asked.

"Not to visit. I brought Randy by when I was home for our parents' funeral, but I just dropped him off and then picked him up later. We were both on bereavement leave. Madeline wanted me to go have dinner at her mother's house that night. Randy refused to go — he and Madeline never did get along — but he didn't want to keep me away from my wife the whole time I was back. He said he'd like to come hang out at the station with his friends for a little bit."

He stepped out of the vehicle, gravel crunching beneath his feet, and paused a moment to study the back of the fire station. "We used to visit Grandpa a lot when he was at 16's," he said.

Wren came around to join him. "Why do you say it like that? I've noticed it before. All the firefighters seem to do it."

"Like what?"

"Plural. Sixteens and Forty-ones."

"Ah." He grinned a small grin and put an arm around her shoulder as they walked to the building. "It's not plural, it's possessive."

"Okay . . . ?"

"It's an old fire department tradition. Engines are personified. Some of them even have names instead of numbers. And the station and crew assigned to that station belong to the engine. This is Engine 41's house. Her squad and her ALS are parked here, too, and the firefighters that are assigned here are her firefighters. Understand?"

"Oh, absolutely," Wren agreed, though her wrinkled brow suggested otherwise.

Death chuckled, brought them to a halt beside a side door, and rapped on the window glass. A young firefighter they didn't recognize answered.

"Yeah, we're looking for Captain Cairn?"

"He's here. If you'd like to come in, I'll go find him."

They went through the door into a large, bright kitchen. Another firefighter turned away from the sink as they entered. It was Lance Elgar, one of the men they'd met at Rowdy Tanner's, and he greeted them warmly.

"Look out, everybody! Death is at the door!" He wiped his hands on a dishcloth, draped it over his shoulder, and offered Death a handshake. "Billy," he said to the younger fireman, "you've heard us talk a lot about Bogie. Well, this gentleman is Bogie's big brother."

"Oh, um, right on." Billy offered Death a nervous handshake. "Pleased to meet you. I'm, um, I'm sorry about your loss."

"Thank you. And this is my girlfriend, Wren Morgan."

"Ma'am. Um, I'll just go let Cap know you're here."

He made a nervous escape from the room and Death raised his eyebrow questioningly at Elgar. "Kid's a boot. He's, ah, he's a truckee."

Death nodded. "Randy's replacement."

"Yeah."

"Make sure he knows he has a lot to live up to."

"Oh, we have. Believe me, we have."

Cap came in and warmly greeted them. He ushered them to seats at the kitchen table and offered them coffee. "I wasn't expecting to see you here. Is this a social call or was there something you needed?"

Death and Wren exchanged a glance, then he took the carefully folded newspaper clipping from his pocket.

"We've come across something else that's a bit weird."

"Something else? There wasn't already enough about this that was weird for you?"

Death handed him the clipping and Cap took it, nodding. "Yeah, fire safety day. We do those every once in a while. This was the last one that Bogie . . . the hell?"

"That clipping was on Randy's wall. I have a copy at home, but I'd never really looked that close. Wren noticed it."

"Noticed what?" Elgar asked.

"Bogie's badge," Cap answered. "In the picture, he's wearing the badge with the wrong number on it."

"Anyway, I've been thinking and thinking about what could have happened and I was just wondering if there was any way that, um —"

"You're wondering if I've lost my marbles and if the wrong badge is the one I brought you."

"Well, I wasn't going to phrase it exactly like that, but, kind of. Yeah."

"Come on."

Cap got up and led the way into the vehicle bay. A few feet from the kitchen door the wall was decorated with framed photographs — groups of 41's firefighters posing beside their rigs. He found one of Randy and Tanner, lifted it down, and offered it to Death. Wren stood on tiptoe, trying to see over his shoulder, and he put his arm around her and held the picture low so they both could see it.

Randy's badge number, in this picture, was 4103.

"Let's go in my office," Cap said. "I've got all his paperwork in there. You can see for yourself that his badge number is 4103."

"I'm sorry," Death said. "It's not that I doubt you, it's just —"

"You want to know what's going on. So do I. Come on with me, I've got an idea."

Cap led the way into his office, waved them toward chairs, and settled himself behind his desk. He took out his phone, searched for a number, and hit call.

"Hey, Miriam? This is Jonathan Cairn with the fire department. I have something to ask you. Do you remember late last summer when we did that fire safety day at your school? Yeah, just after the start of the school year. Just before we lost one of our men. Fireman Bogart, yes. You took some pictures before we left . . . that's right. Do you have any that have Bogie in them? His brother is here and he'd really like to have copies of those, if it would be possible. Yes? Wonderful. Listen, if you could just email them to me, I can print them out for him here."

He spoke for a few more moments, thanked the woman on the other end of the phone, and hung up. "Miriam Drake is one of the counselors at Ridgewood Elementary, where we had that fire safety day. She was taking a lot of pictures, too, for the school yearbook."

He had a PC sitting on his desk. He checked it, nodded, and turned the screen so they could all three see it. The browser was open to an email account and it showed a whole series of new messages, all with attachments, from mdrake@rwoodelem.edu. Cap started with the first one on the list and they studied their way through the pictures. Most of the early shots were from too far away to make out Randy's badge number, but then they came to a series of posed pictures of Randy standing beside one or two children.

"And in these, it shows his badge as 4103," Death agreed.

"All the little girls had crushes on him,"

Wren noted with a smile. Cap clicked open another attachment and she frowned. "This is the same picture as the one in the paper."

"Is it?" Death asked. "No, it looks different."

"The angle is a little different. It was taken at the same time, though. Or almost the same time. See, it's got the same children in the same poses. There's the little girl with long hair standing to his left and the little boy in the dinosaur T-shirt on his right side. Can you zoom in on his badge?" Cap did as she asked and they all sat in silence and stared at the picture. His badge read 4103, just as it should have. It was only in the newspaper picture that it was wrong.

"Why am I mad at you?"

Maria Vasquez, dusting the contents of the living room curio cabinet, glanced over her shoulder in concern. Mister Grey wasn't speaking to her, though. He was addressing his wife, Alaina, a tiny, elegant woman with dark hair and dark eyes. His voice was soft, confused rather than angry, and Alaina gently pushed a lock of gray hair back from his temple.

"Sweetheart, you're not mad. You're only confused. You had a stroke, do you remember that? It's made things foggy for you, but you're getting better. You're going to be fine."

Her voice was tender and it occurred to Maria that it was not just Andrew Grey whose personality had been changed by the sudden illness that nearly killed him.

Alaina was a trophy wife, like the four Mrs. Greys before her; a small-town beauty queen from the wrong side of the tracks who married a middle-aged playboy. Until a year ago, Maria would have bet that the marriage was more of a business venture for her than a labor of love. Andrew Grey had been, at best, a difficult man to live with, but he'd covered her in silks and jewels and put her older brother through medical school.

"Are you sure I'm not mad at you? I feel like I'm so angry. All you cared about was money."

"All I care about is you. I promise you. Maria?"

Maria turned at the summons.

"I think it's time for Mr. Grey's sedative. Get it for him, won't you?"

"Yes, ma'am."

Maria bobbed a curtsey before she left. As someone who'd been very poor before she was wealthy, Mrs. Grey was hyper aware of social status and quick to take offense at any perceived slight.

Going up the stairs to fetch the medicine, Maria passed the Greys' oversized wedding portrait. Their tenth anniversary was coming up in less than two week's time. The past ten years had aged Andrew. His hair was completely gray now, where it had only been gray at the temples on his wedding day. Maria turned the corner at the landing, halfway up the stairs. A bow window pierced the wall here, the shelf in front of it filled with potted plants. Beyond the greenery, the front facade of the Einstadt Brewery peeked at her from across the street, black smoke stains still rising from the broken windows.

"I didn't do a lot to that picture."

Death had tracked down the newspaper photographer who'd taken the pictures of the Ridgewood Elementary fire safety day. Ralph Duror was a slight, thin, man in his early thirties, with bright eyes behind thick glasses and early onset male pattern baldness. Duror studied the clipping Death handed him, then opened an expensive laptop and searched through the files for a few minutes. "Ridgewood, right? About ten months ago?"

"Ten months and a couple of weeks."

"Right. Okay, here's the original of that shot."

He spun the computer around so Death could study it.

"I cleaned it up a bit," the photographer said. "There was a lot of wind that day and the little girl's hair was just all over the place." In the original of the picture, strands of the little girl's long hair were blowing across the front of Randy's uniform.

"Can you zoom in on his badge?"

Duror did. The badge number appeared to be 4183, but if you looked closely you could tell that the middle line on the "8" was only a strand of dark hair. Randy pointed out the discrepancy and Duror brought the two pictures up side-by-side.

"Crap. You're right. I guess I didn't look that close and just thought the number was an eight. We'd have been on deadline, too. It doesn't really matter, though, does it?"

"No, probably not." Death fiddled with the folded clipping, not wanting to go into too much detail. "Just a curiosity I wanted to get cleared up."

Duror tapped the screen. "You know, that firefighter died in a fire just about a week after that." He pulled the laptop back and sorted through his files again. "I covered that, too." He turned the screen back toward

Death. "Got some great shots." Death leaned in to study a screen full of thumbnails.

"So, what's your interest?" the photographer asked. "Did you know this guy?"

"Yeah, you could say that. He was my little brother."

"Oh." The man paused and made a visible effort to adjust his expression from enthused to sympathetic. Death got halfway down the page and his breath caught in his throat.

"This picture, here. Can you pull that up?"

"Yeah, sure." Duror brought it up. "Oh, that was my favorite. The composition and the way it brought out the pathos of . . ." he glanced up and colored. "Never mind. Anyway, the editor didn't want to use it. If you'd like, I can print you out a copy."

"Could you do that? That would be great."

Duror hit the print button, left the desk for a minute, and came back with a fresh, glossy 8×10. Death stared down at it, mind whirling.

It was a picture of a firefighter's helmet lying on the Einstadt Brewery parking lot. Three firefighters stood looking down at it with bleak expressions. One man had tear tracks down his face. The hat badge was upside down, but clearly visible. The number on it was 4183.

Randy's bedroom was immaculate, but Wren was pretty sure that was Annie Tanner's doing. From the looks of the clothes packed into his closet, the youngest Bogart had never thrown anything away. She held up a paint-spattered black T-shirt that was almost more hole than shirt, shook her head in sad amusement, and added it to a trash bag at her feet. Death was at the newspaper office talking to the photographer who took the picture of Randy with the wrong badge. She had offered to stay behind and sort Randy's clothes out. It was a task that didn't require Death's input and one she didn't want him to have to face.

Back home in East Bledsoe Ferry, Wren liked to visit yard sales late on Saturday afternoons, when they were closing up. She could often get whatever clothes were left over for next to nothing. Then she'd sort them, wash and mend them, and, when she was done, donate them to local thrift shops. This was a familiar job for her, but still a melancholy one. She shared a common bond with Randy.

They both loved the same man.

The clothes that still had wear in them went into cartons. She set aside a couple of tattered garments that she suspected had sentimental value — a St. Louis Cardinals World Series T-shirt from 1982 and a black-and-gold high school baseball jersey. Things too worn to be useful went into the bag, along with all underwear in any condition. There were things that were suitable to donate to charity and things that were not suitable to donate to charity and used underwear was pretty near the top of the unsuitable list.

The trash bag made it out to the curb just ahead of a lumbering garbage truck. She taped the cartons closed, marked "Salvation Army" on them in black marker, and stacked them in a corner. She thought about going ahead and taking them so they'd be gone when Death returned, but she didn't know where the nearest Salvation Army store was and she wasn't confident enough with city driving to go look for one.

The drawer in the nightstand yielded a package of cold medicine, a box of condoms, a couple of girlie magazines, and a well-read copy of Terry Pratchett's *Night Watch*. There was a small box on top of the nightstand with the flaps folded closed. Wren opened it and found what must have been the smaller contents of Randy's locker at the fire station. It contained a wallet, a set of keys, a tin of shoe polish, a small sewing kit, and a cell phone with the charger wrapped around it. She glanced through the wallet and smiled at Randy's spectacularly bad driver's license photo. The license also showed his full real name, Baranduin Phileas Bogart, and she'd bet he'd hated having to show it. Whatever tactic Death had used to have only his middle initial on his license, he hadn't shared it with his little brother.

The cell was dead, but it occurred to Wren that it could easily contain pictures or information that should be saved. She plugged it in, sat down on the edge of the bed, and powered it up.

It was a smartphone, but the model was one she was unfamiliar with and she had to fiddle with it for several minutes just to get the screen unlocked. When she did, icons came up for new email and text messages and missed phone calls. Most of the calls and texts were from shortly after Randy's death and were from the same people. Wren scanned through them and was glad that she'd found them instead of Death, because they were heartbreaking.

"Dude! Heard someone from 41 was down. What happened?"

"tv sed fyrfytr dyd! ru ok?"

"Bogie ru there?"

"tell me its not true"

With tears in her eyes, she deleted them until she was left with a string of automated text messages reminding Randy that he was overdue to have his teeth cleaned. She copied the number to her own phone and called it.

"Dr. Weableau's office."

"Hi, I'm calling about one of your patients, Baranduin Bogart? You might have him in your files as 'Randy'."

"Of course." The receptionist was an older woman with a soft, Southern accent. "I knew Randy well. What can I do for you?"

"Oh, um, I was just calling to let you know that he's deceased. Your office has been sending reminders to his cell phone about having his teeth cleaned."

"I am so sorry! Those things are programmed in and I just never thought to go in and cancel it. I'll take care of that right now."

"Thank you. It's not a problem. I just don't want his brother to see it."

"Of course not. Poor, dear, Death! We thought we'd lost him, too, didn't we? I'm so glad that wasn't the case."

"Me too. So how long have you known the boys?"

"Oh, ever since they were bitty things. Heavens! We worked on their momma's teeth when she was just carrying Death. Couldn't believe it when she told me what she was gonna name that poor baby, though knowing her it wasn't really a surprise."

"What was she like?"

"You didn't know her?" The woman's voice took on a slightly suspicious tone. "Who am I speaking to? I thought you must be Death's wife . . . Madeline?"

"Death and Madeline are divorced. My name is Wren Morgan. Death's mine now."

The receptionist laughed suddenly. "You say that fierce."

"I mean it that way," Wren acknowledged, smiling at the phone.

"Good girl. Well, to answer your question, Adele Bogart was a free spirit and a bit of an eccentric. If she'd been born twenty years earlier, she'd have been running around barefoot at Woodstock with flowers in her hair. And Liam Bogart was very staid and respectable — a rookie cop and the son of a fire captain and one of the city's first lady DA's. But they were so in love. They were just goofy with it. He never could refuse that woman anything."

"I'd guessed that by the fact that their sons were named Death and Baranduin," Wren said. "I wish I could have met them."

"Oh, sweetie. So do I. It killed me, hearing that little Randy was gone."

SEVEN

The broad expanse of asphalt, baking under the hot sun, sent heat shimmers radiating back toward the pale blue, cloudless sky. The smell of tar in the air reminded Death of other summer days on other tarmacs — the airfield at Langley Air Force Base, the pathways at Six Flags over St. Louis, running laps on the high school track.

Any of them would have been preferable to this place. He leaned against his Jeep, the metal hot through his T-shirt, and tried breathing exercises to drive the spots from before his eyes. The sensation of being short of breath was a familiar one now, but he didn't know this time if it was caused by the hot, humid summer air in his damaged lungs or by the band that seemed to be constricting his heart.

Before him stood the old Brewmaster's Widow. He was standing in the parking lot where the paramedics had tried to save his brother. He held up the pictures that Duror had printed out for him, mentally placing the firefighters and their rigs in the spaces they had occupied.

Here was the door where the firefighters had entered. The same door from which Rowdy Tanner had emerged with Randy's body across his shoulders. The paramedics had taken his burden and laid Randy down *here.* Forty-one's engine and squad were there, 27's farther down. The ALS backed in here to load Randy for his last ride to the ER, leaving behind a helmet that was not his.

Death didn't know what he'd expected to accomplish by coming here. There was nothing left now. It was just an expanse of broken asphalt, a few sad tufts of scraggly weeds poking through here and there. He crouched down on the spot where Randy's body had laid, bowed his head and closed his eyes, as if somehow that would help him feel close to his brother again. When his grandparents died and his parents were killed, he had felt as if they were walking around beside him, especially during the time leading up to the funerals, but also for months afterward. Even now, sometimes, often when he was at his lowest points, he would get a sense of presence, as if one or another of them had entered the room. He'd think he heard the echo of his father's laughter, or catch a faint scent like the ghost of his mother's perfume.

With Randy, that had never happened. Not once.

So caught up was Death in his thoughts that he didn't hear the quiet motor pulling up beside him. A slamming car door pulled him from his reverie just before a strange man spoke.

"Sir? Are you all right?"

He looked up to find himself the focus of a concerned City of St. Louis police officer.

"Oh, uh, yeah." How to explain himself? It was his grandmother's voice that spoke in his head, dry and wry, repeating a phrase he'd heard from her a thousand times. *Best go with the truth, dear. It's the easiest story to keep straight.*

"My brother was a firefighter. He died in a fire here last summer. I just wanted to see where it happened."

"You mean Bogie?" And, of course, the cop knew him. Cops and firefighters worked together and often hung out together. "You must be Death."

"Yeah, that's me." He climbed to his feet with some difficulty and offered the other man his hand. "Pleased to meet you. Were

107

you a friend of Randy's?"

"Everybody was a friend of Bogie's. And boy, have we ever heard stories about you."

"Oh, I wouldn't believe half of them," Death laughed ruefully. "Especially the ones that make me look bad."

The cop snorted derisively. "According to your brother, you walk on water."

"Now that I really wouldn't believe! So, uh, listen, were you here the day it happened?"

"No, I was off that day. Out on the river with my family. I heard about it on the radio, before they released his name, and then I heard through the grapevine that it was heart failure. I figured it was probably Lakeland at 18's. Good old guy, but he does love his barbecue. Never in a million years would I have pegged it as your brother. I had no clue the kid had heart problems."

"Yeah, neither did we." Death sighed and glanced around at the brick and concrete landscape, unforgiving in the summer's heat. "See, the thing is, there's something weird going on."

"Oh?"

"Randy's captain drew it to my attention. He was wearing a badge with another firefighter's number on it when he shouldn't have had any badge at all. He'd broken the back on his own that morning. Also, the helmet that got left behind where they were working on him wasn't his. It matches the wrong badge." He took out the close-up Duror had given him and showed it to the officer.

"Okay, that's — seriously weird. What do you think happened?"

"I don't know. That's what I'm doing here, looking for anything that might give me some clue as to what really went down. I was wondering — is there any way I could get inside? I'd like to see the spot where he collapsed."

"That's not something I could help you with. It's private property and locked up tight to try to keep kids and vagrants out. There are windows broken out and obviously you could climb through one, but I'd have to arrest you for trespassing if you did."

"Yeah, I was afraid of that. Do you happen to know who owns the building?"

"No, but I could maybe find out for you." The cop went back to his car and Death waited impatiently. It was only a few minutes before he returned, but it felt like hours.

"We have contact information on file, in case something happens and we need to get a hold of the owners. The contact listed is for an attorney." He gave Death a blank ticket with a name and phone number on the back. "The actual owner is a descendant of the Einstadt family, through a granddaughter. He and his wife live in one of those big, old houses across the road. His name's Grey. Andrew Grey."

The television was on, but Andrew wasn't paying any attention to it. The noise was a constant in the background, but, if asked, he couldn't have said if it was a game show or a soap opera or a sporting event. The room he was in was beautiful, but it felt like a prison. His breath hitched in his throat and he hauled himself up, leaning heavily on his cane, and stumbled awkwardly to the window.

His fingers felt thick and uncooperative and he had to struggle with the latch for several seconds before he was able to loosen it and open the sash. The air that came in was hot and moist and carried with it the scents of a city in the summertime: dust and hot asphalt and car exhaust. But they were familiar smells and he settled into a nearby chair and breathed them in. He couldn't even remember the name of the maid who made his bed and brought his meals and his medicine. It seemed to surprise her that he even tried, and that just felt wrong.

He was married — had been more than once, apparently, and his wife was a tiny beauty named Alaina. He'd written it down on a napkin and kept it in his pocket for when he forgot. She was kind and gentle, solicitous of his every need and her presence filled him with a rage that frightened him even more because he could not justify it. He *knew* she'd done something reprehensible. He just couldn't remember what.

There was a memory there, hovering just at the edge of his subconscious, dark and tantalizing and constantly out of reach.

His doctor — another name he couldn't remember — was leaving the house through the front door. He locked it behind him and started down the brick path, but stopped when a gray vehicle drew up on the street and parked beside the lilac bushes, just out of Andrew's line of sight. Andrew heard a car door slam, and then a conversation drifted up to him where he listened, unseen behind the curtains of his second-floor bedroom.

"Excuse me, but are you Andrew Grey?"

"Gregory. Dr. James Gregory. I'm Mr. Grey's physician. Mr. Grey is indisposed, I'm afraid."

"I see," there was disappointment in the tone.

"May I ask what business you have with Mr. Grey?" There was a pause and then the doctor continued. "In addition to being his physician, I'm Andrew's brother-in-law."

"Oh, right. Well, I was hoping to ask him for permission to go through the old brewery building. I called the attorney's office that the police have for a contact, but his secretary said he's in court today and won't be available until at least Friday. I've made an appointment to see him, but I knew the Greys lived right over here, so —"

"Well, Mr. Grey won't be able to help you. He had a stroke a little more than a year ago now and is still completely incapacitated."

"I'm sorry to hear that."

"You know, there's nothing in that old building worth seeing anyway. I've been inside myself a time or two. Just a lot of dirt and rubbish."

"Yeah, I can imagine. But I'd like to see it just the same."

"For heaven's sake, why?"

"Because it's where my brother died."

"You know, most people, and I think, especially most attorneys, would be really alarmed to learn their secretary had made them an appointment with Death." The attorney who acted as contact for the Grey family was a charismatic man in his mid-fifties, with white hair and a light scruff of beard. The grin he gave them seemed genuine and Death wondered if it was or if he was simply a skilled actor.

Death offered a polite if insincere smile for the inevitable joke about his name. "Most people, but not you?"

"Actually, I've been expecting to hear from you. This thing with the helmet and the badges is just bizarre. Do you have any ideas about what might have happened?"

"No, at this point I just, um, I'm sorry but — you know about the confusion with the badges and Randy's helmet?"

"Oh, sure. I read it in the paper."

Death and Wren exchanged a glance. "In the paper?" Wren asked.

"Yeah. This morning. Didn't you know?" The attorney took a folded newspaper from one of the drawers in his desk and offered it to Death across the expanse of polished wood that made up the surface.

Franklin Barrows of Barrows, Fine, and Innsbruck, had the corner office on the thirty-first floor of an upscale office building less than three blocks from the Gateway

113

Arch. The walls were a light shade of sage green, the floor was marble or a close approximation, and heavy, cream-colored drapes in an expensive weave let sunlight in through the floor-to-ceiling windows that made up an entire wall.

Death took the paper, noted that it was opened to the fourth page of the metro section, and read the headline.

"MYSTERY SURROUNDS FIREFIGHTER'S UNTIMELY DEATH"

"What the hell?"

Wren leaned in to read it with him, her cheek pressed against his upper arm.

"They've got everything," Death said. "The whole story. Even things I only just figured out, like the fire safety day picture and the helmet badge left at the scene."

"It must have been the photographer you talked to yesterday, don't you think?" Wren asked.

"I didn't tell him all of this. I just asked him —"

"You asked him about the fire safety day picture and then you asked for a copy of the picture with the helmet. All he had to do was look at those two pictures and he'd have gotten an idea what was going on.

114

Newspaper people are good at that sort of thing. They're kind of like detectives too." She rubbed her small hand across his taut shoulder muscles. "Is this a bad thing?"

Death thought about it, sighed. "No, I guess not. There's really no reason for people not to know. It just seems, I dunno, like an invasion of privacy. He was my brother. It's my business. It isn't a curiosity for the world to goggle at."

"Nothing that can be done about it, I'm afraid," Barrows offered. "It's a legitimate news story. Freedom of the press and all that, you know?"

Death set the paper on the desk, careful to put it down gently because he felt like slamming it down. "I know."

"I think, though, that maybe there is something I can help you with?"

"Yeah, right. I'm sorry. We're taking up your valuable time."

"I'm not worried about that. I have more than an hour until my next appointment. But I do know what you came here to ask me."

"Oh?"

"Yes. James Gregory called me. He tells me you'd like a chance to look through the Einstadt Brewery building."

"Yes, if it would be at all possible. I'd like

to see where my brother died."

"It's a big old monstrosity of a building. Do you think you'd be able to find the right place?"

"Yes, sir," Death said with certainty. "The fire department has floor plans for all the major structures in the city, and the fire-fighter who was working with Randy when he collapsed went over the brewery plans with me. He was able to show me exactly where it happened."

"I see. Well, Dr. Gregory encouraged me to tell you no. He's concerned that you could get injured in there and sue Mr. Grey. Now, he has no actual say in the matter, nor, indeed, does his sister, Mrs. Grey, but I have to admit that his objection has merit."

"I promise you, that isn't going to happen. And I'd be happy to sign a waiver, absolving the Grey family of any responsibility in the event that I were to be injured."

"So would I," Wren added.

Barrows gave her a slightly patronizing smile. "Oh, my dear! That dirty old building really is no place for a young lady such as yourself."

Wren smiled a brittle little smile and fingered her necklace and Death hastened to intervene.

"Wren is as tough, as capable, and as

116

intelligent as anyone I've ever known. Her participation, in any endeavor, is invaluable."

"Huh." Barrows shrugged. "Very well. Suit yourselves."

"So you'll give us permission to go in?"

"Well, I can't very well justify just handing over the keys to you," the attorney said. "But, if you'll both sign waivers as you've offered, I'd be willing to take you in myself after I finish at the office today."

"Could you do that? We'd appreciate it."

"Sure. I'd be glad to. Actually, truth be told, I'm awfully curious about the helmet and badge thing myself."

EIGHT

"Did you know that I'm psychic?" Wren asked.

"Oh, really?"

They were back at Randy's, sharing a pizza for lunch and passing the time until they could meet Barrows that evening. Wren had set the table with Death's grandmother's best china and tossed a salad in her crystal salad bowl because, as she'd explained, "Things are meant to be used, not hoarded. You save them and save them for a special occasion and in the end they wind up sitting idle in a cabinet forever. Life is a special occasion, sometimes we just need to remember that."

Death had been brooding since they came back from the attorney's office and she was trying to lighten his mood. "Really. Do you want me to tell you what you're thinking?"

"Try me."

"You're thinking about the newspaper

story. You're annoyed they wrote about Randy, but you're most upset because you think they must have talked to his friends — the guys at the station and maybe Sophie Depardieu. It hurts to think that Randy's friends would gossip about him to a reporter, and you're annoyed that they didn't ask you first or even give you a heads up."

"Nah."

"Nah? Really?"

"Okay, so I was at first. But then I reread the article. They actually don't have everything, and they would have if they'd talked to Captain Cairn or any of the guys at 41's. For example, they said Randy was wearing the wrong badge when he came out of the fire, but there's nothing about how he shouldn't have had a badge on at all. They talked to someone at HQ, but there's actually nothing in here they couldn't have gotten from public sources or their own archives. Even the stuff about how we lost Mom and Dad and the fact that Randy was my last remaining relative. There were stories in the paper back at the time of the accident plus, of course, the obituaries. All they had to do was search the name Bogart. It's not like there's gonna be *another* Baranduin Bogart who had a brother named Death."

"So if it's not the newspaper article, what is it? You've been a grumbly old bear all morning."

"I'm sorry."

"Don't apologize! If you feel like a grumbly bear you're allowed to act like a grumbly bear. I just don't want you to *feel* like that." That drew a smile from him.

"I suppose it is the article a little," he admitted. "It's my brother and my mystery and my tragedy. I'm jealous about who I share it with. I'm kicking myself for not being more circumspect when I spoke with Duror. And, of course, I'm also kicking myself for being so caught up in all this that I didn't even notice your necklace before. I wonder if Barrows will ever have any idea how close he came to losing an eye this morning."

Wren cackled a laugh.

"That depends on if he talks down to me again. Do you like it?"

"Very clever."

Her necklace was a simple length of black cord strung with polished rocks, with a "Y" of rough wood as the focal point, accentuating the gentle rise of her breasts. The effect was very primitive and artsy and it was only when he really looked at it that Death saw it for what it was. "So I see the handle and the ammo, where's the sling?"

"I've got it hidden in my bra," she grinned.

"Oh." He gave her a sideways, speculative look. "Maybe I should strip search you, just to make sure it's hidden well enough."

"You think that might be a good idea?"

"Well, you said you wanted to improve my mood, didn't you? I think that just might do the trick."

In Missouri, in the high summer, twilight lasts forever. A low sun shone in from across the river, gilding the western faces of the buildings even as it lengthened their shadows, long fingers of night reaching out to grasp the city. Light and dark stood in stark contrast. The Brewmaster's Widow faced north. Death and Wren were parked near the entrance, caught in the never-never land between sun and shadow, waiting for Barrows to arrive as promised.

"I'd rather we could go in alone and search the place without an audience," Death said. "But I suppose this is better than nothing."

He was carrying a flashlight and a measuring tape and Wren had a good camera. Death had considered taking a crowbar in with them, in case the fire crew that overhauled the building had scattered debris in their way. With Barrows along, though, he'd decided against it. If they were blocked, he'd deal with it when it happened.

A busy road circled past to the west, between the brewery and the Mississippi. Shading his eyes with his hand, Death tracked a late-model, expensive sedan as it turned onto the web of smaller roads that lay like a net around the neighborhood. He lost it for a few seconds behind the line of tall, Italianate mansions that included the Grey home, and then it came down the street toward them and turned into the lot to park beside his Jeep.

Barrows had changed into jeans and a polo shirt and he got out of his car with his alarm fob in his right hand and a bulky ring of keys in his left. Death approached him with his hand outstretched and Barrows beeped his car locked and pocketed the key before coming to meet him and shake his hand. "Sir," Death said. "Thanks for coming. I appreciate this, really."

"Glad to do anything I can to help. Ms. Morgan," he acknowledged Wren and nodded toward the building. "Shall we?"

The heavy entry door was made of wood, gray and splintering, with paint that was bubbling and peeling away. The lock and handle were heavily rusted iron. The lock had been broken recently, probably by the fire department the previous summer, and a shiny new hasp and padlock were fitted above the handle. Barrows searched through his keys. He had probably twenty on the ring, each encased in a colored cover and labeled in a neat and impossibly tiny script. A tag on the ring read, "Grey."

"We have a few clients who have property we're responsible for. We keep each client's keys on a separate ring," he explained, trying one key after another. "Normally, that's not a problem, but Andrew Grey has vast holdings and right now I'm in charge of them all."

"You said his wife doesn't even have a say?" Wren asked, curious and dismayed.

"Ah, no." He found the right key, pulled the padlock off, and pushed the door open. "I can't go into details, naturally. Attorney/client privilege. But it's been in the paper, so it's hardly a secret. The current Mrs. Grey is Andrew's fifth wife. She's considerably younger than he is. He has a living will and according to the terms, as long as he is medically incapacitated, I am responsible for administering his estate."

The door opened into a cavernous chamber. Skylights pierced a roof that arced twenty feet or more overhead. Tall, narrow derring windows lined the walls on the north and south. The west wall, which separated the malt house from the grain silos, was blank. Shaded from the sunset, the brewery lay in an eerie twilight.

It had been a surprisingly elegant building. The ceiling was pressed tin, with traces of color still clinging to the raised flower and scroll motif. A balcony surrounded by wrought-iron railings ran around the perimeter of the room. The staircase leading up to it rose in a graceful curve. Huge pipes protruded from the floor. A trio of massive vats crouched in one corner like overgrown mushrooms and the room was littered with obscure, fantastic machinery, all wheels and cranks and spigots worked in rusting iron.

The firefighters' presence was still evident in the paths trampled through the heavy grime on the floor. Where the floor had been washed clean by high-pressure fire hoses, blue and white decorative tiles showed. The paths the water had taken stood out like dry river beds, snaking across the filth. Barrows wrinkled his nose.

"I came in here right after the fire," he said. "I had to see the damage and decide what to do about it. Whether it was worth filing a claim with the insurance company and if it was bad enough to warrant demolishing the building. In the end, I decided not to file. Given the state of the building before the fire, it would be hard to put a monetary value on the amount of damage done. The rates would have gone up because we'd filed. Plus, with the fire being arson, I didn't want the police to think I was trying to burn it down for the money."

"The fire was arson?" Wren asked, glancing around. She looked at the place, Death knew, with an auctioneer's eye, seeing salvageable antiques among the junk and estimating possible uses for the building.

"Yeah, honey," Death said. "Didn't you know?"

"I don't remember anyone ever mentioning it. Did they find out who set it?"

"No. They figure it was probably just some kids looking for a thrill. It's still an open investigation."

"You said you knew where your brother . . . ?" Barrows' voice trailed off; he was unwilling to finish the sentence.

"Back here," Death said, nodding and gesturing toward the warren of offices and storage rooms at the east end of the building. "Randy and Tanner were searching the building."

In the center of the east wall a single door, wooden with a frosted-glass window, hung open in a doorway that had once held two. They passed through and the feel of the building changed.

It was darker back here. They were standing in a long hall with only a single small window at the far end. The walls were different — smaller bricks in a more ornate pattern — and the stone and tile floor of the big room gave way to hardwood, dried and cracked and splintering with age. Charred bricks made strange designs on the walls and the ceiling was dark with soot. Even all these months later, the smell of smoke hung heavy in the air.

Death pointed out the burn marks on the walls. "See that? That's arson. Someone sprayed accelerant over the walls. Brick doesn't burn, of course, but the fire from the accelerant burning off darkened it." Doors opened on either side of the hall, some with windows and some without. It smelled of dust and age and mold and, Death thought, ever so faintly yet of beer.

He led the way past the first three doors and stopped at the second door on the right.

"This is where they split up. They thought they heard a sound but they couldn't decide where it had come from. Rowdy went to the left, into that storage room, and Randy went in here."

They entered the room and the first thing Death noticed about it was the cold. The rest of the factory was stuffy in the summer evening, but here it was fifteen to twenty degrees cooler than it had been outside. Wren shivered in her light cotton blouse but took out her camera and began snapping pictures. Barrows rubbed his upper arms and retreated to the hall to wait.

This had been an office once. At one time the desk in the middle of the room had probably been expensive and imposing. Now it tottered off-kilter, with one leg broken off shorter than the others. A many-paned window in the wall behind it was intact. Death crossed the room and checked to see if it had been opened recently. An old bird's nest clung to the outside of the sill and the lock was rusted closed.

The floor in the back, right-hand corner had apparently decayed at some point and been replaced with plywood. It had been done long enough ago that the plywood was gray with age and buckled at the edges. Rust-ringed nails held it down, gleaming in the low light.

Death looked around for some mark or track or sign that Randy had been there; that Randy had died there. There was nothing. The floor was swept clean, any tracks had been obliterated and only a light, even coating of dust remained. The bookcase that had fallen on Randy and burned his body so badly was gone. The other firefighters had dragged it away, chopped it up and destroyed it vindictively.

The only thing out of place was the strange, preternatural chill that seared his lungs and settled in his bones.

He returned to the warmth of the hall, Wren tagging along behind him, there if he needed her but letting him take the lead. He dropped one arm around her shoulders for a brief hug. Her skin was smooth and soft and cold under his palm and he thought of death and held her closer and for a few seconds longer than he otherwise might have. Two feet farther down the hall he opened the door to the room Rowdy had searched. It was a store room, darker and dirtier than the office had been. He didn't go in, but shone the light from his flashlight along the floor and around what he could see of the interior.

"Rowdy said the floor isn't safe in here. He could feel it trying to give beneath him when he was searching." The room was crowded with shelving units, many of them still stacked with crates holding dusty bottles. A few of the bottles had been broken and the beer and mold smells were stronger in here. Dust had begun to fill them in again, but large footprints were still visible in the grime on the floor, full prints going in, but only the front half of the boots visible returning.

Death crouched to study them more closely. "He went in carefully, ran back out when he heard Randy's alarm. That's why only the toes of his boots touched, and his stride was longer coming out than going in. It fits what he told me." He paced down the hall to the end, trying two more doors as he passed, then came back and looked briefly into the rooms between the office and the factory floor.

"I don't want to rush you," Barrows said hesitantly, eyeing the doorway to the office. "But —"

"It's okay." Death clipped the flashlight to his belt and scrubbed his palms against his jeans. "I think we've seen everything there is to see here."

They returned to the factory floor in silence. Barrows crossed it at such a fast walk that he was almost running. When they were outside again and he turned the key in the lock, he took a deep breath. "So . . . do you think it's haunted then?"

"Haunted?"

"Yeah, um. I mean, I've never been one to believe in ghosts or anything, but they do say that haunted houses have cold spots. And that cold in there is like nothing I've ever felt before. Walking into that room is like stepping into a refrigerator. I've gotta be honest. I'm just a little bit freaked out here."

Death looked around, at the darkening sky and the abandoned buildings that made up the rest of the brewery complex and the white, Italianate mansion across the road where the Einstadt heir lived. He slipped his hand into Wren's.

"You and me both, pal. You and me both."

Wren waited until they were in Death's Jeep and well away from the brewery to speak. The vehicle was hot, the leather seats almost to the point where they would burn bare skin, but, for once, she welcomed the warmth, soaked it in. The cold in the room where Randy died was uncomfortable and creepy. "Did you find what you were looking for?" she asked Death finally.

He glanced toward her, one eyebrow raised. "You think I was looking for something?"

"I know you were. I just don't know what."

He smiled slightly and, without looking,

reached across the vehicle to brush a wild lock of red hair from her cheek to tuck it behind her ear.

"You know my mom was an English literature professor. Dad was a cop and Grandma was a district attorney, but Mom was the detective in the family. She taught me everything I know. Have you ever heard of the Kipling Method?"

Wren wrinkled her nose in thought. "Well, I know who Kipling *was* . . ."

"It's a method for gathering facts, called that because of one of his poems. It's also known as 'five W's and an H'."

"Oh! You mean 'who, what, when, where, why, and how'? Cameron calls it the 'journalistic approach'."

"Bingo! Well, I've been applying that to the problem of Randy's badge and helmet. The 'what' is switching Randy's helmet for another and pinning a counterfeit badge on him. The main questions I want answers to are 'who' and 'why,' but I can't see any easy way of finding them. So instead I tackle the other questions — 'when,' 'where,' and 'how.' Now, according to Captain Cairn and the guys at 41's, Randy left the station without a badge. I presume he was also wearing his own helmet, though I can't actually verify that at this point. None of the guys were looking at his helmet. He was in the truck with Rowdy until they arrived at the fire and they went in the building together. The only time he was alone and the only place he was alone was for three minutes in that room where he died."

"Have you considered that," Wren hesitated, treading lightly. "Have you considered that maybe Rowdy was, I don't know, mistaken somehow or . . . ?

"Or involved?" Death asked, glancing her way. "Yeah, of course I've considered it. I just can't see it though. Rowdy and Randy had been friends for years. Randy was Rowdy's best man at his wedding and his kids' godfather, even though we were never very religious. And I can't think of any motive, nothing. No reason for him to have done it. But, yeah, it has occurred to me. That's why I looked at the room he was searching, checked his footprints. It checked out. So, for now anyway, I'm going to rule him out."

"Okay, but if he didn't do it, then that means someone else had to have. That's what you were looking for, isn't it? Some sign that someone besides Randy and Rowdy was in that building."

"Yup."

"And did you find it?"

"Maybe." They came to a stop sign. Death was taking a leisurely route back to Randy's house, avoiding the city's main arteries in favor of small side streets that traversed residential neighborhoods. "What do you think of Barrows' theory? Is my little brother haunting the room where he died?"

"The brewery isn't haunted," Wren said certainly without even stopping to think about it.

Death gave her a sideways, speculative glance, returned his eyes forward, and paused before speaking again. "So you don't believe in ghosts?"

"You know I do." She rubbed her arms, remembering the cold in the room and other rooms, some cold and some not, that had made her shiver. "I've seen too many things, and heard things and *felt* things. People who think they're smarter than I am or more sophisticated than I am can laugh at me all they want to. Yes, I do believe in ghosts."

"But?"

"*But* that room wasn't haunted." Death just nodded encouragingly and waited for her to continue. "Most of the auctions we do are estate auctions. You're going into houses where dead people lived, sometimes for years, sometimes for their whole lives.

And sometimes they're the houses where they died. You go into their houses and you go through their stuff, you drag it out into the yard and you sell it off to strangers. And it doesn't happen very often, but sometimes — they just don't like it very much."

She looked over to see if he was laughing at her. He wasn't so, emboldened, she continued. "Sometimes it's things moving by themselves, or disappearing just to show up again somewhere you've searched a thousand times. Sometimes it's noises, footsteps where no one's walking, or indistinct voices in the next room when you know you're alone. It's rare to actually see anything, but the one thing that you almost always notice is a feeling. A presence, like someone walked into the room with you. There was this one house once, nothing fancy, just a little, run-down, two-bedroom bungalow with a fenced yard and an old utility shed. Sam and Roy forbade anyone from going in alone. Not that anyone wanted to."

"Mmhm." He turned down a narrow alley. They had come up the street behind Randy's without her realizing it and now he pulled up and parked behind the garage. He turned the key off and opened his door, but paused before getting out. "And in the brewery? In the room where Randy died? Did you feel a presence there?"

"All I felt was cold," she said. She got out of the Jeep and circled to meet him at the front of the vehicle.

"What about here?" he persisted. "Do you feel anything here?"

She hesitated. "Not in the house," she said. "Or, at least, not all the time. And nothing bad. I got out your grandmother's good dishes today because I felt like she wanted me to. I could have been imagining it, of course."

"Maybe. Maybe not. So, if not in the house, then where?"

Wren shrugged, sheepish. "I probably sound like some kind of loon."

Death grinned. "That's never turned me off before," he said, and ducked away from her playful punch. "No, but seriously. If not in the house, then where?"

She walked over and stood beside the garage. "I feel like there's a dog in the yard. A female. She's about yay high," she held her hand out, palm down, about two feet off the ground. "And she wants me to pet her."

Death went over and put his arm around her shoulders. "Her name was Lady. She was my grandpa's Dalmatian. She lived to be almost twenty and she's buried right next to where you're standing. Come on in the house. I know a nice little Italian place that delivers. We can order dinner and I'll tell you what I saw in the Einstadt Brewery."

NINE

Wren downloaded the pictures from her camera to her laptop while Death called the restaurant and ordered their dinner. She let him order for her — he knew the establishment and he knew what she liked. That secretly delighted her — that he paid close enough attention to know what she liked. When he came back, she was studying the photos again. "What do you see?" he asked.

She shrugged. "You're looking for a way someone could have gotten into and out of the room quickly without being seen by Rowdy or the guys from the other station."

"Yeah. I'd thought maybe someone could have hidden in the room itself, then waited until Rowdy took Randy out to leave. They'd have had all the time in the world, then. But there's nowhere in the room to hide."

"Could they have simply used the door and hidden in one of the other rooms?"

"Possible but unlikely. The doors were all pretty stiff when I tried them. The hinges rusted and grime built up on the floor behind them. You didn't go all the way down the hall, but there's a cubby at the end with a stairway to the second floor. It's blocked with junk that, judging by the dirt, has been there for decades."

"Right. Okay, so . . ." Wren looked back at the pictures she'd taken. "The window's out."

"Rusted closed. And that bird's nest looks like it's been there for years."

"I did notice that the floor was too clean. I don't know if that's significant, though. Could the fire department have done that? If there was an investigation into Randy's death, maybe?"

"I doubt it, but we'll ask Captain Cairn. Notice anything else about the floor?" he hinted.

Wren frowned. "Do you mean the plywood?"

Death reached over her shoulder, found a picture that showed the square of plywood in the corner, and brought it up. "Why is there a piece of plywood in the corner?"

"I figured the floor got damaged at some point and they pulled up the broken boards and stuck a piece of plywood over the hole."

"Sounds reasonable. But, tell me, what do you think this room was used for?"

"It was an office. There was a desk."

"Whose office?"

"Somebody important. That desk is beyond salvage, unfortunately, but it was a really nice piece of furniture at one time. It was solid oak, did you see? And those scraps on the floor? That was a leather inlay. I'd say it was the office of the head of the company, or at least a vice president."

"Right. So you've got this successful brewery. Do you let the big shot's office floor deteriorate to the point where it caves in and then patch it with cheap plywood?"

"No, of course not. It must have been done after the brewery closed."

"When?"

Wren turned to blink at Death in bemusement. "You say that like you think I should know."

"Think about it. You've read the same articles about the history of the brewery that I have."

She went over it in her mind. The factory was built in 1873 to replace a smaller building a few blocks away. Business was booming, and they built the main malt house and the family mansion at the same time. They expanded it in 1897 and again in 1908. It operated until Prohibition passed in 1919, then Aram Einstadt locked the doors and walked away. He died three years later and, by the time Prohibition was repealed, there was no one in the family interested in re-opening the business. That's why people started calling it the Brewmaster's Widow. They said he'd been married more to the brewery than he had to his wife. Some of the other buildings were sold off or rented out for other purposes, but the malt house has been sitting idle ever since.

"So when did someone slap a piece of plywood over a hole in the president's office floor?"

"You think it was done recently? They just used an old piece of plywood so no one would notice?"

"No, it was done several decades ago at least. There's dirt built up in the cracks between it and the normal floorboards. Someone put it there for a specific reason."

"So what do you think the plywood is covering? Is there something in the hole in the floor?"

"You could say that. I think it all ties together, the company president's office, the plywood, and the fact that the room feels like a refrigerator."

"Aaaannndd . . . you're going to tell me

some day?"

He grinned. "I think there's an opening to the Cherokee Caves. It's the cold air coming up from the caverns that chills the room. They were used to keep beer cold, remember? I've heard of other brewing families having private tunnels from their houses to their breweries. It let them go to and from work in bad weather without going outside. There's probably a stairway with a door into the caves at the bottom. When they abandoned the brewery, they decided for some reason to cover the stairwell. Maybe they were afraid vagrants would get into the building through the tunnels and they wanted an extra layer of protection beyond just the door. And someone else disturbed it in the last year or so." He pulled up another picture and zoomed in close. "Look at the nails."

"They're new!" Wren realized.

"They're new and they're driven into existing nail holes left by rusty nails with larger heads. See the rings of rust around each one?"

Wren sat back and thought about it. "Okay, so there's a way that someone could have come into the room and switched Randy's helmet. But I still can't think of any reason for it. *Why?*"

141

"Yeah, that's where I keep getting hung up, too. The only thing I can think to do is find the person responsible and ask them, as forcefully as necessary."

"So what's our next move?"

"Well," he shifted, put his feet up on the coffee table, and shrugged. "It's not exactly legal and it's not exactly safe, but I know a way to get into the caves. Randy and I went in once when we were teenagers." He huffed a laugh, remembering. "If Dad had caught us, he'd have skinned us alive. Anyway, I think that's the next thing. I want to see if I can find that tunnel. I want to know exactly where it leads."

"It's time for your medicine, Mr. Grey."

Andrew Grey was sitting in the luxurious bedroom, next to the open window, breathing in the scents of hot asphalt and car exhaust that came in between the burglar bars. He had an open book on his lap, but he was staring at it more than he was reading it. He tried in vain to recall the maid's name. He knew he asked her every day and every day she gave him his pills and he swallowed them and slept. When he woke up, he'd forgotten again.

"I've never read this book," he said, bemused.

She took it from his hands, closed it, and set it aside. "You can read it in the morning."

She handed him a glass of water and he swallowed several mouthfuls. He handed the glass back and she set it on the tray she'd brought and reached past him to close the window. "Do you need me to help you to the bed to lie down?"

"I need to visit the restroom. Where's my cane?"

She gave him his cane and helped him rise. Slowly and awkwardly he made his way across the room and into the bathroom. When the door was closed behind him, he put his hand to his mouth and spit out the pills he'd tucked under his tongue.

When he'd been in the Corps, Death had run every morning, at least a mile. Before active duty, he'd run his way through basic training and before that he'd put in miles and miles on the high school track and baseball diamond. He'd never particularly enjoyed running, but it was a basic part of his fitness regimen so he did it. It was familiar — working the night's kinks out of his muscles with the early sun on his shoulders and the new day fresh in his lungs.

He stopped at the corner and leaned

against a street sign, pretending to check his phone and trying to look casual.

The first six weeks after he was released from the VA hospital, he'd had to carry an oxygen tank with him wherever he went and he'd needed to use the electric shopping carts to make it through one of the big retail stores. It had been one of the most humiliating experiences of his life. The breathing exercises he did faithfully had helped a great deal, but his doctors had warned him that he would never get back to full lung capacity, or even get close.

It had probably been a mistake to walk to the convenience store for coffee and donuts, but it was only three blocks. Mule-headed pride prevented him from driving that distance.

He pushed off the sign and crossed the street. As he did, an older-model, light-brown sedan cruised slowly past him, then sped up when he glanced in its direction. His gut tingled with unease, and he told himself not to be melodramatic. Sometimes Afghanistan, with its ever-present dangers, intruded on Missouri. He had a tendency to be hyper-alert and constantly schooled himself not to jump at shadows.

GasMart was on the corner. The light-brown car pulled into the lot and parked next to the building. As Death passed the gas pumps, the driver got out and they approached the glass door at the same time from opposite directions. The soldier in Death went on alert.

The figure coming toward him was short and slight, with a deep tan and dark eyes, a pencil-thin black mustache, and a baseball cap pulled low. In the warm, humid morning he was wearing a sweatshirt jacket that hung open over a heavy sweatshirt and a pair of leather gloves. The right pocket of his jacket hung lower than the left and swung like a pendulum. He'd left his car running.

Death instinctively tapped at his own hip, but of course he wasn't carrying. He'd left his gun back in East Bledsoe Ferry with Chief Reynolds. He was unarmed and winded and he was about to get caught in a convenience store robbery.

The best course of action would be to stay outside and call 911, but one glance at the robber and he knew that was out of the question. The man was watching him, his hand in his pocket. If he suspected Death was onto him, all he had to do was point and pull the trigger. A smart shooter wouldn't even take the gun out of his pocket first. If Death had had the option of running away, he'd have taken it. Shooting didn't necessarily mean killing, or even hitting. Most people weren't nearly as good a shot as they thought they were. But running was out of the question and, as close as they were, even a lousy shot was apt to be deadly.

He reached the door first and went inside, feigning unconcern and watching the gunman in the reflection on the door. In his mind's eye, he reviewed what he could expect to find in a convenience store that could be used for self-defense.

The counter was to the right. On his left were rows of shelves full of snack food and the odd assortment of groceries and sundries stocked by such establishments. The front wall was entirely windows with low shelves underneath displaying motor oil and engine additives. The back wall was taken up by a row of refrigerated display cases — soda pop and beer and sandwiches behind glass doors that served as poor mirrors.

At the end of the counter was a glass-sided grill full of breakfast sausages and hot dogs roasting on metal rollers. Beside the grill stood a condiment bar with salt and pepper, individual packets of relish and onions, and squeeze bottles of ketchup and mustard. Death crossed to it eagerly, grabbing the bottle of mustard, and turning to trade the faint reflection in the cooler doors for a direct view of the robber. As he did, the man pulled a .38 from his pocket and the teenage boy behind the counter screamed.

The gunman ignored the teenager and spun immediately toward Death, raising his gun as he turned. He held it in both hands, the butt of the gun cupped in his left hand and his right index finger tightening on the trigger. Death read his intention to fire in his body language and dropped, falling to his left as the shot rang out. The bullet passed over his right shoulder and shattered a cooler full of bottled beer.

He'd popped the top off the bottle as he fell and he came up spraying mustard at the gunman's eyes. The gunman ducked away reflexively, still firing, and bullets shattered random targets and took chunks out of the wall behind Death. Leading with the squirting mustard, Death aimed for his assailant's nose and mouth. The thick, yellow paste covered the man's airways and he clawed at his face in a blind panic, dropping his gun in the process.

"Stop or I'll shoot!"

Startled, Death and the gunman turned to the teenager behind the counter. In the heat of their fight they'd both forgotten him. He had a gun of his own, an ancient revolver he held in both hands. He was trembling so badly that the barrel danced like water drops on a hot skillet. The gunman gave up and ran for his car.

Death dropped the mustard bottle and leaned against the counter, trying to drag in enough air to calm his heartbeat. "Kid," he said, "just don't, okay?"

Wren came out of the bathroom toweling her hair dry. Randy's home had a central air conditioner that was ancient but well-maintained and efficient, causing her to shiver in the chilly room. She'd been thinking about Death and his theory about the caves.

If he was right about the Einstadt family having a private entrance to the brewery through the caves, it made sense that the passage would lead to the Einstadt mansion. It had been built at the same time as the brewery. It could have been situated over a natural entrance to the caves, or an artificial entrance could have been dug.

That didn't mean the current occupants were involved, or even that they knew the passage existed. Their end of the passage could exit in a remote location, such as a garden shed, and there could very well be some way to get from the passage to the main network of caves. In fact, there'd better be, or she and Death would find nothing on the clandestine caving expedition he was planning for later that day. If that happened, she had a strong suspicion they'd end up trespassing and making an unlawful entry into the brewery before the night was over.

Still, she was curious about Andrew Grey and his wife. With Andrew incapacitated and his wife effectively cut off — and wasn't that an alien concept? — they had no part in allowing Death to see the inside of the brewery. It would be transparently disingenuous of her to bring them a small thank you gift as a pretext to meet them and get a look inside their home. Back home in East Bledsoe Ferry it wouldn't be a problem. If she didn't know someone, she was certain to know someone who did. And then, of course, there was Cameron and his connections through the paper. He knew everybody and everything that went on in a three-county radius.

Cameron. Hmm. He had been the first to find the picture of Randy at the school fire safety day, even if none of them had seen the significance at the time. Maybe he could snoop long distance.

The easy chair Wren curled up in still smelled faintly of a delicate, floral perfume and she knew without asking that this had been Death's grandmother's favorite seat.

I hope you don't mind me sitting in your chair, she thought. *And I hope you don't mind me falling in love with your grandson. I'll give up the chair if you want me to, but Death's mine.*

The A/C unit cut off and the room warmed around her ever so slightly, but perhaps it was only coincidence. She fished her phone out of the pocket in her dressing gown and dialed Cam. He picked up on the second ring. "How's St. Louis? Have you knocked the Arch over yet?"

"Knocked over as in 'robbed it' or knocked over as in 'boom'?"

"Have you done either?"

"Well, no."

"Then what's the difference?"

"Ha ha. Very funny. Have I ever told you how much I love a comedian in the morning?"

"I think you may have mentioned something once or twice. Something about dry heat and telemarketers and little kids leaving jacks and plastic building blocks in the carpet?" Wren growled for form and Cameron laughed.

"So to what do I owe the pleasure of your grouchy attention this morning?"

"I was just calling to check in," she hedged. "How are my babies doing?" Cameron was watching Thomas, Wren's pugilistic old tomcat, and Lucy, the three-legged hound she'd adopted.

"They're fine. Why are you really calling?"

"What makes you think I have an ulterior motive?"

"Because I know you. I've known you for years. I think I can tell when you're working your way up to ask me for a favor."

Wren sighed. "I'm sorry, Cam. I don't mean to take advantage of you."

"You're not. We're friends, aren't we?"

"Of course."

"Well, that's what friends are for. What do you need?"

"I wondered if you knew anything, or could find out anything, about a man named Andrew Grey and his wife. I don't know her first name. He's the descendant of the Einstadt Brewing family and he owns the brewery where Death's brother died. He's not in control of it right now, though, because apparently he had a stroke about a year ago. His wife is his fifth wife. She's a lot younger than he is and he doesn't trust her to manage his business affairs. He has a living will and, because of that, there's a lawyer in charge of all his property. That's

151

pretty much all I know right now."

"I've never heard of them," Cam said, "but I'll be glad to see what I can find out. Is there anything particular you want to know?"

"No, not really. Nothing I can think of."

"Why do you want to know about them?"

"I don't know. It's not important. Just idle curiosity. You don't have to do it if you don't want to."

"Hello? Newspaper reporter? Idle curiosity is my SOP. Give me a day or two to see what I can dig up and I'll get back to you."

They chatted for a few more minutes before saying goodbye. Death had been gone a long time on his coffee and donut run and she was starting to get worried. As much as she respected his independence and his determination to overcome, as best he could, his disability, she knew he tended to push himself beyond his limits. She dressed quickly, pulled on a pair of sneakers, and was just heading out the front door when a police car pulled up in front of the house.

Her breath caught in her throat and her heart froze, but then the passenger door opened and Death got out.

A middle-aged police officer got out of the driver's side and came around the car.

He was laughing and Death looked both perturbed and amused. Wren waited on the porch as they made their way up the uneven walkway, the cop trying to take Death's arm and Death impatiently slapping him away. They came to a stop at the foot of the steps and Death looked up at her. "I have the worst luck in the history of the universe," he said.

"I wouldn't say that. The guy missed," the cop said.

"Who missed?" she asked, alarmed. "Missed what?"

"Your boyfriend here just walked into the middle of a convenience store robbery."

"Oh my God!"

"It's okay, sweetheart. He didn't get me."

"Not for lack of trying," the cop said.

Death glared at him. "I'm trying to re-assure her. You're not helping here."

"Oh. Right. Sorry. I was distracted by try-ing to figure out how I'm going to write up my report with a straight face."

Wren went down the steps, got Death by the arm, and dragged him back up onto the porch, as if by her side was the only place he could be safe. "Why is it going to be hard to write up your report with a straight face?" she asked.

"It's just not every day that a would-be

armed robber gets taken out by a badass former Marine armed with a bottle of mustard."

TEN

Wren, mindful of having asked a favor, convinced Death to let her call Cameron and give him the convenience store robbery story. He was as delighted with it as she'd thought he would be. "This is awesome! 'Mustard-Wielding East Bledsoe Ferry Resident Thwarts Armed Robber!' That's a front-page headline right there. Go over the description of the robber for me again."

Wren glanced at Death to see if he wanted to take that question, but he'd nodded off. She switched off the speaker and took the phone into the kitchen so as not to awaken him. "Police are looking for a Hispanic male, slight build, pencil mustache, mid- to late-forties, wearing jeans and a sweatshirt. He's driving a late-90s model Oldsmobile Cutlass, tan or light brown, and he has mustard all over his face." She giggled as she said it and Cameron laughed.

"Okay," she conceded, "so he's probably

washed that off by now."

"Can I get a closing quotation from the Colonel?"

"The Colonel? Oh, Lord! Colonel Mustard!" She slapped a hand over her own mouth to keep from waking Death. All at once her laughter morphed into tears and suddenly she was sobbing into the phone. Cameron didn't speak but waited her out. "That man was shooting at him. He tried to kill him, Cam! He could've *died* this morning!"

"I know, sweetie. Where is he? I thought he was there with you."

"He's in the living room. I'm in the kitchen. He fell asleep. He hasn't been sleeping well since we found out about the thing with Randy's badge. This fight this morning just took everything out of him. Poor thing! He didn't even get his coffee and donuts!"

"You could make him some."

"I don't have anything to cook with. I'd have to go to the grocery store. I guess I could — I probably should. I know the way now. I just hate to leave him alone."

"Will it take you long? Is it very far away?"

"No, there's a little store a couple of miles from here."

"He'll be fine. You could make him some

spudnuts. And maybe a nice hazelnut latte to go with them."

Wren laughed again, less hysterical now that the first storm of emotion had passed. "He's a Marine, Cam. He takes his coffee black and strong enough to double as metal polish."

"Blech. Well, to each his own, I guess. Listen, I haven't had much chance yet to look into the Greys. It's Jubilee Days this weekend and I had to cover the turtle races. I did find out that Andrew Grey is loaded. After Prohibition shut down the brewery, the family switched their focus to medicinal liquor they made at another location. From there, they went into pharmaceuticals. Andrew's worth billions. He had a stroke fourteen months ago. There was a big stink at the time because one of his ex-wives tried to get a court order to force his current wife to allow her access to him. It dragged on for several months before they eventually settled the matter out of court. There hasn't been anything in the news about him since. I'll go further back and see what else I can find after the weekend."

"Thanks! I appreciate it."

"I appreciate this great story! I'd say give the Colonel a kiss from me, but that would probably weird him out. I guess, instead, I'll just tell you to take care. Of *both* of you."

Wren and Madeline were two different women with different backgrounds and upbringings and outlooks on life. It wasn't at all fair to compare and contrast them and yet, sometimes Death couldn't help but do just that.

If the convenience store robbery had happened while he was married to Madeline, she would have gotten hysterical. It would have taken all his energy and focus to calm her down. She'd have blamed him for going into the store in the first place and she'd have been embarrassed by the police bringing him home and mortified by the publicity afterward. Wren had fussed over him. She'd settled him on the couch and brought him water and ibuprofen. She'd bragged about him to her hometown newspaper and when he'd fallen asleep, she'd braved the city traffic he knew she hated so she could shop for him.

He took another spudnut from the bowl on the table. Wren's lightly glazed potato donuts were dark brown on the outside and creamy on the inside with a silken texture. She refilled his coffee and he studied her face. He could tell she'd been crying after he fell asleep, but she'd hidden the traces as best she could with powder and makeup and he didn't call her on it. When Madeline abandoned him it had felt like the end of the world. Now it seemed the greatest blessing he'd ever received.

"We're going to need clothes to wear down in the cave," he said. "I didn't bring anything suitable and I'm betting you didn't either. We'll need jeans and sweatshirts, the older the better. This is apt to be a messy expedition. We should probably hit the thrift shops and see what we can find this afternoon."

"Oh. Okay." Her gaze drifted past him toward the bedroom. He knew she was thinking of the boxes full of Randy's clothes that were stacked in a corner, waiting to be delivered to charity. The idea of taking that step hurt his heart.

"Not today, okay?"

She glanced at him, caught his meaning, and nodded. "There's no hurry. You don't have to be the one to do it at all."

"I know." Death sipped his coffee. This had been his grandfather's place, the head of the table. Grandpa had always seemed decisive and authoritative — the man who knew what needed to be done and how to do it. Sitting in his chair now, Death tried to assume that mantle of capability, but he just felt like a little boy wearing oversized shoes. "I'd like to talk to Sophie Depardieu again, too," he decided. "I just —"

"You're just not completely convinced that it was really Randy?"

"I am," he said, "but . . . but there's so much about this that doesn't make sense. I know my brother's gone. I've accepted that. I have. I don't like it. I'm not happy with it. But that's the way it is. Captain Cairn and the other firefighters saw his body. Sophie saw his body. They even matched his dental records. I should let it go."

"But you never saw his body." Wren's voice was understanding and not patronizing. (Madeline would have been patronizing.) "You never even got to go to the funeral. Of course you're having a hard time finding closure."

"You know, I didn't come here on purpose." He read confusion in her eyes and tried to explain himself. "To St. Louis. After I was out of the Marines and out of the hospital. I knew I should come, visit my family's graves, talk to my brother's friends, make sure that everything was taken care of. But I didn't. I deliberately stayed away. I made excuses. The drive was too long. I couldn't spare the time. I couldn't afford the gas money. And, yes, there was some truth to all those things. But under all that, the bigger truth was that I didn't come back because it hurt so bad."

Without a word, Wren rose. She circled the table and planted herself on his lap, laying her head on his shoulder and wrapping him in her arms. He returned the embrace, resting his cheek on her soft, red hair. "Wherever I was, for months, I was always conscious of where St. Louis was. It sat like a bruise on the eastern horizon and I didn't dare look at the sunrise for fear of the pain."

"We'll go talk to Sophie again," Wren said. "We'll find out why he was wearing that badge. We can get a boat and go out on the river where they scattered his ashes. Have another service, if that's what you need. We'll do whatever we have to do and then, when it's all over, you'll come home with me and I'll do everything in my power to keep you from ever being sad like this again."

The thrift shop Death took them to was enormous — it had a footprint bigger than the courthouse back home. Half an hour of digging through tables of footwear and racks of used clothing netted a pair of battered sneakers for Death and faded jeans and tattered sweatshirts for both of them. Wren, whose job might include tromping through barns and outbuildings at any time, had a pair of old, worn work boots in her truck.

"I'm washing this stuff before we wear it," she informed him as they left, clothes stuffed into secondhand plastic bags.

"You know it's already been washed, right? And we're just going to get it dirty again."

"I don't care. I'm washing it anyway. With bleach. Especially those shoes."

Death had called Sophie to set up an appointment before they left Randy's house and, after they killed forty-five minutes at a fast-food joint, he drove them to the Medical Examiner's building.

There were handicapped parking spaces available and Death had a handicapped tag buried way in the back of his glove box, but Wren didn't say anything when he drove past and found an empty slot halfway across the lot. They met at the front of the Jeep and she put her arm around his waist, both offering herself as a crutch if necessary and anchoring herself to him. The city was so big, so crowded and so busy, that she felt at times as if she were drowning in it. She had an irrational fear of getting lost and never being found again.

The warm, humid morning had given way

to a cloudy afternoon. East winds brought in cooler air and the scent of rain. Lazy thunder rumbled on the horizon. "Is it going to complicate our caving if it rains?"

Death screwed up his face in dismay. "It could, if it rains hard. Parts of the caves are probably flooded anyway. We'll keep an eye on the weather. We might need to postpone it, but I'd like to at least get ready, so we can go as soon as it's safe." He held the glass door for her and they went into a small lobby. The young man at the reception desk looked up and his face lit up.

"Hey! It's the walking dead guy again!"

"You're hilarious," Death said drily. "I think Ms. Depardieu is expecting us."

The guy checked his computer. "Yup. You remember where her office is?"

"I think I can find it."

"OK, you can go on back. She might be a few minutes late. She's performing an autopsy, but she should be about finished." He pushed a button to unlock the double doors and Death led Wren down the hall to Sophie's office.

At her door, he paused. "We should probably wait out here."

Wren tried the door, found it open, and led him inside. "I don't think she'll mind if we come in and sit down." Death fidgeted and Wren looked around the office. "That's a nice picture of Randy."

"Yeah. She had a flat tire on the freeway and Randy and Rowdy stopped and changed it for her."

They'd only been sitting there for a couple of minutes when Sophie Depardieu came in. Death and Wren rose to meet her. "The door was open," Death began. "I hope you don't mind . . . ?"

She waved aside his concern, shook hands with Wren, and made a beeline for the coffee maker. The carafe was empty, so she started a pot, then circled her desk and sat down. Her hair was wet and she carried with her the scents of commercial disinfectant and blood and a hint of decay.

"Have you figured out what happened with Bogie's badge and helmet?" she asked.

"No, I haven't. Honestly, the more I find out, the less sense it all makes. That's why I wanted to talk to you again. I know you positively identified his body —"

"We did, Death." She reached across the surface of her desk to lay her hand over his. "I saw him myself. His captain saw him, his friends saw him, we matched his blood type and dental records."

"I just wondered if there were anything else you could do. Could you run his DNA maybe?"

"From what?"

"I'm sorry. I thought," Death floundered and Wren moved her chair closer to him, offering silent support. "I thought maybe you could check his DNA against mine. Just to be thorough, because of the mystery surrounding his death."

"But where would we get his DNA?" Sophie asked gently.

"Don't you keep blood and tissue samples when you do an autopsy?" She was shaking her head before he'd finished speaking.

"In cases of murder or suspected murder, sure. In death by natural causes, no. Bogie died of an aortic aneurysm. That's about as natural as it gets, barring death by old age."

"But he was so young, and in such good condition —"

"And that makes it unusual, but hardly unheard of, I'm afraid."

"Oh." He drooped a bit, disappointed.

"What if we could get some of his ashes?" Wren asked.

"They were scattered in the river," Sophie said. "I went to the memorial."

"But, maybe if we could find out what happened to the container they were kept in. There could still be trace amounts —"

"It wouldn't do any good." The assistant

medical examiner's voice was sympathetic, but definite. "You can't get DNA from cremains."

"Oh."

"If you'd like to," Sophie offered, "I can help you put in a request for the full autopsy report."

"I wouldn't like to," Death said, "but I think I need to, if only to be thorough."

"Of course. I've got a copy of the paperwork you'll need to fill out. When the report comes in, I'll go over it with you and answer any questions you may have."

It rained while they were in the Medical Examiner's office, but only a little. The sky was still overcast, but it was a pale, milky cloud cover. The first wave of storm clouds had moved on across the river to Illinois and toward the distant Atlantic.

Dressed in their new old clothes and carrying a bulging, red backpack, Death led Wren across the wet grass of a small park. A deep gully passed through behind the playground, its walls covered in thick underbrush. At the bottom of the gully ran a small stream. A high chain-link fence across the top of the opposite side protected the back lot of a large factory built of dark red brick, unmarked by any company logo or indication of purpose.

"Randy actually found this entrance," he told Wren. "I went in after him. If he'd gotten caught, I'd have been the one in trouble for not keeping an eye on him. I dragged him out kicking and screaming but then, about a week later when Grampa was on duty and Dad was out of town at a seminar, we grabbed a couple of flashlights and snuck back in."

He hunted among the brush and weeds until he found what he was looking for. Half buried under collected soil and greenery, a narrow stone staircase was cut into the side of the steep slope. He made his way carefully down the stairs, mindful of the slippery grass underfoot and confident that Wren was following. For a fleeting second he imagined leading Madeline down into this dark, dirty hole and almost laughed aloud.

"When these caves were open and being used, there was all kinds of stuff down here. The Lemp family had a swimming pool and a private theater in their section of the cave and there were biergartens and ballrooms and even a section that was designated as an air raid shelter during the Second World War, when they thought mainland America might see enemy air strikes. All those things would have taken labor to maintain, and they wouldn't have wanted the hired help using the same entrances and exits as the wealthy owners and paying customers. I figure this was a back door, an employee entrance for the waiters and bartenders and pool boys and whatnot."

Three-quarters of the way down to the bottom of the gully, the steps ended on a natural ledge about five feet wide at its widest point. Death turned left and pulled aside a curtain of hanging vegetation. A dark opening led down into the earth. It was a little wider than a normal door and tall enough for Wren to walk through upright, though Death would have to duck. On both sides of the opening, empty bolt holes bled long, red stains against a backdrop of pink and white limestone.

"There used to be an iron gate across here," Death said. "I imagine somebody probably stole it for scrap. It was rusted and broken down even back when we were here."

He clicked on his flashlight and ducked inside, turning broad shoulders to pass through the narrow opening. Inside, the path dropped sharply. The passage was claustrophobia-inducing for the first ten yards, then opened out. They stood in a roughly octagonal room formed by a strange marriage of karst topography and old brick-work. The natural stone ceiling ten feet above showed scars where stalactites had been broken off and an intricately laid brick arch framed another doorway at the opposite side of the room. Through the doorway, a staircase led down into darkness deeper than the reach of his flashlight beam. These steps were carved into the rock, soft edged and beginning to wear down from the effects of age and erosion.

In the middle of the room, Death paused to shine his light back on Wren's face, pale in the darkness below startlingly red hair. "Miss Morgan," he said formally, "allow me to welcome you to Cherokee Caves."

ELEVEN

On the surface, Wren had been too hot in the secondhand jeans and sweatshirt. Inside the cave, she was quickly glad she was wearing them. Even on the ledge outside, the cool air poured from the opening. The chill intensified the deeper they went. By the time they stopped in the octagonal room, she felt like she was in a refrigerator. Her sweat turned cold and clammy and she tucked her hands into her armpits and wished she'd thought to bring gloves.

As if he were reading her mind, Death slung the backpack down and rummaged through it, handing her one pair of work gloves and pulling a second, larger pair on his own hands.

"I brought along some caving gear," he said. "I didn't want to put it on outside because I didn't want anyone to figure out where we were going. I'm pretty sure we're trespassing, and I really don't want to get us arrested. I did leave an email message to Captain Cairn, telling him where we are and asking him to arrange a rescue party. If we're not out in four hours, it'll send automatically."

"Good thinking." She crouched at his elbow and peered into the backpack. "What else you got?"

"Hats." He took out two hard hats, each with an LED light, and set one on her head and one on his own. "This isn't exactly a wild cave, but that doesn't mean it's not dangerous. I've got extra batteries for both the headlights and the flashlights, a first-aid kit that I hope we won't need, water, protein bars, a rope. And," he reached back into the backpack and came out with a pad of paper, a detailed map of the area printed on translucent paper, a marker, a protractor, and a small device.

"We're mapping the cave?" Wren asked. "What's the gizmo?"

"A laser range finder with a built-in compass."

"Neat. You learn this in the Marines?"

"I learned lots of things in the Marines," he said, giving her a good-natured leer.

"Yes," she said, voice dry. "Believe me, I know."

He opened the drawing pad. There was a

rough sketch on a scrap of paper clipped to the corner of the top sheet. "I found this map of the caves online. It's not precise and it's not aligned with surface features, but I figured it could help us keep track of where we are. It's actually called the Lemp and Cherokee Caves. It's all one cave system, but part of it was heavily developed by the Lemp family."

The sketch showed a system of connected passages. There was a section on the left that looked, to Wren, like a highly stylized lobster. Linked to its right claw was a long, roughly rectangular loop. "Where are we now?"

"I can't say exactly. This entrance isn't on the map. The loop is no longer complete, though. The lower corner got lopped off by road construction when they built I55. That's here," he pointed it out on the sketch, "and here," he pointed it out on his street map. "I'd say that puts us somewhere near the juncture of the Lemp and Cherokee sections. The Einstadt Brewery is here, southeast of where we entered, so I'd expect an entrance to be somewhere on the far side of the loop. The thing is, though, it could be a completely separate passage. If so, it could connect to this caving system anywhere."

Death lifted his hard hat to scrub a hand

through his short hair. Wren could see the discouragement settling over him even as he spoke. "Hell, it might not be connected at all."

"It might not," she agreed. "But this was kind of a social hub for the brewing community, wasn't it? If he was going to all the trouble to build a passage from his home to his brewery, don't you think old Aram Einstadt would have wanted his own private entrance to the Beer Guys' Club, too?"

"I hope so. Anyway, I guess we won't know until we look, will we?"

He picked up the laser range finder and returned to the opening by which they'd entered. "How can I help?" Wren asked.

"You ever do any mapping?"

"No, afraid not."

"That's okay. Tell you what. Why don't you get a pen — there's a couple extra in my pack — and a sheet of paper. I'll call out my readings and you write them down for me, then I'll show you how to plot them on the map."

"We saw this when we were here before. Randy wanted to try to shimmy up it and I had to smack him down. That boy had more sense of adventure than self-preservation sometimes."

Death's chest hurt. He didn't know why — if it was the dank air in his bad lungs, strain from overexertion, crushing disappointment, or the weight of old memories, long forgotten and suddenly too vivid. He felt lightheaded, disconnected from these surreal surroundings. It was as if he were two different versions of himself, the carefree teenager who had explored these caves with his little brother and the worn-down ex-Marine, relying on the woman beside him much more than she probably knew.

"It's the central support of a freestanding spiral staircase," Wren said, bemused. "It looks like a spine. Or a giant corkscrew."

The rusting, rotting iron pole twisted up through a hole in the ceiling, climbing a brick-lined, cylindrical shaft. Here and there, the fin of a stair support remained, though all of the actual steps were gone.

"Why is there a freestanding spiral staircase here? It couldn't have been a very pleasant way to go in and out. You can see how tight the spiral was and how tiny the steps were. And that shaft it runs through looks positively claustrophobic."

"This chamber was the Lemp family's private theater. They had all the stalactites and stalagmites knocked down and replaced them with a stage and fancy decorations

174

made of plaster and wire." He pointed out a heap of trash in the middle of the floor. "The damp down here hasn't been kind to it. Anyway, from what I've read, the stage was tiny and there was no room backstage for the actors to change costumes between scenes. This staircase was here for them. Any time they had a costume change, they'd have to climb 34 feet to a dressing room on the surface, change as fast as they could, and then climb back down."

It was two and a half hours into the four-hour window Death had allowed for them to explore and they'd covered the whole of the caverns. It had been a strange journey, here where mankind had trespassed and faltered and gone. Nature was slowly reclaiming its own, but the scars of human interlopers remained.

The floors were mostly paved, worn steps and rusted ladders leading up and down when the elevation changed. The walls were sometimes rock and sometimes masonry. Moldy plaster and the sharp scent of limestone gave the air a musty, aged feel. The only illumination was what they brought in with them, and the circles of their lights fell randomly on stone and old brick and iron; a decaying playground within a living cave.

They'd waded through shallow water

where pale little fish swam. Water dripped in the distance somewhere and the high sound of liquid droplets echoed and carried, but the softer sounds of their voices and footfalls died unnaturally in the dank atmosphere.

Death found himself imagining the passages thronged with the lost and disillusioned ghosts of the old brewers, seeking and mourning their erstwhile splendor. Randy passed among them, his gaze distant, his face pale and his eyes as cold and dead as they had been in the autopsy photo.

They found the point nearest the Einstadt Brewery — almost underneath it, in fact — and then again a place where the caverns passed by within a few yards of the Einstadt mansion. They'd marked them on the map and searched the areas thoroughly, but there was nothing in either location to suggest there was or ever had been another passage. Wren lay a small, gloved hand on his right arm.

"Are you okay?"

Death responded by reaching his left hand over to take hers, anchoring himself to her. She was his rock, his light in the darkness, his hope for the future, and his reason to go on. Though he hid it as best he could, Death sometimes suffered from bouts of depression. It would be as if he'd hit a wall, and the depths to which his spirit sank frightened him. He wondered, sometimes, how he'd weathered his losses before he met Wren, and if he'd still be around had she not come into his life when she did.

"Why don't we rest here a bit?" she suggested. "We're not that far from the entrance. We've got plenty of time to get back and delete your email before Cap shows up with the cavalry."

The ache in his chest and his difficulty in speaking was telling him he needed to slow down. They found a relatively dry spot on a boulder that had fallen from the wall and snuggled close together. Death dug through his pack and brought out water bottles and protein bars and they ate and drank in silence. By the time the water was gone, he was feeling better. He snuck an arm around Wren's waist and gave her a squeeze.

"You wanna make out?"

She giggled, an incongruously bright sound in the oppressive atmosphere, and the cave warped it and tossed it back as a creepy, demented echo. "It *is* a terribly romantic spot," she agreed, "but I don't think I'd want to get naked down here. It feels too much like the walls are watching us."

"The walls," he said, "or something creeping along the walls. Low to the floor, maybe, and invisible in the darkness."

She half shrieked and buried her face in his chest and Death laughed. "I have got to find a Tunnel of Love to take you through!"

"Very funny, Smart Guy! I think, if you don't mind, I'm ready to leave now."

They stuffed their wrappers and empty water bottles back in Death's backpack and headed for the entrance they'd used. Death was almost back to the top of the long steps that led to the octagonal room when he realized Wren was no longer following him. He turned back and found her frozen on the stairs, her gaze fixed on a point beyond and above his left shoulder.

"Oh, that's cute," he said. "You're trying to make me think there's a monster or something creeping up behind me. It won't work, you know. I have nerves of steel." His voice was steady, but, in reality, he was fighting not to spin around and reach for the gun that wasn't at his hip.

"What?" She blinked. "Oh, no. No, I wasn't. That would have been funny, though. No, Death. *Look!* There's an opening in the wall behind you."

He turned and looked where she was pointing. On the right wall, not quite 90

178

degrees from the entrance, an arched doorway built of brick broke the surface of the stone about five feet above floor level. A natural stone outcropping had hidden it from them as they entered. Even now, he wouldn't have noticed it had Wren not pointed it out. "I stumbled a little," she said, "and my light just happened to hit it."

They climbed the last few stairs and crossed to the opening. Holes in the walls dripped red-orange streaks where iron bolts had rusted away. The passage had worked-stone walls, a paved floor, and a brick ceiling.

"There must have been steps here," Death said. "Probably somebody stole them for scrap." He shone his light into the tunnel. On the back wall, directly across from the opening, something had once been painted in bright colors. Most of the picture had worn and flaked away, but you could still see a few details, changes in the wall's pigmentation, scabs of paint clinging here and there. He picked out what might have been part of an ornate capitol "E," the curve of an "S," and a "dt" at the end.

"Do you see what I see?" he asked. "Does that say what I think it says?"

"I think it says 'Einstadt'," Wren said at once. "I think it was their logo."

■ ■ ■ ■

The boulder was heavy, but Death had gone out into the gully — it was raining lightly again, he reported — and brought back a stout tree limb to serve as a lever. They brought a smaller rock over for a fulcrum, wedged the end of the limb under the side of the boulder, and Wren clung to the lever and dangled her whole body weight from the end. Death added his not-inconsiderable muscle to the effort and the large rock rolled across the paved floor and came to rest against the wall under the Einstadt doorway.

Wren climbed up first, then turned back to help her Marine. He was winded from the effort. She had already been worried about him. There was a faint wheeze to his breathing and she couldn't tell if his pallor was real or a product of the odd lighting. Finding this doorway had mentally and emotionally recharged him, but he was still physically exhausted. She was afraid the combination didn't bode well.

The passage they had found was paved, with worked-stone walls and brick arches every ten feet or so supporting the ceiling. There was nothing natural about this tunnel. Every inch of it had been dug out by man. "Why would they have a tunnel leading all the way over here?" she asked, as much to slow Death down a little as because she was curious.

"I don't know. And it looks like it was a fairly elaborate doorway into the octagonal room. I wouldn't think you'd paint a fancy logo on the wall if no one was going to see it but the hired help. Hell," he shrugged, "maybe I was wrong about that being a service entrance. It seems really inaccessible to me, but maybe back in the 1920s, before it got all overgrown, it was more obvious."

"We can research it after we're done here. We can look online and there's probably a library somewhere that'll be open tomorrow. Heck, even the Rives County Library is open on Saturday until five."

Death chuckled a little at that but didn't answer. His laugh sounded heavy and the wheeze in his breathing was worse. Wren tugged at his arm to stop him and pulled the backpack away from him. "Sorry, sweetheart. You need something?" he asked.

"Yeah. I need to carry this for awhile and you need to slow down. Here," she took a bottle of water from the pack and offered it to him. "Drink a little of this and get your breath back. We're not doing a marathon.

Did you want to get out the compass and range finder and map this?"

He paused to take a drink and leaned against the wall, letting his breathing even out. "Nah. We can on the way out, if it looks like we need to, but so far there aren't any offshoots. I just want to see where this leads us. This is a well-built tunnel, did you notice? It's not wet, for one thing, even though it's raining outside. That tells me there probably aren't any open exits to the outside."

"I'd noticed it was drier up here," Wren said. "I hadn't thought about what that meant, though."

When Death was recovered to Wren's satisfaction, they went on. The tunnel ran in a straight line, heading southeast. After some twenty minutes of walking they came to a T. The tunnel they intersected was built in the same manner as the one they had been following. To the right, it disappeared into darkness beyond the reach of their headlamps. To the left, it went only ten or fifteen feet before ending at the remains of a steel door in a concrete wall.

The rusted and barely legible "Keep Out" sign on the wall was no longer necessary. The ceiling beyond had fallen and the passage that direction was filled with rubble and impassible.

"Take that as a reminder," Death said. "We need to step lightly and keep an eye out for any place that looks unstable. This is well-built, but it's still man-made and probably a lot less secure than the caves below."

Walking more gingerly, they followed the path to the right. It led on for about a hundred yards and ended in another doorway. A rusted door lay to one side, another sign visible on it. This one said, "Authorized personnel only." Beyond the door the passage became a landing where two staircases met. The one coming in from the right was wide and broad and made of concrete. The rise was shallow and a ramp almost as wide as the steps climbed beside it.

"A freight entrance," Wren surmised. "They brought cases of beer this way on dollies to go down to the biergartens, or whatever else was going on down in the caves."

The other staircase was narrower and steeper, built of intricately laid brick with wrought-iron railings still attached to the walls on either side. It was still wide enough for them to climb side-by-side. Holding hands, they followed it up slowly. With ten or fifteen steps left to go, they could see the way was blocked. The staircase's exit had been covered over by a square of ancient plywood.

TWELVE

"Take your time and just call out if you see anybody who looks familiar."

Death turned the big pages slowly. "Not seeing him so far."

He and Wren had come into the police station at the request of the detective investigating the attempted convenience store robbery. "I know it's Saturday morning," he'd said apologetically. "Crime fighters don't get weekends, I'm afraid."

Wren, sitting beside Death and peeking over his shoulder, took a sip of coffee from a cardboard cup and shuddered. "I always thought it was a joke about cops and bad coffee."

The middle-aged detective sitting across the desk from them grinned at her good-naturedly. "I wish it was, believe me!" He fiddled with his own coffee in a ceramic mug with a cartoon cop on it. "So, I gotta ask, you're Lieutenant Bogart's kid, aren't you?"

Death glanced up, gave him a faint grin. "That'd be me."

"Yeah, I thought so."

"Did you know Dad?"

"Not personally, no, but I've heard stories. Your mustard-as-a-weapon thing makes a lot more sense now." He turned his attention to Wren. "You know, his dad took out a fleeing gunman with a horseshoe once."

"That doesn't surprise me. How'd he do that?"

Death grinned to himself but let the detective tell the story. "Guy had been stalking his ex-wife."

"Nasty piece of work," Death interjected. "I don't know why women get involved with creeps like that in the first place, but —"

"She had a restraining order against him, but he showed up anyway and forced his way into the house. She ran out the back and into a park across the street. He was chasing her, holding the gun but not firing it, when this guy's dad shows up. The lieutenant wanted to take him down as quickly as possible, before he did shoot somebody, but the park was crowded and he didn't want to fire his own weapon if he could avoid it. He was chasing along, just a few yards behind the guy, and the chase led through a game of horseshoes, so he snatched up a horseshoe and nailed the guy with it. Three-point ringer, right to the head."

"Dad was big on improvising," Death said.

"And it seems he passed it along to you. Hey, listen, I wanted to tell you I was really sorry to hear about your brother last year."

"Thanks." Not really wanting to have this conversation again, Death changed the subject. "So, were you able to trace this guy's gun?"

"It was a dead end. Registered to a woman named Elena Vasquez, a night manager at a fast-food joint. Reported stolen the night before your little adventure. Someone broke into her car when it was in the back parking lot where she worked, stole the gun and her stereo and a twenty-dollar bill she kept hidden in the console. No witnesses, no cameras in the area, no fingerprints but her and her sister-in-law."

The Grey house had an honest-to-God elevator.

It was an old-fashioned affair, an elaborate, gilded cage no more than four feet square but tall enough to allow for a miniature chandelier to hang from the ceiling.

The floor was polished hardwood parquet and the walls of the elevator shaft had been painted a rich, dark red. Ceramic buttons, yellowed with age, were set in a polished brass plate beside the door. S, G, 2, 3, 4.

Since he'd started spitting out the pills, Andrew's level of lucidity had improved daily. Paranoia kept him from revealing that to Alaina or the doctor, or even to the maid. A little voice in his head pointed out to him that paranoia could be a side effect of not taking his medicine, and even be a part of the reason he needed it. To that, another voice replied that, if he were being drugged unnecessarily, paranoia was probably a reasonable response.

Affecting a harmless, bumbling demeanor, he was using his improved balance and stamina to explore the house. The first thing he'd determined was that it was a fire trap. There were two staircases — an elaborate grand stair that coiled down to come out in the foyer and a narrow, steep servants' stair that led to the kitchen — but they rose within a few feet of one another. A fire in that part of the house would cut them both off, and he'd seen no sign of fire escapes, though the old building had been retrofitted with a very good fire-suppression system.

Leaning heavily on his cane, Andrew hobbled into the elevator and eased the cage door closed behind him. He still tired easily. Propping himself on the wall next to the control panel, he chose button number four first. The cage glided up, the shaft wall sliding past a few inches from his shoulder, slowly passed an opening into an enormous, elaborate ballroom and came to a stop in a narrow hall.

He opened the door and looked both ways, but didn't step out. The room across from the elevator stood ajar. It was a tiny, spartan bedroom. The mattress on the twin bed was bare, the mirror above the plain little dresser speckled with age.

Servants' quarters, he thought, for live-in servants they no longer had. A heavy coating of dust on the floor testified that this part of the house was not in use. It was cramped and stark, with the ceiling only inches above his six-foot frame and the walls at either end of the hallway slanting to follow the gables. He ducked back into the elevator and considered the control panel again.

He knew now what was on three — a ballroom — and he'd spent what seemed like forever confined to two. "G" was undoubtedly the ground floor, where he was apt to be intercepted and sent back up to bed. That left "S," which he was guessing stood for "sub-basement" or "subterranean" or "sub-something."

"Let's see what's in the basement," he said to himself and punched the button.

Alaina was in the parlor on the ground floor, watching TV, doing her nails, and talking on her phone. He could see her through the open doorway, off to his left, as the elevator cage descended. He held his breath, but she didn't look up and notice him. The light dimmed as he dropped lower and he sighed and wondered where he could get a flashlight, reasoning that the basement would be dark.

It was in deep shadow when he came to a stop, but there were windows along the top of the wall, long, horizontal slits heavily fortified with burglar bars. He could see the lower branches of shrubbery through them, but they let in enough light that the blackness wasn't absolute.

The elevator had landed in a short, paved passage that led to an old, wooden door emblazoned with the Einstadt logo. Andrew recognized it because it was on bookplates in all the books in the first floor library and he'd asked about it. It seemed to him that something so intimately connected to his family should feel more familiar than it did, but there it was. A second, simpler door stood ajar on his left. As he passed it, he noted that age and humidity had warped the wood so that it no longer sat firmly in its frame.

He tried the Einstadt door first, but it was locked and solid so he turned to the second door. It led to a typical basement room, with a furnace and A/C unit squatting in the far corner and the rest of the space crammed with broken and cast-off belongings from the house upstairs. One of the windows was almost unblocked and the light was stronger here than out in the passage.

Andrew's nose caught the scent of smoke. Mindful of his earlier observations about the house being a fire trap, he went looking for the source. Like a bloodhound, he followed his sense of smell to a battered metal footlocker shoved against the wall to his right. He felt the sides for heat first, but it was cool to the touch. It was also unlocked. He popped it open and knelt next to it, pulling out the contents so he could examine them.

It was a heavy set of clothing. There was a bulky coat and a pair of pants, boots and a firefighter's helmet. The name "Bogart" was stenciled on the back of the coat and on the helmet was a leather badge, number 4103.

Death's cough, even as he tried to stifle it, echoed like thunder in the quiet library. Wren, sitting beside him, pressed her arm up against his. "You're starting to get a fever," she said, without looking up. "That damp cave wasn't good for you."

"It's just a cold," he said dismissively. His attempt to play it off was undermined by another cough. He could feel Wren's eyes on him and, when he looked over to meet her stare, he shuddered. "Jeez. Don't do that. That's the same look Gran used to give when she was in District Attorney mode."

"Do you have a doctor in the city you can see?"

"It's just a cold," he tried again.

"And what would your grandmother say to that?"

He found himself imagining the cross-examination he'd get from Gran if she were still alive. A bittersweet pang of nostalgia joined the ache in his chest. Wren's stern face softened and she gave him the gentle, loving, doe-eyed expression he could never refuse anything. "Gah! Don't look at me like that! You know I can never resist when you look at me like that! If you looked at me like that and asked for a pet grizzly bear,

I swear, I'd go out grizzly bear shopping!"

"Grizzlies are pretty high maintenance," she said. "A koala would be adorable, though. What are we going to do about that cold?"

Death glowered, then brightened as a thought struck him. "Maybe use it to our advantage?"

"How so?"

"Andrew Grey's brother-in-law, you remember I told you I met him outside the Greys' house? He's a doctor. If I can get an appointment with him, it'll give me a chance to ask him about his sister's husband. He's close to the family; maybe he can give me some inside information."

"You think the Greys are involved?" Wren's voice was doubtful. "The passage that must have led to their house was blocked a long time ago. Anyone could have found the opening into the octagonal room."

Death glanced around quickly before answering. They were in a library; he expected someone to shush them, or at least give them a dirty look. There was no one there, though. They were at the University of Missouri-St. Louis library, sitting at a table by a window in the stacks — the 800s. It was a Saturday afternoon during summer semester and they might well have been the only people in the building.

"Anyone could have found the passage, yes, but think it through. Someone had to get into the brewery before the fire to take the nails out of the plywood so it could be opened, and someone had to get back in afterward, to nail it down again. I looked at the windows when I went there alone and later when you and I went in with Barrows. There are some broken windows, but they're pretty high. There are shards of glass still in the frames. If someone entered the brewery before the fire last year, chances are it was someone with a key."

He fiddled with the heavy local-history book that lay open before him. "Besides, finding the passage and the staircase wouldn't tell someone where it led. The Einstadt Brewery sign on the wall is so faded, you almost have to know what it says in order to read it."

"You argue a compelling case," Wren conceded. "But it's Saturday. His office will be closed. And even when you can call, it can take weeks to get a doctor to see a new patient. What are you going to do in the meantime?"

Death gave her a worried, sideways look and wondered if she really was, somehow, channeling his grandmother. "I can hold out until Monday morning. I'll try to talk him into fitting me in. I can pay cash, I've found that's very persuasive. If I can't get in to see him Monday, and if I'm still coughing, I'll go find a walk-in clinic. Happy?"

"Delirious."

"I know that," he teased. "But are you happy?"

She punched him lightly in the arm and he made a show of pretending to be hurt before they settled back down to their reading.

"Got it!" Wren said finally, a note of triumph in her voice. She slid the book she was looking at closer to him and they bent their heads together. It was a compilation of old newspaper articles, put together sometime in the 1940s. "That gully was part of a water ride. There was a water channel running through there and around the park, with swan-shaped boats. It wasn't a service entrance. The steps led down to a landing for the swan boats and a gate into the underground attractions."

"Huh," Death said. "I'll be damned."

Wren leaned against him, eyes distant and hands clasped under her chin. "It must have been so romantic! The gentlemen in their top hats and tails and the ladies in their summer frocks, gliding through the park on a summer night, like riding on the back of a giant swan. And then they'd go down into the caves. They must have looked fantastic, all lit up, with jazz and laughter and voices echoing through the passages."

"Would you like to go dancing?" he asked suddenly. "I've never taken you anywhere really nice. This is a big city. We could find someplace fancy, get dressed up, and make a night of it."

Wren put her arms around him and rubbed a palm against his chest. "Someday," she said, "that'd be nice. But not when you sound like you're trying to breathe through mud and gravel."

When they returned to Randy's house they found Captain Cairn, dressed casually in jeans and a T-shirt, just getting ready to drive away. "I thought I'd missed you," he said. "Though I could see you were still in the city." He nodded toward Wren's truck parked in the driveway. "I was wondering if you'd done anything toward getting your brother's estate settled? You know, I can give you any help you need with that."

Death gestured toward the house, unlocked the front door, and ushered Cap and Wren inside before answering. "Honestly, I've been more focused on trying to figure out what's going on with Randy's badge than anything."

"Who wants what to drink?" Wren asked. "I can make coffee or there's a pitcher of iced tea in the fridge."

"How about a beer?" Death suggested.

She gave him a long, appraising look. "Are you taking over-the-counter cold medicine?" His chagrined look answered for him.

"Uh-huh. That's what I thought. How about coffee or iced tea? Or soda pop? Lemonade?"

"Tea will be fine. See?" he complained to Cap. "She doesn't let me get away with anything."

"Yeah, I'm a real dominatrix," Wren agreed, straight-faced. "You can have a beer if you'd like, Cap. Provided you're not on medication, of course."

"Thanks," the firefighter laughed, "but it would be cruel to drink in front of him when he can't. Tea would be great, thanks."

Wren brought in the tea and a plate of sugar cookies and the three of them settled down around the coffee table. Cap sipped his tea and looked around the room, pensive and sad. "Place looks bare without all Bogie's crap all over the walls," he said. "Rowdy tells me you're planning to sell. You could do a good business as a P.I. in the city, you know?"

"I know," Death agreed. "I've already made a fresh start in East Bledsoe Ferry, though. And that's home to Wren. I wouldn't want to try to drag her away."

"I can understand that. This city's going to miss you, though."

"This city won't even know I'm gone."

"It might not *know* it misses you, but it'll miss you just the same. The Bogarts have done a lot of good for this place."

"That was more the rest of my family than me," Death said, "but I appreciate the sentiment."

"So have you figured anything out about that badge, then?" Death and Wren exchanged a glance.

"We've done a little digging around," Death admitted. "Put together a few things. I swear, the more we learn, the less any of it makes sense."

"How so?"

With Wren chiming in from time to time, Death outlined for the captain everything they'd learned. Cap's eyes narrowed when the former Marine admitted to going down into the caves, but he let them finish without comment.

"So you're thinking . . . what? That someone used the fire as cover to sneak into the brewery through the old tunnel and climb into the room just as your brother suddenly and unexpectedly died of natural causes, just so they could switch his helmet and pin a counterfeit badge on him? And did so before the bookcase collapsed? And then got away before we reached the room?"

"Well, when you say it like that, it sounds farfetched."

"Say it so it doesn't sound farfetched."

Death grimaced. "Yeah. That's the hard part."

"Could it have been smuggling of some kind?" Wren suggested hesitantly.

"Helmet smuggling?" Cap asked. "Badge smuggling?"

"How about something hidden in the helmet? In the lining, maybe? Drugs or, I don't know, top-secret, spy-type information? Microfilm or microdots, perhaps?"

"Microfilm is pretty outdated, spy-wise, don't you think?" Death asked gently.

"That might make it a better method for passing secret information than ever. Who'd look for microfilm nowadays?"

Death glanced to Cap. "She's got a point. And, weird as it is, it's better than any theory I've come up with."

"This is true. But how would Bogie have gotten microfilm or microdots on his badge or helmet?"

"Maybe he rescued a spy," Wren said.

Death raised his eyebrows, thought about it. "Keep going."

"Okay, so, he rescued a spy. And as he's carrying him — or her — out of the fire or car wreck or whatever, the spy sticks a microdot to his badge without him noticing. Then, they tell their contact or their enemy finds out or something, that the microdot is on Fireman Bogart's badge. Now the new spy has to come up with a way to get it back."

"Why not the original spy?"

"Because whoever was trying to get it didn't know which badge it was on. That's why they had a regular badge *and* a helmet badge made."

"Go on."

"Well, they had the new badges made, but they got their information for the badge number from the newspaper picture of Randy from the school fire safety day. Because of the photographer's error, the number was wrong, but they didn't realize that until it was too late. Maybe they didn't realize it at all. They set the fire — you did say it was arson, right?"

Cap nodded.

"They set the fire and waited for Randy

to come into range. Probably they were planning to knock him out or something. Obviously, whatever they were doing they didn't want anyone to notice."

"Wait," Cap interrupted. "How do you figure that?"

"If they'd just wanted the badges and didn't care who knew they had them, they'd have just stolen them at gunpoint or something. They had to take them without anyone finding out."

Death drank some tea, rattled the ice in his glass. "Cap, would whoever set the fire at the brewery have known that 41's was going to show up?"

"It's a reasonable assumption. They could have even figured out, with a little research, that we'd likely be the ones sending a search team through the building. That's a job for truckies, and we have truckies. But how would they know Bogie'd be on the truck and not the box? And how could they be sure that he'd be the one to go into the room with the tunnel and not Rowdy?"

"Rowdy always goes left," Wren said triumphantly. The two men looked at her.

"What?" Death asked.

"Rowdy always goes left," she repeated. "It was in the fire safety day article. Randy gave a talk to some of the kids and the writer quoted him. Hang on." She went to rummage through a box stacked in the corner with half a dozen other packed cartons, and came back with the fire safety day story. Settling cross-legged on the sofa next to Death, she paused to take a sip of tea, then read from the paper.

"He said, 'the best thing you can do to help yourself and your friends in an emergency is have a plan ready in advance. Think about things that could happen and figure out ahead of time how you could best respond. For example, my friend Rowdy and I are responsible for searching for victims in burning buildings. We try to always stay together, but if we have to split up — say, if there are two victims in two different rooms — Rowdy always goes left and I go right. Because we know in advance who's going which way, we don't have to stop and talk about it. Also, it makes it easier to keep from getting lost in the smoke and confusion.' "

"Yeah, that's right," Cap said. "Rowdy always went left. Bogie went right. They made a great team."

"You said they thought they heard a noise but they couldn't decide where it came from, right?" Death said. "The spy, or whoever, could have hidden something that would make noise in both rooms, to get them to separate."

Cap considered. "It's possible, I suppose. But if that's it, how are we supposed to ever find out what happened or who's responsible?"

"Well, if it was on his hat badge, they've got it and are probably gone by now. But we've got Randy's badge. We could always search it for microdots."

"I'll get it," Wren said. "You stay put."

"Yes, ma'am!"

She went to get the badge, still in its frame beside Death's bed, and Cap drained his tea and rattled the ice thoughtfully. "If whatever it was *wasn't* on his hat badge, why haven't they, whoever they are, tried to get his other one back from you? It's been almost a year now."

"Maybe they don't know what happened to it."

"That's reasonable, I suppose."

Wren came back and the three of them bent over the little object. "What does a microdot look like, do you suppose?" Cap asked.

"Like a dot," Wren offered, "only . . . micro."

Death pinched her and she yelped.

They looked closely at every millimeter of

the badge and checked the frame in case something had fallen off, but nothing presented itself.

"You'd think," Cap said, "that if all they wanted was Bogie's badges, they'd have just broken into the fire station while we were off and one of the other shifts was out and taken them then. It would have been a hell of a lot simpler."

"Yeah, I know," Wren agreed. "The spy theory is farfetched, at best. But the whole situation is farfetched, and right now that's the only explanation I can think of."

THIRTEEN

On Saturday evening a car pulled up and parked on the street in front of Randy's house. Death was lounging on the sofa, feeling rough and trying to play it off. Wren, returning from the kitchen, stepped over and pulled back the curtain to look out. Her eyes grew wide and she clapped a hand over her own mouth.

Death frowned. "Who is it?"

Wren shook her head and held up one finger. Her face was red and her eyes danced. A knock sounded at the door and she went to open it, pulling it wide and stepping back so he could see out.

Madeline stood on the porch, dressed in a seductive little black dress. She wore spiked heels, her hair was swept up off her neck in an elegant French twist, and the rubies on her ears accentuated her dark-red lipstick. She wasn't alone. She had one arm possessively around . . .

Eric Farrington?

Death bit the inside of his cheek and resisted the urge to check the alcohol content of his cough medicine. He recognized this game, of course. He'd known Madeline too long not to. She'd done this before they were married. Any time they had a minor disagreement or she didn't feel he was paying her enough attention she'd pick up the first guy she met and flaunt him in Death's face to make him jealous.

Back then there'd been a couple of differences. One was that Death had *cared* who she dated. The other difference was . . .

Eric Farrington?

Death pulled himself up into a sitting position. "Come on in. Pull up a chair."

Eric dropped into the nearest recliner and tugged on Madeline's hand so, off balance, she half fell into his lap.

Wren closed the door and came over to perch next to Death on the sofa. "So," she said brightly, "you two are a couple now?"

"I wouldn't say a 'couple'," Madeline hedged.

"You betcha," Eric spoke over her. "I got *my* saddle on this little filly now and I'm going to ride her *all night long!*"

Madeline looked horrified.

Wren's shoulders shook with suppressed

laughter. Death put his arm around her, tucking her in close beside him. "And what brings you to St. Louis?"

"Business, actually," Madeline hastened to answer. "Eric has a seminar to attend next week and, since he offered me a ride, I thought it would be nice to visit my mother and let her see the baby."

"What kind of seminar?"

"Telecommunications in modern police work," Eric said. He puffed up his narrow chest. "The chief is always sending me to these training opportunities. He can tell I'm gonna be a key player in the future of law enforcement."

"Eric," Wren said, "he'd send you to Mars if he could figure out how to sneak you onto a rocket ship."

"What would he do on a rocket ship?" Death asked, interested.

"Well, if they ever wanted to study the effects of stupidity in space, Eric could be a payload specialist."

"You shut up. You just don't know a good man when you see one. Not like my sexy little Maddykins, here." He jiggled his knee and pinched her ass and she jumped and shot him a look that was more rictus than a smile. "He does have a certain *je ne sais quoi,*" Madeline offered lamely.

207

"Oh, *je* sais quoi," Wren said. "But I'm not going to *say* quoi. Death still thinks I'm a lady and I'd hate to disillusion him."

"So!" Death said. His cheeks were starting to ache from trying not to laugh. "What brings you to our door this evening?" Madeline and Eric glanced at one another awkwardly.

"Oh, well, you know," Madeline said. "We're going out on the town tonight and we thought we'd see if you'd like to make it a double date. Wren probably doesn't have a thing to wear, though, does she?"

"That's okay," Death said. "I like her even better when she doesn't have a thing to wear."

Madeline pressed her lips together and turned red. Wren was already pink and shaking slightly and Death didn't know if there was a greater danger of her laughing hysterically or throwing punches. Eric tipped his head speculatively.

"Are you . . . suggesting some kind of orgy?" he asked, interested.

Death and Madeline both froze, speechless. Wren, though, erupted at the small man. She jumped up, got him by his lapels, and shook him. "NO!" she bellowed in his face.

"Well, jeez. You don't have to go all Godzilla on me. I was just asking."

"Don't! Don't ask! Not ever again! Don't even think about asking. Don't even think about thinking about asking. Don't even think about thinking about thinking about . . . crap! I lost track of my thinkings."

"It's okay," Death said, laughing. He pulled her back down beside him. "I think he gets the picture."

Madeline rose, trying to gather the tatters of her dignity. "Maybe we should go," she said.

"That sounds like a good plan to me," Eric agreed. He pinched her again, making her jump. "All this talk about orgies has got my engine running. I say we should just skip the restaurant and head back to your mother's for a little nookie in the basement."

"Nookie in my mother's basement —" Madeline echoed with a sort of horrified fascination.

"Yeah! We can always order Chinese when we're done. We can ask your mom if she wants to join us."

Death put his hand over Wren's mouth before she could say "for what?" and in a few minutes East Bledsoe Ferry's newest and oddest couple had gone. Wren closed the door behind them and turned to lean against it, finally laughing out loud. "You know what that was?" she said finally, and Death could hear a hint of vulnerability under the humor. "They were trying to make you jealous. They were both trying to make you jealous."

Death smiled at her and let the warmth he was feeling seep into his words.

"The only way either of them could ever make me jealous would be if one of them somehow got you."

"How long have you had this cough?"

Talia pushed Death's shoulder, signaling him to lean forward on the couch, and pulled up his T-shirt so she could position her stethoscope against his bare back.

Wren was torn. On the one hand, she was relieved that an actual medical professional was taking an interest in Death's health. On the other hand, the pretty, blonde paramedic was climbing all over her boyfriend.

"Wren, could I get you to help me bring in another round of beer and junk food?"

With a reluctant glance at Death, now with his shirt completely off, Wren followed Annie Tanner into her bright, airy kitchen. She and Death had been invited over on this Sunday morning for a day of rest. Practically the whole fire crew was there, most with their families or significant others. There were plans for watching a string of baseball games on television and Rowdy and a couple of the other guys had set up three grills outside in the shade, ready to light when it got a little closer to midday.

"Tal's not hitting on your boyfriend," Annie said, as soon as they were alone. Her voice was warm and slightly amused.

Wren looked back dubiously. Talia was practically sitting in Death's lap now, peering down his throat with a tongue depressor in one hand and a penlight in the other. "I promise," Annie said. "She's in a committed relationship."

"She's got a boyfriend?"

"Girlfriend, actually."

"Oh." Wren studied the pair in the living room again, reevaluated. "And you're sure she's not considering switch hitting?"

That made Annie laugh openly. "Believe me, I'm sure. Normally her girlfriend would be here, too. Trinka. She's a sound tech for a radio station and she's at work right now, though she may show up later. She likes to make inappropriate jokes to embarrass Tal and try to get the boot to blush."

"She sounds great. I'd like to meet her." Wren worried her lower lip with her teeth. "So, do you think she thinks Death is really

211

sick? Talia, I mean? He's promised me he'll see a doctor tomorrow, but I can drag him to the ER right now if I have to."

"She'll say if she thinks he needs to go," Annie said, "but I wouldn't worry yet." Her voice turned sad and introspective. "I think she's looking for redemption. She blames herself for losing Bogie, you know. Because she worked with him for years and never realized he was sick. Because she couldn't keep him from going down and couldn't get him back when he did."

"It wasn't her fault," Wren said, compassionate but yet a little exasperated. "There wouldn't have been any warning signs. There was nothing anyone could do."

"I know. But she and Bogie were good friends. The guys at our station are all pretty cool, but not everyone on the fire department is thrilled to be working with a woman, let alone a lesbian. Bogie stood up for her. He never let anyone give her any crap. Besides, she's a paramedic, that's just how they are."

"That's how big brothers are too." Wren sighed. "Death was halfway around the world when it happened, critically injured, hiding in a dirty cellar from some really nasty people who wanted him dead on principal. But he blames himself for it, too.

So does Cap, I guess because he was in command."

"So does Rowdy," Annie said. "He was Bogie's partner, and he was there when it happened. Hell, for that matter, I blame myself. He spent his last night on Earth under my roof. I cooked his last meal and made him eat it and I never noticed anything wrong with him." The two women stood in silence for a long moment.

"Wow," Wren said, finally. "This got really depressing, really fast."

Annie wiped her eyes. "It did, didn't it? Here, let's get the mongrels fed and then we can find something else to talk about." She started dumping assorted chips and snack foods into large bowls and Wren took over ferrying them in to set them on the coffee and end tables. When there was food on every available surface, Annie looked askance at a large cooler sitting under the table.

"I need to get one of the guys in here to take the beer in the other room."

"It's in the cooler?"

"Yeah, but it weighs a ton."

"I can probably get it. I'm stronger than I look." The cooler was heavy, but Wren put her legs into it and managed to drag it into the other room. Annie followed her, looking impressed. Wren dropped the cooler at the end of one of the sofas and then she and her hostess retreated to the kitchen.

"Thank you," Annie said. "You know, it's awfully rude of me, inviting you over and then putting you to work."

"It's okay. I don't mind. I like being useful, and I like being strong enough to do things like that." She laughed suddenly. "Death's ex came by his office last week when I was there and he wasn't. She tried the old 'helpless female' routine. 'I've got something for Death, but I'll have to wait for him to come carry it because it's heavy and I'm just a poor, weak, girl.' Thing didn't even weigh ten pounds, I bet."

"I've heard stories about Madeline, but I never met her. What's she like?"

"She's hot," a new voice said.

They turned to find Talia standing in the doorway.

"Sorry," she said. "I just came in to see if I could get a glass of milk?"

"Oh, honey. You don't even have to ask. You know where it is. Help yourself." Talia got a glass and poured herself some milk.

Wren sighed. "She's right, you know. Madeline is hot. Really hot. Like a super model, even."

"I didn't know you'd met her," Annie said

to Talia, a bit accusingly.

"I haven't met her, but I've seen her. Bogie pointed her out at their parents' funeral, and he used to print out pictures of her a lot."

"Really?" Wren asked.

"Oh, yeah. When their parents were killed, she pretty much just stepped back and left Death to deal with it all by himself. Bogie never talked to Death about it, but he took offense in a big way. For months afterward, if he was a little bit down about something or missing his brother, he'd cheer himself up by printing out her picture and finding creative ways to destroy it. He'd draw fangs and horns and tails on her, use it for a dartboard, blow it up with firecrackers —"

"Wow." Wren smiled. "You know, the more I hear about that boy, the more I like him. Talia," she said suddenly, worried, "is Death really sick?"

Talia smiled and it lit her face. "He's not that bad. I think it's just a cold, but, with his medical history and the state of his lungs, he needs to be extra careful. He said he promised you he'd see a doctor tomorrow." Wren nodded.

"He should be fine until then. Don't let him wriggle out of it, though." She sipped her milk. "Y'know, I'm surprised. I'd expected to find the two of you in here talking about auctions. Annie's an auction buff," she explained to Wren. "Though I understand she's no longer allowed to bid on antique pump organs."

"It's a long story," Annie said ruefully. "Do you like auctions, Wren?"

"Didn't anyone tell you?" Talia smiled. "Wren's an auctioneer."

"You're on vacation," Annie said. "I shouldn't be dragging you away to go bargain hunting with me!"

"It's okay," Wren assured her. "I enjoy watching other auctioneers work. If they have a good technique I can always learn something. And if they don't, I can make fun of them later, behind their back."

"Ooh. How catty! I like that."

The Sunday paper was spread over the Tanners' kitchen table and Wren and Annie were poring over the auction listings. Death was settled comfortably on a couch with three paramedics keeping an eye on him. Rowdy had given their outing his blessing, if that's how one chose to interpret a vague wave and an absentminded, "Sure, Honey. Whatever."

"So where shall we go?" Annie asked.

Wren scanned the ads and her eye fell on

a familiar name. "Einstadt Road! Like the brewery. It must be named after the brewing family, too."

Annie leaned over to look. "Oh, yeah. That's the road that runs past in front of the brewery, actually. The factory's on one side and there are a bunch of fancy old houses on the other. The auction must be at one of them."

"We should go to that one, then!"

"Are you sure?" Annie frowned. "I try not to go to that part of town. I haven't been by there since . . . you know?"

Wren touched her shoulder sympathetically. "I know. But Death thinks the Greys, the Einstadt heir and his wife, are involved in the thing with Randy's badge. They live on that road. The auctioneers will have spent time there getting ready for the sale, and probably some of the neighbors will stop by out of curiosity. This could be our chance to learn something." The fireman's wife looked dubious, but acquiesced.

"Don't tell Death exactly where we're going," Wren said. "If he knows, he's apt to want to come with us. I'd rather have him here taking it easy and being looked after."

The auction looked and smelled and sounded like a thousand other sales Wren had been to in her life, though it was a little weird to be part of the crowd rather than part of the staff. It was well under way by the time they arrived. Annie parked in the brewery lot amid a flock of other vehicles and kept her eyes averted from the dark, looming building as they made their way across the street and followed the sound of calling and the inevitable scent of barbecue.

An hour and a half later, with the afternoon sun beating down on their heads, they made their way to the cash tent. Annie had scored a nice wooden toy chest for her children's play room, several boxes of toys, a 1970s-era record player, and a random collection of odd records. Wren had a jar of assorted buttons; a small jewelry case; and a vintage 1930s tuxedo with tails, in excellent condition, that she was positive would fit Death with only a few small alterations.

The line was short and after they'd paid Wren struck up a conversation with the women working the cash box. "I'm an auctioneer myself, from the other side of the state."

"Are you looking to transfer?" the older of the two women asked. Her name tag read "Madge" and her tone was a mixture of skepticism and interest.

"Oh, no. I'm just here on vacation with

my boyfriend. I work for a small, family run business, Keystone and Sons out of East Bledsoe Ferry."

Madge perked up. "Good Lord! Roy Keystone?"

"Uh, yeah. Roy and his brother, Sam. You know Roy?"

"I was at the Missouri State Auctioneers' Association potluck dinner year before last. Yeah, I know Roy."

"Oh," Wren grinned. "The crawfish pie. Right."

"Crawfish pie?" Annie asked.

"Once or twice a year, usually, the state auctioneers' association gets together for a big meeting/convention kind of thing. Year before last they did a potluck dinner and asked everyone who attended to contribute a dish. Roy promised them a crawfish pie they'd never forget."

"He was right about that," Madge said wryly.

"The night before the dinner, Roy and his wife Leona made up a pie crust. They put the bottom crust in the pan, filled it to heaping with dried navy beans, and then draped the top crust loosely over it, after scoring the rim to make it look like it had been sealed. They baked it and then dumped the beans out and wound up with a beautiful, empty pie shell with the top crust loose. They took it to the dinner and, just before they got there, they filled it with live crawdads and put the top back on. Then they just set it in the middle of the table and waited."

"Bob DeVrie was one of the association officers that year," Madge said. "You probably don't know who he is. He's from down south somewhere and he was running for some minor public office at the time. He decided to give an impromptu benediction and campaign speech while he had a captive audience. So everyone's standing around waiting to eat, and the food's getting cold, and no one's really happy, and then somebody's little boy called out, 'Look, Mommy! The pie has legs!'"

"Naturally, everyone looked to see what he was talking about. Leona had cut ventilation holes in the top crust," Wren explained. "Real pretty ones. They looked like flower petals. And, if you looked, you could see things moving inside the pie. Then a long, black, insect-like leg came poking out of one of the holes. Then the whole top crust started shifting."

"It was pandemonium." Madge was giggling and she had to stop and wipe her eyes on her sleeve. "People were running and screaming. It was like a scene from one of those old Japanese horror movies."

"The Thing That Came Out Of The Pie!" Wren gasped.

"Oh, that's classic," Annie said. "Hey! Do you think they'd mind if I stole their idea? There's a fire department picnic coming up in a couple of weeks."

"Knowing Roy and Leona," Wren said, "I can assure you they would be honored if you used their special crawfish pie recipe."

A delicate but very pointed cough interrupted their conversation and Wren turned to find another woman had entered the tent. Wren had noticed her earlier, standing a little apart from the rest of the crowd, carefully not touching anything and looking over the items on sale with an odd mix of longing and disdain. "Excuse me," she said now, "but is this where I pay?"

"Yes, ma'am," Madge said. "What do you have?"

The woman offered the square of card stock with her number on it and Madge checked their records. "I'm only seeing one item, an antique steamer trunk. Is that all?"

"Yes, that's it."

Annie made as if to move toward the tent opening, but Wren caught her arm and gave a tiny shake of her head. They hadn't found out anything about the neighbors or the neighborhood yet, but her senses were tingling. They waited quietly while the woman paid by credit card. Wren had to bite down on a triumphant grin when Madge handed over the receipt and said, "Thank you, Mrs. Grey. You have a nice day, now."

Alaina Grey just stood there, looking bewildered. "Don't you need to know where to deliver it?" Madge blinked and exchanged a brief glance with her coworker.

"Ah, ma'am, this is an auction. We don't deliver. You're responsible for removing your own purchases."

"But that's absurd. How am I supposed to get it home? Do I look like a delivery man to you?"

"Look, it's right there on the auction bill. 'All items must be settled for before being removed.' "

"Right. And I settled for it. Now remove it for me."

"We don't do that!"

Wren nudged Annie and stepped into the conversation. "Excuse me, but maybe we can help. Where do you live?" Alaina tipped her pretty head delicately to the west. "Three houses that way."

Wren turned to Madge and gestured

toward the back of the tent. "If I could borrow that two-wheeler and a cargo strap, we could help this lady get her — steamer trunk? — her steamer trunk home."

Madge, relieved, waved a hand in the general direction of the hand cart. "Go for it."

Wren fetched the two-wheeler and she and Annie followed Alaina out of the tent and across the yard to where a steamer trunk stood open on the grass. The sale had been and gone from this section of the property and the display was reduced to a random assortment of holes where merchandise had been and a scattering of things waiting to be called for.

"This is a nice trunk," Wren commented. "Good exterior without too many dings or abrasions and the lining is faded, but completely intact. Did you notice that it's been modified to hold a larger-than-normal selection of cosmetics and accessories? If I had to guess, I'd say this was used by a vaudeville performer. It's the right era. These trunks were popular for that and an actor or actress would have needed the extra space for props and stage makeup."

"Yes, it's very nice," Alaina said. "That's why I bought it. Can we go now?"

Annie scowled but Wren just bit the inside

of her cheek to keep from laughing, more amused than insulted by the woman's hauteur.

"Just give me a second to get situated," she said. It was standing upright, on one end, and it took a bit of maneuvering to get it closed without trapping too much grass and dirt inside. "Give me a hand here, Annie?" she asked, when she had it latched. "I'm going to tip it forward. If you can push the two-wheeler under the back, I'll use the cargo strap to fasten it on and it should be quite manageable."

It was heavy, but not terribly so, and when she had it strapped to the two-wheeler she could move it easily.

"I can't see a thing from back here," she said. "I'll push the trunk, but you'll have to guide me and keep me from running over anyone."

They left the auction in a group, down the walkway to the sidewalk and then up the sidewalk to the mansion three doors away. The yard was ringed by a wrought-iron fence with an elaborate gate and a white brick gazebo was visible in the backyard. The walk led up to a set of stone steps that proved a challenge, but with Annie's help Wren got the trunk up on the porch and Alaina unlocked the door to let them inside.

"Careful," Alaina said. "Try not to scratch my floor with that . . . thing."

"Right," Wren said cheerfully. "So, where do you want it?"

The smaller woman considered. "Probably best to just leave it in the foyer. I'll have the gardener fumigate it before he takes it upstairs."

Wren set it down gently and was unbuckling the strap when she heard Annie give a small, pained gasp. A quick glance showed her friend staring at something out of Wren's line of sight, so she maneuvered the trunk around and set it down gently in such a way that she could look where Annie was looking and Alaina, for the moment, couldn't see her face. She followed Annie's gaze and felt herself grow a little light-headed.

"So," Alaina said, a trifle awkwardly, "is there a fee for the delivery?"

Wren swallowed hard and forced herself to act normal. "We don't work for the auction company," she said. "We're just helping you. To be nice." She tipped the trunk away from her and slid the two-wheeler free, draping the cargo strap over the handle.

"Oh. Okay. Well . . . thank you?"

225

"Right. You're welcome. So, um, that's a lovely picture. Is it your wedding?"

Alaina turned to look up the stairs and smiled. "Yes, that's my husband and I. I was a lovely bride, wasn't I?"

"Yes, very. Hey, maybe your husband can move the trunk for you when you need it moved again."

"Andrew can't do physical labor. He had a stroke. He's been very ill, poor dear."

"Oh, I see. Well, I'm sorry to hear that. I hope he gets better soon."

"Thank you. So . . ." Alaina was looking between Wren and the door, clearly wondering how to get rid of them.

Annie had tears in her eyes and looked like she was about to burst into hysterics. Wren got her by the arm, turned her toward the exit, and beat a hasty retreat, dragging the two-wheeler behind them. Out the door, down the steps and the walk and up the sidewalk they went, the handcart rattling on the concrete behind them. She didn't stop until they were back in the yard of the house where the auction was, huddled out of the way among the low branches of a young peach tree.

Annie leaned against the tree trunk. She was gasping for breath and Wren wished she had a paper bag in case the other woman hyperventilated. Her own mind was working a mile a minute.

"Did you see?" Annie demanded. "Did you see what I saw?"

"Yes, I saw. Listen! We can't tell Death about this. Okay? Not yet. We've got to figure out what it means first. He's been through too much already. I'm not going to let him get hurt again."

"But you saw it, right? Tell me you saw it."

"Yes. I saw it." Wren squeezed Annie's shoulder, put her other hand on the back of Annie's neck, and made the other woman look her in the eye. "I saw, okay? Except for his hair color and that silly little beard, when that picture was painted Andrew Grey was an absolute dead ringer for Randy Bogart."

FOURTEEN

"What brought this on? Do you have any idea?"

Death shifted on the exam table and the paper cover crinkled beneath him. In the last year, he'd seen a lot of doctors' offices. James Gregory's was pretty average, with oil paintings and plants in the waiting room and the examination rooms sterile and barren of personality.

"My girlfriend and I went caving over the weekend," he admitted a bit reluctantly, paranoid that Gregory would guess which caves they'd been in and why. His cough had worsened in spite of Talia's administrations and the infection had climbed up into his upper respiratory passages. Gregory stared at him.

"Caving?" he asked. He swiveled his chair to look more directly at Death and tapped the tablet computer on his knee. "Caving in the Mississippi River Valley? With your lungs? Really? Do you have a death wish, Mr. Bogart?"

Death blinked. "What's the big deal about caving?"

"Have you ever heard of caver's lung?"

"I cannot say that I have. What is it?"

"The proper name is histoplasmosis. It's a fungal infection caused by coming into contact with bird or, especially, bat guano. Most cases occur in the Mississippi or Ohio River Valleys."

"Is it serious?"

"Normally, no, but under some circumstances it can be and it can even prove fatal. The damage to your lungs puts you at a greater risk for things like this. You really need to put more thought into things. If you're going to go caving, for example, wear a filter mask and make it a point to avoid any chambers that have been colonized by bats."

"I didn't know that," Death said. "I'll be sure to be more careful in the future."

The doctor fiddled with his tablet for several seconds, scrolling up and down, frowning here and there. Death waited and tried not to fidget.

"I'd like to go ahead and run a couple of tests to see if there's any evidence of histoplasmosis. I'll forward the results to your regular doctor and you should follow up with him, especially if this infection doesn't clear up within the next couple of weeks. I'm also going to give you a prescription for an antibiotic. Histoplasmosis is usually asymptomatic in the early stages, but it can co-exist with a bacterial infection, and you almost certainly have one of those."

He scrolled up on his tablet and read some more.

"Are you still doing your breathing exercises and cardio?"

"Of course."

He nodded, touched his finger to the screen. "I see you have a prescription for an antidepressant. How's that working?"

"Oh, that." Death shifted uncomfortably. "Yeah, I don't need that anymore."

Gregory lowered the tablet and gave him his full attention. "Mr. Bogart, this is a new prescription. It's just over a week old."

"Uh, I told my doctor that I was coming to St. Louis to settle my little brother's estate. He thought the drugs were a good idea." That wasn't exactly the truth. Certainly not the whole truth. But it was enough, in Death's estimation, to be sharing with Gregory. "It didn't do anything but make me sick to my stomach, though. And, anyway, I got a better antidepressant. A redhead."

"Having supportive people in your life is excellent, but it doesn't mean the drugs can't help you, too. Depression is an illness. You've got to understand that. It's not a sign of weakness or something to be ashamed of. Clinical depression involves specific chemical imbalances in your brain. That's what this medication is for. To correct that concrete, physical problem."

"I just don't see how puking my guts up is supposed to cheer me up," Death countered, a bit defensively. Discussing his mental health wasn't on his agenda this morning. He'd gotten the prescription after the incident at the shooting range, taken it twice, given it up, and forgotten about it.

"It'll take your body a week or two to get used to the medication. You have to give it time to work." He fiddled with the tablet, tapping it on his knee, turning it in his hand. "Your redhead, does she know you're supposed to be taking antidepressants?"

"Of course not."

"Why 'of course not'? Don't you think she'd like to know?"

"I just don't want to worry her, that's all."

"If she cares about you, don't you think she's worried anyway?"

Death had no answer to that and the

silence stretched out between them for several seconds.

"You know," Gregory said finally, "I have conversations like this with my own sister. Her husband isn't doing well. Frankly, I don't expect him to be with us much longer. At this point, I'm just trying to make him comfortable and prepare her for the inevitable."

"I'm sorry to hear that."

"My point is, life hands us difficult times, sometimes, through no fault of our own, and all we can do is use whatever means are at our disposal to get through them." He sighed. "You know, I remember when your brother passed away. Alaina and I attended his memorial, in fact."

"I didn't know that."

"He died on her husband's family property. It seemed a show of respect was in order. It was a lovely ceremony. I understand you were unable to attend yourself?"

"Yeah, I was in a military hospital in Germany. In a coma."

"Several of the firefighters gave eulogies and a charming little girl of about seven sang James Taylor's 'Fire and Rain'."

"That was his goddaughter, Miranda."

"She has a lovely singing voice for one so young. It's a pity you couldn't be there.

Funerals and the like are for the living, Mr. Bogart, and I think you're probably the one who needed it most of all."

"Ohmigod!"

Wren winced and moved the phone away, putting it on speaker. Cameron shrieking like a little girl had her ear ringing.

"Wren! Ohmigod! You're not going to believe what I found!"

She exchanged a glance with Annie Tanner. While Death was at the doctor's office, she and Annie were at the Tanners' house, she on her laptop and Annie on her PC, researching Andrew and Alaina Grey. "You found a picture of Andrew Grey and he looks like Randy," Wren guessed.

"No! I found an old picture of Andrew Grey and he looked just like Death's brother! Wait . . . you knew?"

"My friend Annie and I talked our way into the Greys' house yesterday. We saw a painting on the wall. We're trying to find out everything we can about Andrew Grey now."

"Annie who? And how? And what did Death say?"

"Annie Tanner. Her husband was Randy's best friend. I'm at her house now and I've got you on speakerphone. Cam, this is Annie. Annie, this is my friend Cameron. He's a newspaper reporter back home in East Bledsoe Ferry." Cameron and Annie said hi to one another and Wren gave Cam a quick rundown on how she and Annie had gotten in to see Alaina and Andrew Grey's wedding portrait.

"What did Death say?"

"Uh, yeah. About that. We didn't tell him."

"*What?* You have to! This is his brother you're talking about. I mean, there's got to be a connection! You know that!"

"Yes, I know. And I'm going to tell him. But I want to find out everything I can about Andrew Grey first, try to figure out what's going on. Death's been hurt so much, Cam. I'm just trying to protect him as best I can. That's why I'm not going to tell him for now. And that's why you've got to promise not to tell him either."

"I think you're making a mistake," he said. "But, if that's what you want, okay. You've got to let me in on this, though. Or else I'm telling."

"Blackmail?" Wren asked, amused.

"Absolutely!"

"Well, it isn't necessary. We're counting on you to use your journalistic skills and contacts here."

"Do we have any theories about what happened?"

"I suggested they murdered Andrew," Annie said, "then switched him with Bogie to get rid of the body without anyone suspecting anything. But Wren pointed out that Bogie wasn't murdered. He died of natural causes. And they'd still have to get rid of Bogie, so they wouldn't have gained anything."

"Bogie?"

"Randy," Wren clarified. "His friends here call him Bogie."

"Oh. Got it. Hey! Andrew Grey's kind of a local celebrity, isn't he? How come no one ever noticed how much he and Randy looked alike before?"

"I thought about that," Wren said. "I think it's because they didn't look the same at the same time, you know? That picture where Andrew looks like Randy is ten years old. In current pictures they don't look alike at all, really. Andrew's gone completely gray, for one thing, plus I think he's had some plastic surgery and it's kind of distorted his features. And when he did look like Randy, Randy was in high school and then he didn't look like Randy."

"Maybe Randy was really Andrew Grey's secret son," Cam suggested excited. "And they set up the whole thing with the fire and the secret tunnel to kidnap him so he could take over Grey's empire after Grey had a stroke?"

Wren stared at the phone. "Cameron, that theory doesn't make any sense at all. And I'm sure Randy wasn't Andrew's son. Death's parents were totally in love. There's no way his mom would have cheated on his dad. Besides, you've seen the pictures. Death and Randy both look like their dad."

"Not as much as Randy looked like Andrew. And maybe she didn't know she cheated on him."

"You mean, like, she didn't notice it wasn't her husband she was having sex with? Are you saying Andrew disguised himself as Liam Bogart, like Zeus disguised himself as Alcmene's husband to father Hercules?"

"What?" Cam asked.

"What?" Annie asked.

Wren sighed. "Classical mythology? Never mind."

"Maybe he made a clone of Liam, but with his own DNA." Cameron was on a roll. "The Grey family is into some pretty cutting-edge medical research — cell splitting and cryobiology and such. Maybe he made a clone and it fathered Randy and when Randy hit a certain age they needed to study him — for science — so they made another clone and dressed it up in a fire-fighter costume and switched it with the real Randy so they could take him back to their lab and experiment on him. Only they got the badge number wrong."

"It would have to have been a clone that had the same dental work done that he did," Wren pointed out, exasperated. "They ID'd Randy by matching his dental records, remember?"

"I like it," Annie said unexpectedly.

Wren stared at her.

"Oh, I don't believe for a minute that that's what really happened," she agreed. "But I wish it was, because then Bogie might still be alive."

With Cam enlisted and sworn to reluctant secrecy, Wren and Annie settled down to their research.

"Andrew Grey has a Wikipedia entry," Wren said. "I've never actually known of anyone in real life who had their own Wiki entry." She read, "Andrew Stephen Grey, son of . . . grandson of . . . blah, blah, blah, three times great-grandson of 19th century brewing icon Aram Einstadt. Sole heir to the Einstadt family fortune, married five times. He has two children, I didn't know that."

"Right, by his third wife," Annie said. "She was the one who lasted the longest. Ten years and two days. His kids would be," she did the math in her head, "the boy's fifteen and the girl's eleven. Their mother has full custody. He doesn't even have visitation rights."

"That's a little unusual, isn't it?" Wren asked. "I wonder why not."

"Well, according to this, she divorced him for infidelity and conspicuous cruelty after he was caught in a scandal involving an orgy at an S and M fetishist party."

"They were at an orgy or he was at an orgy? There's news stories about orgies? Where are you finding this?"

"In *On the Scene Magazine*."

"Oh, I saw some links to articles on that in Google, but they were in the archives and you had to be a member to access them."

Annie blushed. "Okay, so I'm addicted to trashy celebrity gossip magazines."

"Well . . . great! Only, um, how reliable are they?"

"Probably not terribly, at least if you take them individually. For example, if you believe this magazine, Kate was pregnant for about two and half years before Prince

George actually popped out. If a story is repeated across a lot of the magazines, though, there's a lot higher chance that it'll be true."

"So we need to see if the orgy story is repeated elsewhere."

"It is. I actually found it first on *Look at the Starz.* I came here to double check. It's all hearsay and anonymous sources, but the story is pretty much identical. Andrew already had a reputation as a playboy. His first wife was a socialite, like him. They got married in their early twenties, all satin and lace and respectability. A couple of years later she filed for divorce on the grounds of infidelity. As soon as the divorce was finalized, he married his mistress, but that one only lasted three years. Then he married wife number three. She was a model like numbers two and five. Four was an actress."

"So what was the scandal? Just that he got caught having an orgy?"

"It was a kinky, S and M fetish party, and the hosts called the police on him after he refused to honor one of his partners' safe word. When they investigated, it turned out that the girl he'd brought to the party with him had a fake ID. She was a minor. He claimed he didn't know how old she really was, but no one believed him. I think that's what lost him custody of his kids."

"He sounds like a charming fellow."

Wren went back to her laptop, adjusted her search terms, and tried again. "The third wife was Leilani Moran, right? She's the one who sued for access to him after he had a stroke." She clicked the link. "This is confusing. I'm getting the news stories all out of order."

"Yeah, same here. Only with me, I'm getting the wives all out of order."

"Apparently, the Grey family is worth a fortune. Cam's right, they're not only into pharmaceuticals, but they have a lot of connections with advanced medical research."

"Yeah, and they're very careful to guard that fortune. I remember an article from back when Andrew and Alaina first got married. Let me see if I can find it."

"You remember a ten-year-old gossip article about a couple that isn't even really famous?"

"I only remember it because it struck me as so weird at the time. And it was about their wedding and I was planning my wedding to Rowdy at the same time."

They read, each pursuing their own line of inquiry, in silence for several minutes.

"Here it is," Annie said. "They had a prenup."

"A lot of couples get pre-nups," Wren pointed out. "Even Death and Madeline had a pre-nup, fortunately."

"Yeah, Bogie mentioned that. Their grandmother was a lawyer. But this was a really weird pre-nup. For one thing, it pretty much assumed that the marriage was going to end in divorce."

"Pessimism or realism?"

"Yeah, I don't know. Anyway, according to the terms of their pre-nup, if this article is right, if he filed for divorce, he would have to pay her alimony until and unless she remarried, *unless* he could prove infidelity, in which case she wouldn't get anything. If she filed for divorce, she wouldn't get anything *unless* she could prove infidelity or cruelty, in which case she'd get either a lump sum or monthly alimony, depending on the circumstances and how long they'd been married. And it also said that, if the marriage ended for any reason, she had to return all gifts he'd given her and repay any moneys that she'd been advanced as his wife."

"That's mercenary."

"Yeah, that's what I thought. I was marrying my high school sweetheart at the time, for love and for forever, and the contrast stuck with me, though I hadn't thought of it in ages."

Wren's phone rang and she answered to find Death on the line. She talked for a couple of minutes and then hung up.

"He's back at Randy's," she said. "The doctor gave him a prescription for antibiotics and he's going to take it easy for the rest of the day. I need to get back there and keep an eye on him. I don't like leaving him alone when he's sick, even if it's not supposed to be serious. Madeline did that. I'm not Madeline."

"I can understand that," Annie said, still reading. "Oh, wow!"

"Oh, wow?"

"Wife number four tried to kill him. With a stiletto heel. Prada." Annie sniffed. "That's such a cliche."

"A cliche?" Wren asked, eyebrows raised.

"Well, as much as killing someone with a shoe can ever be a cliche, yeah, I'd say so."

"So you'd use, what? A Reebok?"

"Ha ha. Very funny. *Obviously* I'd use a pair of Mary Janes. Give it that certain, extra-creepy, kinky overtone."

"Why'd she try to kill him, I wonder?"

"I don't know. They were only married two months. She was the actress, so maybe she had a more violent temperament than the models did."

"Maybe," Wren conceded. "I know, I was in the drama club in high school and let me tell you. The drama taking place on the stage was the least of it!"

"She pled innocent by reason of insanity," Annie said, still reading. "Spent a few years in a rehab facility and now she works as an instructor at an acting school in," she snickered suddenly, "the San Fernando Valley."

"Why is that funny?"

"Well, you know what the San Fernando Valley is known for?" Wren just shook her head, bewildered.

"The San *Porn*ando Valley."

"Good heavens! Really? How do you even know all this stuff?"

"I read, like, fifteen of these magazines a week."

"So it's possibly not a, shall we say, prestigious acting academy?" Wren asked.

"Well, it might be. But it also might not. Why?"

"I don't know. I just thought she might be someone we could talk to who actually knows Andrew Grey. Though I'd really like to talk to Leilani and find out why she was so determined to get in and see him. Apparently, she tried to get in to see him in the hospital right after he had his stroke, but

Alaina wouldn't allow it. She filed the suit on the grounds that she was concerned about his welfare and that, as the mother of his children, she had a right to know how he was doing. She also claimed it was unethical for his brother-in-law to be his physician and tried to get the court to appoint another doctor to care for him."

"What happened?"

"It dragged through the courts for just over four months. She finally dropped it when Alaina let her in to see him."

"So it didn't amount to anything after all?"

"Probably not," Wren agreed.

"You sound like you're not too sure of that."

"It's just that the timing is funny."

"How?"

"Alaina let Leilani in to see Andrew in the hospital three days after Randy died."

FIFTEEN

When Madeline showed up again — alone this time — Wren answered the door with a finger to her lips.

"Death's not feeling well. The doctor gave him some antibiotics and he's sleeping right now. I don't want him to wake up. What do you need?"

"What do you mean he's not feeling well? He looked fine the other day."

"You couldn't hear him coughing and sounding all congested?"

"Well . . . I guess. So he's got a cold. So what?"

Wren sighed, impatient. "His lungs are damaged. A chest cold is a lot worse for him than it is for other people."

"Oh." She frowned. "I never thought of that."

"What did you want?" Wren asked again.

Madeline shrugged, seeming at a loss. "I was just bored. My mom's got the baby.

Eric's at his seminar and I have his car. I thought I'd see if Death'd like to look up some of our old friends from high school or visit some of our old haunts."

"I see." Wren felt her hackles rise. Madeline was trying to reconnect with Death. Apparently she thought she still had a shot at getting him back.

Over her dead body, Wren thought. *Still . . .*

"You grew up in St. Louis, didn't you?"

"Yes, we both did. One of the many things we have in common."

Choosing to ignore that, Wren opened the door wider. "Why don't you come in? Have a cup of coffee and tell me about it." Madeline followed her into the kitchen, looking around curiously.

"What's Death going to do with the house?"

"Sell it probably."

"That's good. I never did like this place. I never felt welcome here. I never got along with Death's family, you know. I don't know why. I really felt we were perfect for one another, but they kept trying to pull us apart."

"Is that how you remember it?"

"That's how it was. I mean, we were *the* most popular couple in school. I was head cheerleader. Death was captain of the

246

baseball team. We were homecoming king and queen our senior year. Obviously we belonged together."

Wren smiled a fake little smile and wondered where Randy had kept his firecrackers. "So, I was wondering," she said. "You're from St. Louis. Do you know anything about the Einstadt family?"

Madeline shot her a shrewd, calculating look.

"Oh, so *that's* your angle. Well, I can tell you right now, you're wasting your time."

Wren blinked, nonplussed. "What are you talking about?"

"The Einstadts. Or, rather, the Greys now. That relationship is far too distant. There's no way Death's ever going to see any of that money."

"Any of that . . . ? Madeline, are you saying Death is related to the Einstadts?"

"Sure. Isn't that why you were asking?"

"No. I didn't know they were. Does Death know?"

"He should know. I told him. I suppose he might not have been paying attention to me. I always hated the way he'd just tune me out sometimes."

Wren thought about it. "Okay, I'm not following you. How would you know they were related if Death didn't know they were related?"

Madeline sighed. "Like I said, it's a really distant relationship. My mom found it because she's into genealogy. Do you know who Nonna Rogers was?"

"Yeah, Death's mother's grandmother. She passed away shortly before his parents were killed."

"Right. Well, her maiden name was Terhaar. Her great-aunt was Sarah Terhaar who married Aram Einstadt, so Andrew Grey's three or four times great-grandmother."

"And that would explain the resemblance between Randy and Andrew."

"What resemblance?"

Wren showed Madeline the pictures of the two men and Madeline studied them, pulling at her lower lip. "Yeah, they do look a lot alike. Too bad Randy didn't get Andrew's charm."

"From what I've heard, Randy was the one with charm. You only think otherwise because you equate charm with capital."

"It's as good a measure as any."

"No. No, it's really not."

"Anyway, it isn't like it matters now. You know, I've always figured it was some kind of karma, Randy dying the way he did."

Wren gave Madeline a dubious glare. "What do you mean?"

"You know that he and I never got along, right? Well, he's dead and I'm not. I call that divine justice right there."

Wren scowled at her. "I wouldn't be so quick to cite karma if I were you," she said.

"Why not?"

"Because I'm having dinner with Death tonight and you have a hot date with Eric Farrington."

"Look what I found!"

Death scrubbed a hand over his face and struggled to drag himself upright in bed. His cheeks were flushed with sleep and a low fever and he had an impressive case of bedhead. "Waffles?" he asked, bewildered.

"I made the waffles," Wren said, "I found the tray to bring them to you in bed." It was a pretty metal tray with legs, designed for just this purpose. She set it aside on the bedside table and helped him sit up, fluffing his pillows and piling them in behind him for support. "How do you feel this morning?"

"I'm fine," he said automatically and she clicked her tongue in disapproval.

"Yeah, you look fine. Here, I brought you your meds. Have a few bites of waffle first, so they're not hitting your stomach while it's empty."

She put the tray in his lap and he did as she asked, obedient and still not entirely awake. When he'd eaten a little of the waffles, she put four pills, two antibiotics, and two pain pills in his hand and held out the glass of orange juice.

"No coffee?"

"Coffee would wake you up. I don't think that's what you need this morning."

"I gotta get up," he said. "I gotta get up and . . . do . . . something."

"No, you've gotta rest and get better so you'll be up to doing something."

"You didn't have to bring me breakfast in bed," he said, sleepy and bashful.

"I know I didn't have to. I wanted to. I like this bed tray. Was it your grandma's?"

"Yeah. I don't know where she got it. She had it for years."

By the time he finished the waffles and orange juice he was listing to the side and almost asleep again. He yawned and blinked furiously, trying to wake up. "I don't know why I'm so tired."

"You're worn out. You've been fighting this chest infection and it's exhausted you. Now that you have medicine to fight it for you, your body's trying to crash. It's okay. There's nowhere you have to be today and nothing you have to do. Just take it easy and

250

give yourself a chance to get better." She set the tray back on the bedside table and helped him slide back down in the bed, fluffing his pillows and pulling the light blanket up around his shoulders.

"What are you going to do?" he fretted.

"I'll be right here in the next room if you need anything."

"But you'll get bored."

"Don't worry about me. I can entertain myself. I'm just going to go online and chat with Annie."

Annie was waiting when Wren got online.

"I found a copy of that wedding portrait on the Internet. Not the painting, but the photo it was painted from." She sent a link and Wren clicked on it. "How did you find that?"

"The almighty Google."

"Of course. Silly I asked." She studied the picture. "That beard he was wearing really did look pretty ridiculous."

"Yeah," Annie typed. "What is that? Is it a goatee?"

"A Van Dyke, I think."

"Like Dick Van Dyke?"

"Or the painter, maybe?"

"Oh. Yeah, I suppose. One of my gossip magazines did a story on the wedding. They said the beard was to hide stitches and bruises from when the wife before went after him with the shoe. I don't know if that's true or not."

"How soon after the divorce did he and Alaina get married, do you know?"

"Not very long. A couple of weeks or so. He must have been having an affair with Alaina the whole time he was married to Prada-girl."

Wren's phone rang and she answered it.

"Typing is tedious," Annie said. "Why don't we just talk?"

Wren glanced over her shoulder. Death was curled under the covers and she could hear him snoring. She kept her voice low. "Yeah, okay. That works for me. Hey! I know why there was a resemblance between them. I got it from Death's ex-wife, of all people. It seems Andrew Grey and the Bogarts were shirttail relatives."

"So you're thinking Andrew and Bogie were both some kind of throwback to a common ancestor?"

"Maybe? Yeah?"

"They sure did look a lot alike," Annie said. "One of my magazines has this program online to let you see what you'd look like with your hair and whatnot different. I ran Andrew's picture through it, changed his hair color, and got rid of the beard. You want to see?"

"Sure."

Wren opened the email Annie sent her and found two pictures, side by side.

"My God! If Randy wasn't wearing his uniform, you wouldn't be able to tell which was which."

"You think?"

"Well, yeah."

"Wren, I Photoshopped their clothes. The one in the uniform is Andrew. The other one is Bogie."

There was a long silent stretch while the two women studied the pictures. It was Annie who finally broke it to voice what they were both thinking but what each was afraid to put into words.

"If that man was shaved and his hair dyed, no one could tell him from Bogie. Not you or me. Not Cap or Rowdy or the other guys. Not Sophie at the coroner's office. Nobody. Is it possible? Is it even remotely possible?"

Wren was slow to answer. She felt she was in dangerous waters and wanted to tread carefully.

"This is an old picture. Andrew didn't look like that anymore," she said. "He had plastic surgery, remember? It distorted his features."

"His face was crushed and burned in the fire. That could have been on purpose."

"So what we're thinking here is that it was actually Andrew who died. Alaina, for some reason, didn't want anyone to know he died."

"Leilani," Annie said. "She was the one with the lawsuit. Alaina didn't want Leilani to know he died."

"Why not?"

"I don't know."

"Okay, put that aside for now. Andrew died. It would have to have been right before the fire, don't you think? They did an autopsy. They'd have noticed if the body was dead more than a short time."

"I can't explain that either."

"Right, so we'll come back to that too. Andrew died and Alaina needed him alive. She knew that Randy looked like him."

"How?" Now it was Annie asking.

"Easy. She saw his picture on the front page of the paper when the station visited the school for fire safety day."

"Yes! And that's where she got the number for his badge and why it was wrong."

"Right. So she got a set of turnouts . . . somewhere . . . and a uniform, and had a set of fake badges made. I don't know how she'd have managed that, but she's filthy rich, so that probably helps."

"You can order uniforms and turnouts off the Internet. With expedited shipping, she could have them in a day or two. Hey! Maybe she knew he was dying, so she got all the stuff ready. Then, when he did die, she set the fire in the brewery, lured Bogie into the room with the tunnel entrance, kidnapped him, and left Andrew's body in his place."

"By herself?" Wren was skeptical.

"No, of course not. She's rich. She must have minions."

"Annie, she couldn't even get a steamer trunk home from three houses away. If she has minions, why didn't she just call them to come get her trunk?"

"You're being silly. Minions don't move furniture. Minions move bodies and kidnap people."

"Yeah, what *was* I thinking?"

"So then Bogie's alive!" Annie said, and alarm bells went off for Wren.

"No! Wait! You can't start thinking that! You know how farfetched and improbable this all is. You're only going to get your hopes up for the impossible."

"But I want to think it."

"I know. So do I. But I don't want to see you get hurt again. You see? This is why

255

we're not telling Death about this."

"But it explains the badges! Nothing else explains the badges."

"But it doesn't explain the dental records. It doesn't explain how she managed to time Andrew's death to coincide with the fire, or how a tiny woman could have kidnapped a six-foot firefighter without causing a ruckus. And it doesn't explain why, if he were still alive, Randy hasn't contacted anyone." A thought struck Wren and it left her cold.

"You know, the only way I can think that this would work would be if Randy was in on it."

"He never would have!" Annie answered at once. "You take that back!"

"I'm just trying to point out how unlikely this is. You can't get excited. You can't get your hopes up."

"So we're just going to forget the whole thing?"

"Of course not. This all has something to do with the Greys. It has to. We just have to keep digging until we find out what it is. Can you think of any way we could get in to talk to Andrew?" There was another long stretch where neither of them was saying anything.

"We could pretend to be encyclopedia salesmen," Annie offered finally.

"Really?"

"Okay, no."

"How about this then," Wren said. "Maybe we could find someone else who's seen him or talked to him lately and talk to them?"

"Oh! Good idea. But who?"

"I don't know. Servants? Big house, rich couple. They must have servants. Alaina mentioned a gardener. I bet there's a cook, too, and at least one maid. Maybe people who visit the house, too? Clergy? Delivery-men? Someone to read the meter, maybe?"

"Right! We'll be regular detectives! When?"

Wren hesitated. "Let's wait and see what happens this afternoon. I don't want to leave Death alone when he's sick. Wait until he's up and around and I'll tell him we're going shopping or something."

Wren was in the kitchen cooking lunch when Death finally got up and dragged himself out of bed. He felt hungover and disoriented, but better than he had in several days. He was also hungry again, and he staggered out of the bedroom in his T-shirt and boxer shorts, following the smell of food. There was a salad sitting in the middle of the table, buns warming in the oven, and hamburgers sizzling on the stove. Wren had her phone to her ear and when she saw him she started guiltily and blushed.

"Hey, my invalid's up," she told the person on the other end of the line. "I've gotta go. I'll call you back in a little bit, okay?"

He dropped into a chair at the table and Wren turned the burner off under the skillet and came over to kiss his cheek and feel his forehead. "I think your fever's gone down. How do you feel?"

"Better. Starving."

"I've got just the thing for that." She bustled about the kitchen, fixing their plates and opening the refrigerator to set out pickles and condiments.

Death watched her and marveled, again, at how much his life had changed since she'd come into it. In the months before he'd met her, he'd been fresh out of the VA hospital. He'd been homeless and perpetually broke, dealing with the aftermath of his injuries with scant resources and no one who cared. He was always hungry, often in pain, starkly alone. Now . . . there had been times in his life when he'd had more people who loved him, but he'd never felt more loved.

"Who were you talking to?"

"Oh, Annie. We were thinking of going shopping this afternoon. I wanted to wait and see how you were feeling, and if you had any plans."

"Better. I'm feeling better. I thought I'd just hang around and watch TV, maybe start trying to dig my way through those legal papers Cap brought me. You ladies can go do whatever it is you're wanting to do. I'll be fine."

"Are you sure?"

"I'm sure." He waited while she put the finishing touches on their meal. Weighed his words. "I know there's something you're not telling me," he said. Wren practically jumped and gave him such a guilty look that he nearly laughed.

"It's okay. Whatever it is. It's okay. I trust you."

She brought his hamburger over and set it in front of him, then stood beside him for a moment, leaning against him and combing her fingers through his hair. "How did you know?"

"That you were keeping secrets? You're the world's worst liar. Most honest people are." She sighed and sat down.

"It's just something . . . weird . . . that Annie and I stumbled across."

"More weirdness. Yay."

"I know, right? Listen, we're trying to find out some more information. It's probably just a wild coincidence, but as soon as we have more than crazy theories, I promise, I'll tell you everything."

"I know. I trust you. It's okay."

"Dance with me."

Andrew turned to find Alaina watching him. He'd been exploring again and it looked like he'd been busted. "The room moved," he muttered vaguely, feigning confusion.

"It's probably just the medicine. Do you know what today is? It's our anniversary."

"I don't remember."

"That's okay. Just dance with me."

"But the room moved. The little room. Now I don't know where I am."

"Silly. That was the elevator. This is the ballroom. We have parties here. Or we used to. One day, when you're better, we will again." She crossed the polished hardwood floor. At the far end was a raised platform for a band or small orchestra, but there was also a high-end music system built into the wall. "You like parties?" he asked.

"I love parties." Alaina smiled to herself. "I invite fat women with ugly husbands just so I can watch them be jealous." She fiddled with the music and a song came up. She moved into his arms, tiny, delicate and bird-like, and drew him into the middle of the room.

He recognized "The Lady In Red" by Roy Orbison and an eerie sense of familiarity came over him. For the first time in what seemed like forever, he felt like he'd done this before. Andrew closed his eyes and followed the memory as they swayed in the middle of the room.

He was in a rented reception hall, heavily decorated with flowers and lace. Peach and gold, he remembered. Everything was peach and gold. She was in his arms, exquisite in an elegant and ridiculously expensive wedding gown. He despised her and she knew it, but she'd won. Smug in her victory, she'd demanded that he dance with her. Under the circumstances he couldn't refuse, so he'd gritted his teeth, forced a smile, and complied.

Orbison's voice was rich and haunting and entirely unsuited to his mood as he swayed obediently in time to the music and fantasized about snapping her pretty little neck. So why was he doing this again today?

He stopped abruptly and stepped away. "I don't want to dance with you."

"Do you want to dance to a different song?"

"I think I'd like to go back downstairs now."

Still frowning, but gentle, she helped him to the elevator and they descended to the second floor. They left the cage with Andrew leaning more heavily on Alaina than he really needed to. He didn't want her to figure out that he was no longer quite the invalid he had been. The maid was in the hall and she looked up when they emerged.

"Mrs. Grey," she said respectfully, "the gardener has your steamer trunk ready. If you know where you'd like it, I'll have him bring it up."

"In a little while," Alaina snapped, taking out on the help the annoyance she'd suppressed for Andrew. Unperturbed, Maria bobbed a quick curtsey and went back to her dusting.

They went into the bedroom and Alaina helped him lower himself into a chair. Outside the window, Andrew could see heat shimmering off the black asphalt roof tiles that topped the kitchen ell. The house was heavily air conditioned, though, and he shivered in the cool air. Alaina brought a quilted throw and tucked it around him.

"I think you've tired yourself out today," she said, ruffling his hair and feeling his forehead. "Just rest for awhile and I'll have

Maria get you your medicine."

"I feel like Nancy Drew," Annie said.

"I feel like an idiot." Wren adjusted her sunglasses and peered through the passenger window of Annie's car at the mansions across the street. They were parked, again, on the Einstadt Brewery lot, with the Grey house two doors down to their left. "What are we even doing here?"

"We're trying to get to see Andrew Grey, to see if he really is Andrew Grey."

"But how?" They'd been racking their brains about that all day and came up with nothing that Wren considered a viable idea. Annie's definition of "viable" was a lot broader and she had half a dozen wild plans. "Why don't we just go up, ring the bell, and ask to see him?"

"She's not going to just take us in there and introduce us. Especially if there's something shady going on. She didn't offer to let us meet him yesterday, did she? When we were already in the house."

"Yeah, but we didn't exactly ask, either."

"Not gonna work, Anners."

"Hey, Anners! I like that. A new nickname for Annie."

"Or short for 'Bananners'. That works too."

Annie stuck her tongue out. She was in high spirits and Wren knew, with a deep sense of foreboding, that she'd already made up her mind that Andrew Grey was really Randy Bogart. If this backfired, as it was apt to, she was going to be devastated all over again. "Okay, smartass, you don't like my idea, come up with a better one."

Wren wrinkled her brow in thought. "Maybe we could pretend to be magazine reporters. We're doing a story on . . . the St. Louis brewing families. Death and I have read up on some of the history, you know. It wasn't just the Einstadt family that lived in this neighborhood. That yellow house belonged to a member of the Pabst family, I think, and the Lemp mansion is just a couple of blocks away."

"Ooh! The haunted Lemp mansion! Okay, then. Let's do this!"

Annie opened her car door. Wren caught her arm.

"Annie, wait. Is this really a good idea? Death says I'm a terrible liar."

"Really? I'm a great liar. I lie all the time. 'Oh, no, honey! I don't think your hairline's receding at all!' " She got out of the car and leaned back in to glare at Wren. "Come *on*! Let's *go*!"

Five minutes later they were back on the

sidewalk in front of the Grey house, frustrated and discouraged. Summer had finally asserted itself and Wren felt like she was melting in the damp heat. Her shirt stuck to her back and her hair stuck to her forehead and, even after only a few minutes in the sun, she could feel her fair skin beginning to burn.

The maid who answered the door had been polite, uninformative, and as disinclined to chat as anyone she'd ever met. No, Mrs. Grey wasn't taking visitors at the moment. No, Mr. Grey was not available. No, she didn't know anything about the family history, nor the house's history, nor the brewery's history. Perhaps they could check the library. Good day.

"Now what?" Wren asked.

"I dunno," Annie admitted. "Maybe we'd have more luck with the neighbors."

"Yeah . . ." Wren's eyes sharpened as she watched a uniformed figure approach. "Or maybe we could ask the mail carrier."

The carrier who delivered to Einstadt Avenue was a woman. Wren judged her to be in her late fifties, but fit. She had wiry hair dyed an unnatural bronze; raw, sunburned features; and freckles on her arms. Her uniform shorts showed off a pair of perfectly toned legs and Wren tried not to be jealous as they approached her.

"Oh, yeah. I've been on this route twenty years next October. I used to see Andrew Grey all the time before his stroke. He'd wait for the mail, every day sometimes, for months at a time. I figured he was having affairs and he didn't want his wife — whichever wife it was at the time — to see the love letters."

"Have you seen him recently?" Wren asked.

"Not too often. He's been in the garden a couple of times in the past few weeks. That stroke really messed with his head."

"How so?"

"Well, he's polite now, for one thing. Spoke to me like a human being, and let me tell you, he's never done that before. He asked me who I was and if I knew him. Seemed all vague and discombobulated. I didn't get to talk to him much, though. That wife of his was hovering around him like a little bumblebee. Shooting me dirty looks." The woman cackled. "Maybe she thought I was after her sugar daddy."

When they were back in the car, Annie started the engine and cranked the A/C and they sat for a moment staring at the Grey house.

"Could he be . . . hypnotized?" Annie

asked. "Like, maybe someone hypnotized him ahead of time so that all they had to do was say some trigger word and he'd think he was Andrew Grey?"

"I don't know." Wren thought the idea was bizarre, but then there wasn't much about this situation that wasn't bizarre. "Or drugged maybe? Is that possible? Are there drugs you could give someone to confuse them and make them forget who they are?"

Talia was not happy with the question.

"How can you ask me that?"

She was at home with her girlfriend when they found her. Trinka was a small, spry woman with sharp, elvish features and frizzy hair. She'd greeted them with a broad, puckish grin, but now she watched them all, moist-eyed with sympathy.

"I can understand Wren coming up with these wild ideas," Tal said, "she never knew Bogie. But he was my friend and he died on my watch and you want to make up silly, fantastic stories about him?"

"Tal, honey," Annie said. "We're not asking you this to hurt you. We know it's farfetched, but it's the only thing we can think of that would explain the mystery with the badges and the tunnel to the brewery."

"I know you're not *trying* to hurt anyone.

But that's the only thing that can come out of this. Not just me, but Rowdy and Cap and Bogie's brother, all the guys at the station. Dead people don't come back to life. Bogie's gone. You've got to accept that." She walked away from them, into the other room. Wren gave Trinka an embarrassed, apologetic glance and Trinka smiled at her sympathetically in return.

Tal stopped in the doorway and spoke once more, without looking back.

"Yes," she said. "Yes, they could. There are drugs that would do that. It's possible."

SIXTEEN

"I know why Alaina needs Andrew alive!"

Death frowned. "What?"

There was a long silence from the other end of the phone line. "Cameron? Hello?"

"Wren?" Cam said finally. "Your voice sounds funny."

"This isn't Wren. It's Death. Wren's in the shower. What are you talking about?"

"Why are you answering Wren's phone? This is Wren's phone, isn't it?"

"Yes, it's Wren's phone. I answered it because you've called three times in the last five minutes. I thought it must be urgent and Wren's in the shower."

"Oh. You tricked me!"

"I didn't trick you. You started talking before I could say hello."

Behind Death, the bathroom door opened. He turned as Wren emerged in shorts and a T-shirt, a towel wrapped around her head. She gave him a questioning look and he held up her phone. "It's Cameron. He knows why Alaina needs Andrew alive?"

Wren's mouth tightened and she took the phone. "You suck at conspiracy, Cam." She listened. "Tricked you how?" She tucked the phone against her shoulder and addressed Death. "He says it's a voodoo, ex-Marine, mojo thing."

"Right. Well," he gestured vaguely behind him, "I'll just take my mojo in the kitchen, if you need anything."

He went in the kitchen and started a pot of coffee. He was just pouring out the first cup when Wren came in carrying her laptop and sat at the table. Death gave her the cup of coffee he'd just poured and fixed himself another one. She waited until he took the chair across from her to speak.

"I didn't want you to go off half-cocked, come up with a bunch of wild ideas, get your hopes up, and set yourself up for a fall. That's all."

"And you thought I would?"

"Well, that's what Annie and I have been doing."

"You still don't have to tell me if you don't want to," he said, though the curiosity was eating at him.

"I think it's maybe hit the point where you need to know."

"Okay, then."

She opened her computer and fiddled with the keys for a few seconds.

"That auction Annie and I went to was just up the street from the Greys' house. Alaina was there. She bought an antique steamer trunk and Annie and I carried it home for her. To get a peek inside her house, you know?"

"Nosy girls," he teased. "What did you see?"

"Andrew and Alaina's wedding portrait. This is the photograph it was painted from."

She turned the computer so he could see the screen and Death's breath caught in his throat. He was sure his heart skipped at least one beat. "Randy?"

He took several long minutes to process this. "Andrew Grey looks . . . a lot . . . like Randy."

Wren got up, came around the table, and wrapped her arms around his shoulders. He leaned into her and she rubbed his back. "So what kind of half-cocked, wild ideas did you come up with?" he finally asked her.

"Oh, all kinds. DNA experiments, cloning, Randy being a secret Einstadt heir, space aliens, body snatchers . . ." She went back to her seat and pulled the computer aside so she could look at him directly.

"We've been researching Andrew and Alaina Grey. She's his fifth wife. He has a reputation for not being a very nice person, but she's stayed married to him for almost ten years. Part of that, or all of that, is probably because she signed a really stupid pre-nup. It said that, if she left him, she had to be able to prove infidelity or cruelty on his part or she'd get nothing. And even if she did prove something, she'd have to return everything he'd ever given her and pay back any money he'd let her have. One source suggests that he paid her brother's way through medical school, so we're probably talking a couple of hundred thousand dollars."

Death drained his coffee. He reached back to the counter and snagged the pot so he could refill his cup. He had a feeling he was going to be needing a lot of coffee. "Go on."

"Andrew collapsed at his country club almost fifteen months ago. He was rushed to a private hospital and Alaina's brother was his personal physician. For four months he was kept completely incommunicado. No one saw him but Alaina and his private medical team."

"That's not entirely unusual."

"No, I know. But his third wife, Leilani Moran, thought it was suspicious. So much so that she filed a lawsuit demanding access to him. She's the mother of his only two children and she claimed that as giving her the right to know how he was. They settled the lawsuit out of court when Alaina finally let her visit Andrew, three days after Randy died."

"So you're thinking — let me see if I follow you — you're thinking that Andrew died but Alaina didn't want anyone to know about it. She saw Randy's picture in the paper, saw the resemblance, and arranged to have Randy kidnapped and Andrew's body left in his place."

"There are a whole lot of logistic problems with that. I know there are. But, yeah. That's what we were thinking."

"How would she kidnap him? How would she keep him prisoner all this time? Randy's a smart guy. He'd figure out a way to get out, or to get a message out."

Wren gave him a worried, pitying look, and he knew she'd caught the present tense. He'd used it on purpose though, not so much latching onto a new idea as finally surrendering to an old one. This is what he'd been thinking since the moment he knew about the second badge. It wasn't his brother's body. It was an imposter. His brother was alive.

"Annie suggested hypnosis, but I thought drugs were more likely. We talked to the mail carrier who delivers on that street. She's seen him in the garden a couple of times. She says he acts vague and confused, and he's changed. He seems nice now. But she hasn't really talked to him. Alaina never lets him out of her sight."

"But why would Alaina need Andrew alive?"

"I didn't know," Wren said.

"But now you do?"

"Leilani's lawsuit. Cameron got copies of the transcript from one of the hearings. See, Andrew figured the women were only marrying him for his money, so he decided to make it a competition. He gave Alaina and each of his exes a copy of his will. The one who stayed married to him the longest is the one who inherits."

"And that's Leilani?"

"It is right now. Tomorrow Alaina ties her record and Thursday Alaina becomes the heir."

Wren sniffed. Something was starting to burn. There was flour on the counter and a mixing bowl in the sink and Death's grandmother's rolling pin lay in the dish drainer, wiped clean rather than submersed, to protect the ball bearings. She jumped up and grabbed a hot pad and pulled a pan of biscuits out of the oven. They were a little dark, but still perfectly edible. She found a trivet for the hot pan and set it down to cool.

Death, staring off into space, didn't seem to notice.

She transferred the hot biscuits to a plate and set it on the table, got butter and jam and honey out to go with them, and returned to her seat. "What do we do now?" she asked.

Death shook himself. "We've got to find out if it's really Randy and, if it is, we've got to rescue him. They can't be planning to keep him around as Andrew forever, and after Thursday they won't need him any more."

"You think they'd kill him?"

"I wouldn't take a chance that they might not."

"So how do we find out if it's really him? Couldn't we just call the police and tell them what we suspect? Because if it's really him then it's kidnapping and that's a crime. They'd have to investigate a crime, wouldn't they?"

"Would they?" Death sighed. "It's a far-fetched theory. You said that yourself. Don't you think the police would think I was just grasping at straws? That I couldn't cope with losing my brother and latched on to the physical resemblance between him and Andrew to hatch some wild fantasy that he was still alive."

"Yeah, but —"

"But? Dad was a cop, Wren. Believe me when I tell you this. Cops hear everything, from ghosts to aliens to government conspiracies. They get pretty skeptical pretty fast." He saw the plate on the table in front of him. "Oh, you made biscuits!" he said, snagging one.

"Um, no, actually, you made biscuits."

"Oh, yeah. I did. I forgot." He opened it and buttered it and Wren helped herself to one. "The Greys are rich, too. That gives Alaina a lot of leverage. It probably shouldn't, but realistically, it does. We need to find some way to prove that it's him."

"Maybe we could get Leilani involved?" Wren suggested. "If Andrew really is dead, then she's being swindled out of her inheritance. Plus, she's rich too, so that'd give her leverage."

"Maybe. But I still think a judge is more apt to think she's just being mercenary."

"You're right." Wren fiddled with her own biscuit. "They'd probably accuse her of playing on your grief to further her own ends. I wish Madeline hadn't had the body cremated."

"You and me both."

"There must be something."

They lapsed into a companionable silence, eating biscuits and drinking coffee, both thinking but neither coming up with anything. When Death's phone rang, they both jumped. He glanced at the caller ID and looked up, meeting Wren's eyes.

"Sophie Depardieu." He answered it. "Hello?" Wren listened in on his end of the conversation.

"Yeah, great . . . the sooner, the better . . . okay, we'll be there. See you then."

He hung up and set the phone down carefully. "That might have been our break right there."

"Oh?"

"The autopsy report is ready. Sophie can meet us at two this afternoon to review it. We'll go over it with a fine-tooth comb. If it was really Andrew Grey and not Randy who died, there must be something in that report that will tell us so."

"Before we start," Death said, "we have something to show you."

Wren had printed out Andrew and

277

Alaina's wedding picture and the picture of Andrew that Annie had Photoshopped and she handed them across the desk one at a time.

"The man in this picture is Andrew Grey," Death told Sophie as she studied the first one. "His family owns the Einstadt Brewery and there is a secret tunnel that leads to the room where Randy supposedly died."

Sophie frowned. "Supposedly? Death —"

"Wait," Wren said, "there's more. The plywood hiding the tunnel has been disturbed within the last year or so. Andrew collapsed four months before Randy died and hasn't been seen publicly since. We've also learned that, because of the terms of his will, if he died before tomorrow his third wife would inherit his estate instead of his current wife."

"Rowdy's wife ran Andrew's picture through Photoshop," Death said. "This is what he'd look like without a beard and with Randy's hair color and uniform." Sophie gasped audibly upon seeing the picture, but then she lay both photographs facedown on her desk and clasped her hands on top of them.

"You said that Andrew collapsed four months before Randy died," she pointed out. "Don't you think we would have noticed if we were looking at a four-month-old corpse?"

"We figured he must have just been very ill for that time, or maybe they were keeping him on life support."

She was already shaking her head before he'd finished speaking.

"I can tell you right now, that's not the case. I know how much you want for your brother to not be dead, Death. I understand. But, I'm sorry, frankly I think you've gone completely off the rails. First of all, the aortic aneurysm that killed Randy was not something that would cause a long, lingering illness. It was pretty much instantly fatal. And any sort of long-term medical intervention would have been very, very obvious. Weight loss, changes in skin tone and coloring, needle marks, the presence of a feeding tube . . . anyone in this building would have spotted it a mile away. Hell, even the paramedics who tried to revive Randy would have seen it.

"I'm sorry," her voice was firm, sympathetic but intractable. "It's just not possible. You're going to have to accept that Randy's gone."

"Then there's some other explanation," Death said stubbornly. "That body was

Andrew Grey. It's the only thing that makes sense."

Sophie opened her mouth to argue, but Wren intervened. "Why don't we just go over the autopsy report and see if there's anything in there that stands out?"

The ME glanced at her, then gave her a small nod. She pulled a file folder over to the center of her desk, deliberately placing it on top of the pictures, and opened it. "Well," she said, "first off, Randy was a regular blood donor, so we know his blood type. That matches."

"Randy was O+," Death said. "It's the most common blood type in the U.S."

"True," Sophie conceded. She read farther down the page. "He was in good health apart from the aneurysm. Do you know what that is, by the way?"

Death nodded, but Wren hesitated. "I'm not entirely clear on that," she admitted.

"An aortic aneurysm is when the aorta dilates to more than one-and-a-half times its normal size. This weakens the walls of the aorta and if it ruptures, as Randy's did, massive hemorrhaging can lead to shock and death within minutes."

"Shouldn't there have been some signs or symptoms?"

"He might have experienced a little pain

from time to time, but if he did he probably shrugged it off as a pulled muscle or a cramp or something." She went back to the file. "His blood sugar was really high, but that's probably because he had nothing in his stomach but a little alcohol and a lot of sweet tea."

"No, that's wrong!" Wren pounced. "He spent the night before at Annie and Rowdy's house and they made him eat breakfast."

"They might have served him breakfast," Sophie said, "but he didn't eat it. Wren, it doesn't mean anything. Randy was a champion at getting rid of food without eating it. He came to dinner at my house once when my aunt was visiting. She has this horrible cabbage casserole she always makes and he totally charmed her by apparently putting away three helpings of it. I didn't figure out what he'd done until the next day, when I suddenly had the gassiest dog in the universe."

The sound of rustling paper drew their attention to Death. He had snagged a sheet from the open file and now he sat staring at it, trembling so badly that the paper shook in his hand. He looked up and met Sophie's eyes. "This is the dental record."

"Yes, that's right."

"And you matched this to the body?

There's absolutely no mistake about that?"

"Yes," she said, gently but emphatically. She sorted through the file for another page. "This is the dental X-ray taken of the corpse. You can see that they match."

Death smiled. It started slowly and built, like a tsunami, until he was grinning so broadly that it hurt.

"This is *not* my brother's dental record."

Sophie sat back in her chair and huffed in exasperation. "Yes. It is. We got it from his dentist. You can see his name on it, right there."

"I don't care whose name is on it. This isn't Randy's file." He turned it around so she could see. "You see this? It says his upper teeth are all original, one filling and a crown on a back molar."

"Yes, and?"

"And Randy's left canine is an implant. I still have the scar where the original was surgically removed from my arm." He rolled up his right sleeve and flexed an impressive bicep at them. A small, thin white line slanted down at an angle three inches below his shoulder.

"He bit you?" Sophie was completely nonplussed.

"Not on purpose. We were playing punch football."

"Punch football?" Wren asked.

"It's like touch football, but manlier."

"Yeah, it would be."

"But how could someone have altered the dental record?" Sophie persisted, still not ready to buy into the idea.

"I don't know. I'll find out."

"I don't even know what to say," Sophie said helplessly. "This is all just so fantastic. How . . . ?" She trailed off, holding her hands up with her fingers splayed in a questioning gesture.

"I don't know," Death said again. "I don't know and I don't care. The answers are there and we'll look until we find them. The only thing that matters is, my brother's alive."

Seventeen

It was a total cliche, Death thought, but maybe it was a cliche because it worked. And, he conceded reluctantly, it was also pretty stupid. Careful to avoid the power lines, he clamped himself more securely to the top of the pole, palmed a miniature set of binoculars, and trained them on the back exposure of the Grey house. He wore a hard hat, tool belt, and orange safety vest and he'd set caution barricades around the light pole he'd chosen. No one had given him a second glance.

From this vantage point he could see over the roof of the kitchen ell and down into the back garden, where a large, middle-aged man was working with the roses.

There were three rows of windows above the ell, so he concluded that it was a four-story house. If it came to the point of breaking and entering, that could be important to know. Now that he'd fully embraced the idea that Randy was alive, he was desperate to lay eyes on him.

He could see movement on the second floor. One window stood open and there was someone just beside it, sitting in an armchair reading. He could see a man's left hand and the book it was holding, but not enough of the reader to identify him. A door opened and a uniformed maid came in. She spoke to the reader, then turned and closed the window. A glare of sunlight and the reflection of trees obscured his view and Death cursed under his breath.

Below, a horn honked insistently. He looked down and groaned.

Captain Cairn's sedan was parked behind his Jeep and Cap was standing beside it, reaching in the window to blow the horn. When he saw that Death was looking at him, he pointed sternly to the ground. Death loosened the safety strap he'd secured himself with and climbed down slowly.

"How, exactly, is getting yourself electrocuted supposed to help this situation any?" Cap demanded.

"Wren tattled," he guessed, sadly aware that he sounded about five.

"Wren's worried about you."

"I wasn't going to touch the wires."

"Not on purpose, maybe. What if you'd

285

had a coughing fit while you were up there? Are you still taking antibiotics?"

Death stuck his hands in his pockets and shrugged.

Cap sighed. "It's hot out here," he said. "Come sit in my car and let's talk about this."

They climbed into Cap's car and Death had to admit the air conditioning was a relief. It was hot outside, hotter still in the full sun at the top of the light pole.

"Wren told you Randy's still alive?" Death asked.

"She told me your theory," Cap answered carefully.

"Jeez! Why is everyone so set against seeing this? He's alive. He has to be. It explains everything and it's the only thing that makes sense."

"Death, please try to understand, it's not that we don't want to believe you, and God knows it's not that we don't want you to be right. But it's just so farfetched. And yes, it would explain a lot, but there are also some pretty big questions left to answer. Like, if that was Andrew Grey's body, what happened to him between the time he collapsed and the time we pulled him out of that fire?"

"I don't know yet, but there has to be an answer and I will find it."

"You're going to have to. The only way forward here, that I can see, is to get a court to intervene. If they can order Alaina to allow an independent physician to examine Andrew, we can have them do DNA tests. Or, hell, even getting his fingerprints would do it."

"You think they'd have Randy's fingerprints on file?"

"I know they do. He and Talia had a response at a crime scene a couple years ago and they had to be fingerprinted so their prints could be eliminated from the investigation. The thing is, though, if you hope to convince a judge that there's merit to your claim, you're going to need answers to all those questions, even the hard ones. And you really need some sort of proof to back it up."

"The body came out of the fire wearing a badge he wasn't wearing and the wrong helmet. Isn't that proof?"

"It doesn't hurt," Cap admitted, "but it's a pretty thin thread to hang a wild idea on."

Death sighed. "What I want to do," he said, "is go over there, kick the door down, and take my brother back."

"And Alaina could shoot you for invading her home, the courts would believe you'd gone mad with grief, and who'd there be to rescue Bogie, if it *is* Bogie, then?"

"I know."

Cap tapped his fingers against the steering wheel. "You know, Wren's convinced they want you dead as it is. She's decided that the robbery you walked into was really an attempted hit."

"She's from a small town. Convenience store robberies are a lot more rare there than they are here."

"Still, it is pretty coincidental. The story about you investigating Bogie's death runs in the paper one day, you nearly get killed the next. It doesn't cost anything to be careful, son. At least, don't give them an excuse to get rid of you."

"Yeah, I know." Death ran a hand over his face, tired and frustrated. "I just want to see him. I want to see him so bad."

"That is the wildest idea anyone has ever brought me. And I did the interviews in the 'aliens stole my pencil' case."

"Aliens stole my pencil?" Wren asked.

St. Louis police detective Ray Starbourne leaned back in his chair and laced his hands together behind his head. "Nerd burglary. One nerd stole another nerd's Battle Beyond the Stars memorabilia. Lost his custom-made, engraved mechanical pencil at the

288

crime scene. I asked him to explain how it got there."

"Ah. Aliens stole my pencil."

"Exactly."

"This is not an 'aliens stole my pencil' idea," she said. "I know it sounds farfetched, but it also holds together, and it explains a lot." She had spent the morning tracking down Detective Starbourne. He was in charge of investigating a string of break-ins at area dental offices and clinics. Thieves were stealing X-ray machines. It was part of a larger wave of similar crimes that had hit the Midwest during the summer. The police, and the FBI, which was coordinating the investigations, suspected terrorists, gathering material for dirty bombs.

Randy's dentist was one that had been hit, though in that case the burglars had left without the machine after getting it stuck in the lab door.

"Well, you're right about the break-in at Weableau's office. That was definitely a copycat by amateurs. The MO wasn't the same at all. I figured someone saw the news reports about the other burglaries and figured it'd be an easy way to pick up some extra money."

"Look at this," Wren passed across the copy of the fake dental records Sophie had made her. "This is the dental record sent from Dr. Weableau's office to the coroner's office. I took it back and showed it to Marlene. She's Dr. Weableau's office manager. It was sent because it's the most recently dated of the X-rays in the file, but when she cross-checked it against billing records, Randy wasn't there on the date it was supposedly taken. Then we went through the other records in his file. They're all on this same type of form. But their office changed paper goods suppliers about six years ago. The older records should be on one of the older forms, with different spacing and a different font."

"You make a compelling case," he admitted. "I just don't know that it would be enough to convince a judge to let us intervene. If you could bring me fingerprints or something with DNA on it maybe. A toothbrush, some strands of hair —"

Wren tipped her head to the side speculatively.

"Would you need to know how I got them?"

Starbourne tipped his own head, an unconscious mirror of her actions. "That would depend entirely on whether or not you got caught."

■ ■ ■ ■

Death was waiting in his Jeep when Wren got back to Randy's house. He leaned across the seat and opened the door for her.

"Hop in. I want to show you something."

"Okay. What?"

"You'll see."

Wren shrugged to herself and got in. Death was practically thrumming with tension, the air in the Jeep charged with it.

"So," she said, a bit hesitantly, "I called Captain Cairn and told him what's going on."

"Yeah, I know. He came and found me and made me climb down from my light pole."

"You climbed a light pole?" She turned in her seat to glare at him more directly.

He blushed and cringed defensively. "I didn't get electrocuted." He waited, but she just continued to glare, so he went on. "I was trying to get a better look at the Grey house. The bedrooms are on the second floor. There was a man in one of them reading a book, but I couldn't see enough to identify him. The house is four stories. They have at least one maid and a gardener built like Mount Rushmore."

291

"You're thinking of breaking in?"

"Well, yeah."

"I talked to the detective who's investigating the dental office burglaries," she told him. "He suggested that we try to get fingerprints or DNA. He's interested, but he doesn't think we have enough grounds for a judge to allow the police to intervene yet."

"Cap said the same thing."

Death pulled into a small lot and stopped. "Do you recognize where we are?"

Wren looked around. There was a playground off to her right and a scattering of picnic shelters. "Yeah, this is the park with the entrance to the underground caves."

"Right, now look at the building on the other side of the ravine. What would you say that is?"

"I dunno. A factory of some kind?"

"Yeah, that's what I thought. But then I started digging into what I could learn of the Grey family holdings. Hold on."

He pulled back into the street, drove down to the corner, and turned. They came up beside the building and he turned again, driving past the front facade. A small, discrete sign beside the entrance read, "Lloyd Parkour Research Facility."

"A research facility?"

Death glanced over, eyebrows raised, and gave her a meaningful look. "Medical research. Specifically, they specialize in cryobiology."

"Cryobiology, that's like cryogenically freezing people?"

"Well, they don't do it with the aim of reviving them in a couple of hundred years, like what you're thinking. Mostly it's freezing blood and tissue samples, eggs and sperm, organs. There are a lot of current medical and scientific applications. But they do have facilities for whole-body cryonics. And you know who the president of the board of directors is?" She shook her head.

"Dr. James Gregory — Alaina Grey's brother."

They drove back to Randy's house in silence. Wren waited until they were seated at the kitchen table with a pot of coffee brewing before she spoke.

"You think they froze Andrew when he died and then warmed him back up in time to switch him for Randy, right? Honey, I don't want to throw cold water on your idea, but I don't think it's possible. The freezing would have caused his cells to rupture, wouldn't it? And something like that would show up in an autopsy."

"But they freeze tissue to transplant back

to living people, so there must be something they can do do keep it viable."

"Something that wouldn't be obvious?"

Instead of answering, Death took out his phone and dialed. He waited a minute before he spoke. "Sophie? It's Death. Sorry to bother you. Do you have a minute? Wren and I have a question. We've discovered that Alaina and her brother have access to a crionics facility . . ." He outlined his theory and Wren's objections and listened for a minute. "Yeah, we're staying at Randy's . . . sure, that'd be great. Okay, thanks. See you then." He hung up. "She wants to think about it a little. She's going to come over and talk to us on her lunch break."

By the time Sophie arrived, Wren had put together a simple meal of homemade potato soup and sandwiches. Death thanked Sophie for driving over and invited her to come in and have something to eat while they talked. Sophie took her place at the table, unfolded her napkin in her lap, and sat fiddling with it nervously.

"It's okay," Death told her gently. "Whatever you have to say, it's okay. I promise I'm not going to get mad at you if you're here to shoot down my idea."

She sighed and put the napkin back on

the table.

"I'd actually meant to come shoot down your idea," she admitted. "That's why I wanted to come over here. To let you down gently. But I thought about it, did some research, and talked to some of my colleagues. The thing is, yeah, I think it is possible."

He brightened. "Really?"

"Really. Whole-body cryogenics is done with the intention of eventually reviving the person being frozen. To keep the body viable, they drain the blood and replace it with a solution that acts as antifreeze. That would keep the cells from rupturing during the freezing process. Then they'd have to warm the corpse back up to 98.6 and replace the antifreeze with blood. The subject's own blood could have been preserved for that by freezing it separately. Again, there are substances added to the blood to protect it during freezing, but they wouldn't show up in an autopsy unless we had some reason to look for them."

"So that works," Wren breathed. "It makes perfect sense."

"No, it doesn't," Sophie objected. "If Andrew died when he first collapsed, as he would have had to have, then you're suggesting that Alaina had his body frozen and kept it around for four months in the bizarre hope that she could find a lookalike to kidnap under circumstances that would allow her to leave Andrew's dead body in his place. It's absurd."

"I don't think they kept Andrew's body around because they were planning to kidnap someone," Death said. "They were just trying to hide the fact that he'd died until after the point when Alaina would inherit. It's impossible to get an accurate estimation on time of death, or even date of death, when a body is immediately frozen, right?"

Sophie nodded reluctantly.

"They were planning to make it look like he died after Alaina became his heir, but Leilani was suspicious and pressing them in court. If they were ordered to produce him, they were screwed. Not only would she not inherit anything, but at that point it would become obvious that they were both guilty of fraud. Seeing Randy's picture in the paper must have seemed like divine intervention."

"It wouldn't have worked," Sophie said slowly. "Their original plan, if you're right, it wouldn't have worked. With that much money at stake, the heir's brother as the physician of record and Leilani contesting the will, any judge in the country would have ordered an autopsy. They'd have been presenting a body that had undergone a massive aortic aneurysm and had no signs of major medical intervention and claiming that the aneurysm happened months earlier and the subject had been on life support since. The contradictions would have been glaringly obvious."

"They probably came up with it in a hurry, when Andrew suddenly died on them, and didn't stop to think it through until they were already in it up to their necks. Gregory's a doctor — he must have realized by now that it was a bad plan."

"So," Wren said, "even with all the complications involved in kidnapping Randy and switching bodies, it was still safer than any other option they had available. And there's nothing about freezing the body that would come up in a standard autopsy?"

"There would probably have been trace amounts of antifreeze solution in his veins," Sophie said, "but the most common solution used for that is based on glucosine. I'd imagine it would come back as high blood sugar."

"And that could be covered up by filling his stomach with a large quantity of sweet tea," Death said, satisfied.

■ ■ ■ ■

"What do we do now?" Wren asked, when Sophie had returned to work.

"We've gotta figure out a way to get Alaina and her brother out of the house so I can get in to see my brother."

"And get DNA or fingerprints?"

"Yeah. Absolutely."

Wren sighed. "I know that tone of voice," she said. "If you're planning on throwing him over your shoulder and absconding with him, I'd like to remind you that you'd pass out from lack of oxygen before you made it down the stairs."

"I've been doing much better with stairs," he objected. "And down is easier than up, anyway."

"Not carrying giant young firefighters, it's not."

Death tipped his head in a reluctant concession to reason. "You said the mail carrier has seen him walking in the garden recently though, right?"

"Yeah."

"Well, maybe he's mobile. If so, maybe I can convince him to leave with me."

"Yeah, maybe. And then we could get his fingerprints checked and that would prove if he's Randy. And if he is —"

"He is!"

She rubbed along his upper arm. "*If* he is, we can go to the police and have Alaina and her brother arrested for kidnapping. How do we get them out of the house, though?"

Death's phone rang. He glanced at the number, gave Wren a slight shrug, and answered it in his professional voice. "Bogart Investigations."

His eyebrows rose and he glanced at her meaningfully.

"Yes, Doctor, I'm feeling much better, thanks." He put it on speaker and held it out where they could both hear.

"I hope you don't think it too forward of me to call you," Gregory said, "but I realized after your visit the other day that I'd had a celebrity in my office."

"Me?" Death snorted. "I'm hardly a celebrity."

"A minor one, at least. Your name was quite prominent in the news a couple of months ago. Something to do with missing jewels? Some of them dating back to the Civil War?"

"Uh, yeah. That was a case I was working on."

"It sounds fascinating. Listen, my sister and I are planning to go out on the river tomorrow, if the weather holds. I have a neat little 27-foot pontoon boat that we like to tootle around in."

Wren's eyes danced and she clapped a hand over her mouth. Death gave her a stern look.

"I thought maybe you'd like to come along. We'd be absolutely delighted to hear about your adventures." The doctor sighed, maybe just a bit too dramatically. "I'm hoping to cheer Alaina up, frankly. Her anniversary was a couple of days ago but, sadly, her husband is in no condition to celebrate with her. I know that she'd be charmed to meet you. Plus, of course, she's a woman. Jewels are one of her favorite subjects."

"Gee, I don't know what to say," Death shot Wren a questioning glance and she tipped her head and shrugged. "Yeah, sure, that'd be great, I guess. Thanks for asking."

"Wonderful! And thank you in advance for joining us. Why don't we meet at my yacht club at, say, five p.m.?"

Death agreed and after Gregory had given him the address of the club they said goodbye. He hung up and Wren let out the laugh she was suppressing. "He said tootle!"

"Yeah, I noticed. What the hell was that?"

"They know you're investigating Randy's

'death'. Do you think they want a chance to see how much you've figured out?"

He lifted one shoulder. "Possible, I guess."

"And convenient!"

Death frowned. "Convenient how?"

"You wanted them out of the house. Now you're getting them out of the house. And you'll be able to keep an eye on them and know exactly when they're heading back."

"Yeah, but there's a hole in that plan. I'll be with them. I can't very well go boating with them and sneak into their house at the same time."

"You can't maybe," Wren said, "but as far as I could tell, that invitation didn't include me."

EIGHTEEN

The crowbar clanked against the floor of the raised Einstadt passage as Death tossed it in, the echoes sending chills down Wren's spine. She climbed up through the entrance on her hands and knees and pushed herself to her feet, turning back to help him follow. "Jeez, make some noise why don't you?" she teased to cover her own nervousness. Her palms were sweaty and she felt her heart thump against her rib cage. The light from Death's flashlight danced ahead of them down the tunnel.

Death was quiet and intense. "I really hate this plan," he muttered. "I still think you should just try to talk your way in with the maid."

"You haven't met the maid," Wren replied, letting him lead the way. Their passage stirred up dust and their voices echoed. She resisted the urge to whisper and tiptoe, the nature of their mission making her want to sneak. Down here in the silent dark it would not only be pointless, it would sap her energy and feed her nerves.

She looked forward to this experience with a mixture of anticipation and dread, and the passageway seemed both much longer and much shorter than she remembered. She paced along in Death's footsteps, her brain supplying her with unwanted scenarios of all the things that could go wrong. Before she knew it, they had reached the T in the path and the rusted-out door and pile of rubble separating them from the Grey house was just ten feet away.

"This may not even be possible," Death said, approaching the barrier with a slow, catlike stride, examining it analytically. "If we can't make a path through here, we'll have to scrap this plan and think of something else. I could do a little second-story work tonight after everyone's asleep."

"Don't give up too quickly," Wren scolded. "Have a little faith."

He shot her a quick smile, his teeth white in the dark. "In you? Always."

He studied the rockfall, then carefully inserted the tip of the crowbar under the largest boulder.

"You need my muscle?"

"Maybe. Hang on a second and let me

see what happens." He pushed down experimentally, testing the stone's balance. There was a brittle *pop* and the rock shifted. Death frowned, set the length of iron aside, and moved in to study the rubble pile more carefully. "Well, I'll be damned."

"What is it?"

By way of answering, he picked up the enormous stone and turned around, staggering a little. "Here," he said, "catch!"

He tossed it at her and Wren shrieked and ducked. The rock hit her lightly and bounced away and Death laughed. She stared at him and the stone, completely nonplussed. "What the . . . ?"

"Styrofoam."

"The tunnel's made out of Styrofoam?"

"Not the whole tunnel." He turned back and studied the barrier again. "Not even the whole rock pile. This is really ingenious." Wren moved up to stand next to him where she could see too.

"See?" he said. "The ceiling collapse is real, but someone has cleared a doorway in it. Then they made false stones out of Styrofoam and painted them to look like the rocks and bricks. The fake rocks are glued to a screen door." He found a handle in among the rubble and pulled and the wall of fallen stones opened outward. Moving more quietly now that they were so close to their destination, they passed through.

Beyond the rocks, the tunnel extended for another eight feet or so and ended at a wooden door. Death leaned down and put his mouth close to Wren's ear. "You can sneak now if you want."

"Thanks," she whispered back. "I was trying not to earlier."

"I know. I could tell."

They snuck up on the door and Death crouched beside it and took a small metal tube from his pocket. It opened out to a miniature telescope. "Woah! Cool," Wren said softly. "Where did you get that?"

"On eBay."

"Of course."

He put it to the keyhole before looking through it.

"Okay, there's just a little bit of natural light coming in, probably from a ground-level window somewhere. There's a short passage on the other side that leads to an elevator. One door on the right side of the passage and a second door just left of the elevator. One of the doors probably leads to a staircase. You'll have to decide which one is less conspicuous, the elevator or the stairs. You wanna look?"

"Yeah!"

He handed over the tiny telescope and she peered through the keyhole and noted the things he'd pointed out. When she was done she tried to hand it back but he closed her hand over it. "Hang on to that. You can use it to make sure the coast is clear before you go in."

She nodded and tried the door handle, but it was locked. Death pulled out a set of lock picks and made short work of getting it open. "You're just prepared for everything, aren't you?"

He winked at her. "Boy Scouts ain't got nothing on the Marines." He put the lock picks back in his pocket, then took a small can of penetrating oil from his other pocket and oiled the hinges. He looked at his watch and sighed. "I need to leave soon if I'm going to meet Alaina and Gregory at five. His yacht club is up in St. Charles. Walk me back to the entrance?"

"Only if you hold my hand," she said.

Death took her hand obediently, casting a longing look on the wooden door before they turned away. Wren knew, without him having to say it, what was going through his mind. He believed his brother was alive and was just on the other side of that door. After all the long and lonely time he'd spent mourning him, Randy was alive, possibly injured, painfully close. And now Death was supposed to just walk away and leave him in her hands.

She squeezed his hand. "It'll be okay," she said. "I know it's hard and I know it seems like it's taking forever. But it won't be long now. We're going to bring him home." The smile he gave her in return was bright and brittle with need and she could only pray that she was telling him the truth.

"The diamonds or the pearls with this blouse?"

James Gregory, lounging in his sister's bedroom while she finished dressing, sipped his drink and tipped his head. "Which would you least mind losing if it fell in the water?"

She gave him a brief, irritated glance.

"I'm not planning on throwing either of them in the water."

"No. But we're going to be on the river. There's always the chance of something going overboard."

Alaina turned back to her dressing table, set the pearls aside, and gazed down at the diamonds cupped in her hand.

"Andrew gave me these for a wedding present," she said. Leaning toward the mirror, she fastened them in place. "So what do you know about," she paused and glanced to the open hall door, lowering her voice, "about this man we're meeting?"

"I know he's smart. Dangerously so. No longer as physically powerful as he once was. Currently fragile, even. His lungs were damaged as the result of an injury during combat and he's fighting a nasty respiratory infection. He's suffering from clinical depression as well. Probably a mild case, but still . . . His doctor gave him a new prescription for antidepressants just a short time ago. It's always dangerous when someone starts taking those."

Alaina frowned and turned to look at him directly. "Dangerous how?"

"Depression isn't simply sadness. There's a plethora of symptoms, and they can include extreme fatigue and apathy. Often those suffering depression have suicidal thoughts, but they're too hopeless and exhausted to act on them. The danger is that the medication can give them the energy to kill themselves."

"You think he might be suicidal?"

James raised one eyebrow. He drained his drink and hauled himself out of the low recliner. "Please tell me you're going to put on more sensible shoes."

"It'll take me about half an hour to get to the yacht club," Death said, checking his watch. "I'll call you when I'm sure they're both there. Don't try to go in before then. You're still going to have to get past the gardener and at least the one maid, so promise me you'll be careful."

"I'll be careful," Wren said. "Are you sure this is such a good idea, though?"

"Baby, if you don't want to go —"

"Not for me," she said. "For you. Going out on the river in a boat with those people. I don't trust them. It could be dangerous."

"It's a busy river and we'll be out in broad daylight." She frowned at him and he laughed and bopped her nose. "Okay, broad twilight. Still, it's nowhere near sundown and on a pleasant summer evening there will be other boaters, people fishing off the shore, maybe a riverboat at the landing below the Arch. Alaina and her brother would have to be crazy to try anything drastic."

"Or desperate. Desperate people do stupid things. Just promise me you'll be careful, too."

"Careful is my middle name."

"No it isn't. Your middle name starts with a D."

"Smartass."

She was sitting in the entrance to the Einstadt passage and he was standing on the stone they'd rolled over to climb up on. He leaned forward and brushed his lips against her forehead. "Here's to bringing Randy home. Wait for my call, okay?"

"I will. Just you see that you take care of my Marine."

"And you take care of my auctioneer."

"Mr. Bogart," Gregory said, "I don't believe you've met my sister, Alaina."

"Mrs. Grey. Charmed," Death said, kissing her fingers. The courtly gesture never failed to impress a woman. It also gave Death a chance to look closely at their fingers and hands. He'd used it more than once, when working divorce cases, to determine if this or that woman had a wedding ring or, maybe, a tan line where a ring had been. In this instance, he wanted a look at Alaina's rings. A woman could do a lot of damage with a big diamond and if there was a chance she was going to take a swing at him, he wanted to know ahead of time how well she was armed.

"I call her Lainey," Gregory said.

"He's horrible," Alaina simpered. "I keep telling him that Lainey's a name for a six-year-old with braces and pigtails. You're certainly welcome to call me Alaina, though."

They were in the clubhouse at Gregory's yacht club, sitting around a high table in a corner heavily populated by potted plants. Gregory gestured to the bar. "How about something to drink before we go? They do a Tahitian sunset that's to die for."

"Sounds great."

The waiter was already on his way over with three brilliant orange drinks on a tray. Gregory handed Death the first one, picking it up with his hand across the top of the glass. "Now, you're not taking anything that shouldn't mix with alcohol, are you? As your doctor, I've got to ask."

Death gave him a bright smile that didn't reach his eyes. "Not a thing," he said cheerfully. He picked up the bright, fruity drink, and took a tiny, cautious sip. While far from an alcoholic, as a former Marine he'd had his share of experiences with alcohol. This drink had a bitter undertaste, faint and nearly hidden by the heavy flavors of the tropical fruit and rum, and a gritty texture.

Whatever Gregory put in it had been in pill form, he decided, and it hadn't dis-

311

solved completely in spite of being crushed ahead of time. Letting the little bit that he'd tasted dribble back into the glass, he winced, lowered the drink, and wiped his mouth with the back of his hand.

"Wow, powerful stuff," he laughed. While they were looking at him wiping his mouth with his right hand, he used his left to tip a little of the liquid out into the nearest potted plant. It would take subterfuge and sleight of hand, but he could get rid of the whole drink this way and they'd never guess he hadn't drunk it. With a bright smile, he feigned another swallow of alcohol. If they were trying to drug him, that had to be a good sign. Cheered, he wondered how Wren was doing.

Twenty-seven minutes after Death left her sitting alone in the tunnel, Wren's phone lit up with a text message from him. It was a single word: Go.

Climbing to her feet, she retraced their earlier steps until she came to a stop outside the wooden door into the Grey mansion. Her hands were sweaty but her mouth was dry. She had been raised to respect other people and their belongings. Never to trespass. Entering someone's home without their permission went against her every instinct. But she was doing this for Death.

She would do anything for Death.

Kneeling before the door, she took out the miniature telescope, put the end to the keyhole, and peered once more through the lens. The passage beyond was as dark and silent as it had been before. She put the scope away, scrubbed her hands against her jeans, and took a deep breath. Easing the door open, she stepped inside.

The basement was dry and musty. An air conditioning unit was running somewhere, but otherwise, everything was silent. The door to her right was warped and didn't close completely. A glance inside showed a room full of jumbled junk and broken furniture, with no signs of life. She could look there later, if there seemed a point. Her main goal now was to find a way upstairs. With luck, she could steal a toothbrush and a comb or hairbrush and be gone with none of the occupants the wiser.

The elevator shaft before her was empty, the cage door closed and the car gone. There was a push button to call it down, but doing so would be a bad idea. Even a quiet motor would be loud in the still house.

The door next to the elevator led to a steep, narrow staircase. Wren climbed it gingerly, keeping her feet to the outside of the treads and wincing every time one creaked or groaned beneath her. The door at the top had no keyhole for her to peer through. If it was locked, it was latched on the other side. There was no way for her to pick that, even if she'd known how, and no way to tell if it was open except to try to open it.

She looked for some sign — light around the door, perhaps, where moving shadows could betray the presence of a person on the other side. It was no use, the door sat securely in its frame. She touched the surface tentatively, wondering even as she did what she thought she was doing. In a fire, she remembered, you were supposed to feel a door before opening it to see if it was hot. The door wasn't hot, so the house wasn't on fire.

Okay, that was good to know.

Wren put her ear close and listened, but she couldn't hear anything. She was going to have to go through it on blind faith.

Turning the knob gently, she gave an experimental push. The door yielded easily and she edged it open a crack, peering through at the darkened hallway beyond.

Wren had a story ready in case she got caught but she wasn't confident in her ability to sell it. As Death had said, she was a terrible liar. She wondered if she'd be able to convince the maid of her relative innocence, then remembered actually talking to the maid and wondered if she'd be able to convince the police of her relative innocence.

The door opened to a back hallway. Another, larger hallway met it a few feet to her right. She crept to the corner and, looking around it, found herself staring at the front door. Okay, so she was at the back of the entry hall. In fact, she was standing under the main staircase. The basement stair ran directly beneath it and opened at the back.

Death said the bedrooms were on the second floor, above the kitchen ell. That's where the main bathrooms would also be, and the master bathroom was the most likely place she was going to find DNA. If she could get the toothbrush Andrew/Randy was using, she would have both DNA and fingerprints. There was a plastic zipper bag in her pocket and she was wearing gloves — not rubber gloves, but cheap cotton work gloves that would keep her from leaving fingerprints and be easier to explain if she were caught.

Feeling like a mouse that was tempting the cat, she crept up the staircase. The thick carpet muted her footsteps and she avoided the railings to prevent even the sound of fabric rustling against wood. Halfway up she came to the landing and paused a second to glance again at the enormous portrait of Andrew and Alaina. The resemblance, as always, was startling, but up close she could see the differences between the two men. It was mostly a matter of expression, she realized. Even though she'd never seen Randy except in photographs, she could see that they were nothing alike. Andrew's jaw was set in a hard line. He looked incapable of breaking into the easy, charming grin that Randy always wore. Although he'd been ten years older than Randy when the picture was painted, he didn't have the crinkles of laughter around his mouth that the younger man did. His eyes were cold.

Passing the painting, she continued to the second-floor landing. A hallway ran left and right and she paused a bare second before turning right toward the front of the house. Before she'd taken her third step a mild voice froze her in her tracks. "I've never seen you here before."

NINETEEN

Long, covered docks reached out into the river, surrounded by boats, large and small, that nosed in around them. They reminded Death of swimming in a pond with his brother when they were children, and the little fish that would come up and nibble on their toes.

The docks were too big to shift under their weight, but they bobbed with the wake of passing boats. The movement didn't faze Death. He'd spent enough time at sea while in the military to be used to the feel of water beneath him. Gregory also adjusted well, Death noted. Alaina was less at ease. She'd worn canvas sandals with thick, wedge-shaped heels, and she walked in the middle of the path with her arms tucked in tight against her sides. She was carrying a large, flowered tote bag and she clutched the strap in both hands, taking tiny steps while watching her own feet apprehensively.

The Mississippi at twilight had a smell all its own. It was damp, similar to rain in the air, but with an undertone of the rich, black mud that made up the riverbed, accented with the scent of things that were growing and things that were dead. Dragonflies hovered low over the water, drawing the catfish up to feed. It was quiet at the end of the dock. The soft sound of river water moving relentlessly around and through the man-made obstacles accentuated the silence rather than disturbing it. The bank and the city seemed much farther away than they actually were.

Gregory stopped at the very last berth, where a long and ostentatious pontoon boat was tied up. "I call her the *Zaca*, after Errol Flynn's yacht," he said.

Gregory boarded first, without a backward glance. Death offered Alaina a hand, steadying her as she stepped from the dock to the deck, then followed her on. He waited for Gregory to get the engine started, then loosed the mooring line and they moved out into the current.

The river here ran almost east and west, with a curve to the south three-quarters of a mile downstream. The low sun gilded the tops of the wavelets and cast the river bend in deep shadow. As they left the dock behind, a small aircraft passed low overhead. It startled a murder of crows that had settled in the trees of the west bank and they rose in a raucous cloud and crossed the *Zaca*'s bow on iridescent wings.

The strange girl moved away from the door and the man known as Andrew Grey rose from where he'd been kneeling in the shadows of the basement junk room. Softly he closed the lid of the chest he'd been searching through and silently followed her.

Hidden in the doorway, he watched as she hesitated between the elevator cage and the basement stairs. She chose the stairs and he crept over and peeked around the edge of the opening, watching her until she was more than halfway to the first floor. Satisfied that she didn't intend to return, he went back to look at the door she had to have come in by. The door with the odd logo was unlocked now and stood very slightly ajar. He hesitated beside it, not wanting it to creak and betray his presence. But he hadn't heard the woman enter and he could smell WD40, so he surmised that the hinges had been oiled.

He pulled it toward himself, his touch delicate, and it came open easily. Beyond there was an underground passage, but it was too dark to make out any details.

Deciding that the intruder was more immediately interesting than the secret passage, he carefully closed it most of the way and tiptoed back to the stairs to see what she was doing.

She was lurking at the top of the steps. She touched the door hesitantly, then went through. Andrew waited until she had cleared the stairwell, then hurried up after her with a speed and agility that would have surprised his caretakers.

He peeked out in time to see her disappear around the corner to his right. He waited and after a moment he could hear, only because he was listening for it, the soft sound of her footsteps on the treads of the main stair. He turned left, then right onto the steep, narrow service stair and quickly climbed to the second floor. There was a full-length mirror at the head of the main staircase. Alaina always checked her appearance in it before descending. Andrew used it now to watch the intruder. She had paused on the landing, beneath the wedding portrait. While she studied it, he studied her.

She was a redhead, with short, wild hair and fine, porcelain skin sprinkled with freckles. Thin, black work gloves covered her hands and there was a smear of dirt down her left cheek. She wore jeans and sneakers and a navy T-shirt that was too big on her. When she turned to continue up the stairs, he could see the Marine Corps logo on the front of the shirt. Emotion rose in the back of his throat and closed like a fist around his heart.

She wasn't a thief, he decided. Alaina had abandoned a pair of rings and an expensive wristwatch on the landing table and the redhead passed them over without a second glance. She was chewing on her lower lip and rubbing her palms on her thighs every few minutes. Worried, he decided. She was nervous and didn't want to be here, but she was resolute. Whatever her goal, it was important to her.

He faded back into the nearest doorway when she reached the top of the stairs and waited to see what she'd do. She hesitated, then turned and moved away from him. There was a name stenciled on the back of her shirt in faded letters. Andrew swallowed hard and stepped out into the hallway. He leaned back against the doorframe and forced himself to act casual.

"I've never seen you here before," he said.

Death swiveled idly in his lounge chair,

pretending to take another sip of his second drink. Gregory had fixed this one. It came from the same bottle as the drinks Gregory and Alaina were working on and Death hadn't seen anything to suggest that the doctor was trying to slip him another Mickey, but he wasn't taking any chances.

Gregory's pontoon boat was enormous and ostentatiously luxurious, with reclining seats, a curved bench along the prow on the port side, and a built-in bar. The helm was halfway back to starboard and Gregory lounged in his captain's chair with a generous shot of bourbon, blatantly ignoring the laws against drinking and boating. "It's a lovely evening," Alaina said, tilting her head so that the sun, dipping toward the horizon now, caught her earrings and set them glittering. It was the third time she'd done so and Death wondered if she'd practiced with a mirror to get the angle right. "Shall we go upriver or down?"

"Down, I think," Gregory said. "I told you, Mr. Bogart, that Lainey and I attended the memorial for your brother. I thought perhaps you'd like to visit the spot where the fire department scattered his ashes."

Wren turned slowly to face the man who stood two rooms away, leaning against the doorframe, watching her curiously. He was dressed in jeans and a polo shirt, carrying a wooden cane. His hair was gray but there was a thin, darker line along the part where the dye job had begun to grow out. And here were the laugh lines and the crinkles at the corners of his eyes. For the first time since this whole thing started, Wren was 100 percent certain they were right.

"Randy?"

His eyes were blue-gray where his brother's were green, but they looked like Death's eyes nonetheless. She thought she saw a glimmer of recognition in them when he heard his name.

"Mr. Grey? Who are you talking to?"

Wren turned and groaned to herself as the formidable maid came down the hall carrying a stack of towels. The maid saw her and her eyes narrowed and hardened.

"You! How did you get in here?"

"Uh, yeah, that. Funny story," Wren said, aware that she was talking too fast. She was an auctioneer. It was an occupational hazard. "See, there are these caves and they used to be really fancy and I was exploring them and I found this passage and there was a door —"

"Save it for the police. You can't be up here bothering Mr. Grey."

"She's not bothering me," he said. "I want to hear what she has to say."

"You can't," the maid replied. "You're very ill and she's upsetting you."

"She's not upsetting me. And I can talk to anyone I want to. I am the boss, right? You work for me."

"I work for your family. Your wife and your doctor have instructed me to take care of you. Part of that is that you're not to have visitors. Go back to your room and when I've taken care of this intruder I'll bring you your medicine."

"But I'm not really sick, am I?"

Wren watched, fascinated, as he transformed before her eyes. He stood up straight and squared his shoulders. It added a good five inches to his height and took twenty years off his age. "And I'm also not Andrew Grey." He reached in his pocket and took out a bright rectangle. Wren recognized it even before he held it up to show them.

It was the name tag off a St. Louis County Firefighter's uniform.

"My name is Baranduin Bogart," he said, "and I'd really like to know what the *hell* is going on!"

"Don't fall in," Gregory cautioned.

"I'm just feeding the ducks," Alaina said.

Drifting downstream at a leisurely pace, they'd come across a flock of ducks that surrounded the craft, quacking eagerly. Clearly they were used to being fed by boaters. Alaina had found a bag of popcorn in a cabinet under the bar and she was leaning over the railing, dropping kernels and watching the birds gobble them up. "Lean over too far and you'll be feeding the sharks."

She scowled at her brother.

"We're not in the ocean! There aren't any sharks here."

"Actually, there are. Freshwater bull sharks have been seen as far upriver as Alton."

The siblings both looked to Death. He was still lounging in his chair, the glass in his hand nearly empty. He half shrugged and nodded. "I've heard that too. Fishermen have caught one or two over the last few years, I think."

Alaina edged away from the railing just a bit. "How big?"

"Now that I don't know. Big enough to attack, I think. And bull sharks are one of the most aggressive species."

"I apologize for my sister being such a poor hostess," Gregory said. "Feeding the ducks and not feeding her guest."

"I'm fine," Death said.

Alaina made a face, set the popcorn aside, and went back to the bar.

"You didn't offer him anything either," she pointed out, "and it's your boat." She found some tortilla chips and salsa, poured them into bowls, and set them on a low table between the lounge chairs. "Besides, I'm used to letting the servants worry about things like that. Why didn't we bring any servants along?" Gregory answered her with a disbelieving look. After a moment, her face grew red.

"Oh."

Death watched the exchange with interest.

Flustered, Alaina turned back to the bar. "I think there are some cheeses and cold cuts in the refrigerator, if you'd like a sandwich."

"I'm fine," Death said again. He had no intention of ingesting anything these two had to offer him.

Alaina returned to the rail but the ducks had lost interest when the popcorn stopped and were headed for another craft. Traffic was light this far downriver. A houseboat, headed upstream, passed them on the port side. "Do people ever really live in houseboats?" Alaina asked.

"I'm sure they do sometimes," Gregory's tone was disinterested.

"More often than you'd think, I'd wager," Death offered.

"It sounds icky," Alaina said. "Diesel fuel and chemical toilets all the time, no room for a real staff. And what do they do if there's a bad storm?"

"Storms can be dangerous. I remember reading about one of the big tornadoes that hit St. Louis. In the 1890s? 1896, maybe? The official death toll was in the hundreds, but some historians think the real toll was as much as double that. The tornado crossed the river and capsized and swamped a lot of the river craft. The houseboat population was largely itinerant, so no one would have necessarily missed the people who were lost. Whole families could have been drowned and their bodies never recovered."

"This river is good at hiding bodies," Gregory agreed. He and Alaina exchanged a brief, barely there glance. Death began assessing the potential of chips and salsa as defensive weaponry.

"Yes!" Wren shrieked, delighted. She bounced down the hallway and caught Randy in a fierce hug. "You're Randy Bogart! Only it's Baranduin. Only your family calls you Randy. Oh, and your friends call you Bogie. And you're alive and that's awesome!" He didn't return the hug.

"Do I know you?"

She froze, feeling foolish. "Um, not exactly. Not at all, actually. That would be no. But, um, I know you. Or rather, know of you."

"Oh. Okay." He hugged her then. "An explanation would be nice."

"Right! Um . . . sorry, I know I'm saying um a lot . . . but, um . . . it's complicated. You look like Andrew Grey, who was really rich. He died, but his wife had to hide that because she'd only inherit his money if she stayed married to him longer than his third wife so she had his body frozen and then she thawed it out and kidnapped you and left his body in your place so for, like, almost a year now everybody thought you were dead. But they made a mistake with your badge and also got your badge number wrong so we got suspicious and we figured out what was going on and I came here to try to get proof that you were you and not him because we thought they were drugging you but I guess they're not because you know who you are and that's kind of weird but really awesome because now it's simple and we can just call the police and tell them you were kidnapped —"

She stopped suddenly, sensing that she was being stared at, and looked up to find Randy giving her a look. He had one eyebrow raised and he was frowning down at her doubtfully and she realized she had been talking fast again. Really fast. Like, one long run-on sentence rattled off without stopping for a breath fast. She stepped back and held up a hand.

"Sorry! Sorry. Auctioneer."

"They *were* drugging me. I stopped taking the pills. Did I hear a kidnapped in there somewhere? And something about everyone thinking I'm dead?"

"Yes, but everything's going to be all right now. We'll call the police and you can come home and it's going to be awesome!"

At this point they'd both forgotten the maid. Wren actually jumped a little when she spoke.

"Well," she said, "this is inconvenient." She tossed her stack of towels to the floor, reached in the top of her apron, and came up with a pistol. "Go back in the bedroom and sit down, both of you, or I'll shoot you where you stand."

The farther downriver they traveled, the more relaxed Gregory got and the more agitated and nervous Alaina became. Death remembered promising Wren that they wouldn't be stupid enough to try anything on a crowded river. He chided himself for overconfidence.

He was on his third bourbon, keeping his hand cupped around the glass to hide the level of alcohol. With no convenient potted plants to dispose of it in, he was having to judge his timing and toss it into the river when they were otherwise occupied. Alaina had drifted toward the stern.

"What are you looking at?" Gregory asked.

"Just watching the water churning out in our wake. When I was in the Caribbean with Andrew a few years ago we went boating at night. Our wake glowed in the dark, blue and green."

"Bioluminescence," Gregory said.

"It was very pretty."

"Mmm. Yes, well, don't fall into the propellers or you won't be pretty anymore." He looked to Death. "Did you have to take the Missouri State Water Patrol course on boating safety when you were in high school, Mr. Bogart? I remember it well, but I don't know if they still do that."

Death blinked sleepily, keeping his re-action time slow. The drunker they believed him to be, the greater an advantage his sobriety gave him.

"You mean the one with the pictures of all the dead bodies?"

"Yes, that one. You go into the water at the wrong time or place and the propeller can suck you right in and chop you into fish bait." Gregory sounded mildly amused by the idea, but Death couldn't decide if it was because that was part of his plan or just because he thought it would be a happy circumstance. Gregory fetched himself another drink, then brought the bottle over and refilled Death's glass.

He had mentioned visiting the location where Randy's ashes had been scattered. That had been at the confluence of the Missouri and the Mississippi, still several miles below them. They were passing through the wetlands and conservation areas north of St. Louis now, only the ever-present Gateway Arch on the horizon betraying the presence of a city nearby.

If Gregory and Alaina's plan involved getting him in the water to drown, the confluence would be the place to do it. Where America's two biggest rivers met, the surface was deceptively calm but the current below was deadly. Also, with parkland bordering the river on both sides, if they chose a time when no other craft was nearby there were less likely to be witnesses. Gregory glanced over at Death and his gaze seemed calculating to the ex-Marine. Death gave him a faint nod and saluted him with his own glass. He had no intention of dying on this river. There was too much waiting for him back on land.

Wren stared. "You're a minion? Huh. I didn't see that coming. Alaina does have a minion after all!"

Maria snorted derisively. "I don't work for that airhead. I report to Dr. Gregory. He knows very well his sister can't be relied on."

"But he can rely on you?"

"Implicitly."

"Maria Vasquez, I'm surprised at you," Randy chided.

"Vasquez?" Wren asked. "As in Elena Vasquez?"

"Maria."

"Then I'm guessing Elena's your sister-in-law." Wren said, putting two and two together in her head and coming up with I'm-gonna-kill-this-bitch. "That's where you got the gun, isn't it? Not this gun, the one you lost at the convenience store."

"Well, aren't you just a little Miss Smarty Pants?"

"I'd say you're pretty clever yourself. Was it your idea? Put on a fake mustache, make the police think they're looking for a man?"

"What are you talking about?" Randy asked. The women ignored him.

"How did you like the mustard?" Wren asked.

"Mustard is a flowering plant, you know. I'll be sure to put some on pretty boy's grave."

"Over your dead body."

"You know what?" Maria said, "I'm just going to go ahead and shoot you both. That's the simplest solution to everything. I'll say you broke in here and killed Andrew Grey and then I wrestled the gun away from you and shot you in self-defense."

"Now, ladies, let's not do anything hasty."

"Yeah, that's not going to wash," Wren said derisively. A little bit of her brain was freaking out because — GUN! — but it wasn't the first time she'd had a gun pointed at her and right now she was more angry than she was scared. "The police, the fire department, and the coroner's office all know that we think 'Andrew' is really Randy. He turns up dead, the first thing they're going to do is check his fingerprints and DNA to see if we're right. Then the 'home invasion' becomes a 'failed attempt to rescue a kidnap victim' and next thing you know, you're going down for two counts of first-degree murder."

"You're lying."

"Why do you think I snuck in here? I was trying to get DNA or fingerprints so the police would have enough evidence to start an investigation. See?" Wren pulled a handful of plastic bags from her pocket. "I brought evidence bags. The cop I talked to gave them to me."

"Right," Maria said skeptically. "A cop told you to go breaking and entering for evidence."

"He just didn't want to know how I got it. Missouri's a capitol punishment state, too." Wren smiled wickedly. "Which arm do you like your lethal injections in?"

"Okay, shut up," Maria growled. "Just shut up. I need to think. Get in the bedroom, both of you. Now! Or, so help me God, I will shoot, even if I have to hide the bodies."

Randy got Wren by the shoulder and propelled her ahead of him into the bedroom. Maria slammed the door behind them and they heard the lock click.

They stood for a moment, staring at the closed door.

"She's a genius," Wren said drily, taking

her phone out of her pocket.

Randy rubbed the bridge of his nose. "Who are you again?"

"Oh, right. Sorry. My name's Wren Morgan. I'm Death's girlfriend."

Randy struck like a snake, knocking the phone out of her hand and catching her completely off guard. The phone sailed across the room and out the window. He pushed her up against the wall and growled in her face, voice suddenly seething with fury. "I'm getting really, really tired of people lying to me! My brother's dead. Who the hell are you?"

"This is a nice boat," Death commented. His words slurred together just a little and he slumped in his chair.

Gregory's smile was predatory. "Not getting a little bit tipsy there, are you?"

"Please. I'm a Marine. Takes more than one bottle of booze to drink me under the table."

"Of course." Gregory's phone rang. "Excuse me, I've got to take this," he said. "Doctor and all, you know?"

Death saluted him with his glass and watched from beneath lowered lids as the other man moved to the far end of the boat and spoke over his cell, occasionally glancing at Death.

Alaina was very nervous now, fiddling with her glass and her jewelry and refusing to look Death in the eye. He focused on Gregory's mouth, trying to read his lips. He wasn't as good at it as his great-grandmother, Nonna Rogers, had been, but she'd taught him a few things before she died. ". . . God's sake . . . she's not . . . cell phone!"

Death's heart dropped to his stomach. *Crap!* he thought. *Wren. Busted!*

"He's not dead!" Wren said.

"He is. Don't lie to me." Randy's whole body felt tight as a fist, the grief as fresh and as powerful as it had been when he'd first walked into the captain's office and seen the men in Marine uniforms waiting for him. "I may not have all my marbles in the same coffee can right now, but I remember that. That was the first thing I did remember. My brother's dead. He went off to Afghanistan to play hero. He saved two of his men. He went back for the third."

"He saved him too."

"He didn't! Their Humvee blew up. It got hit with a mortar. I *remember* that!"

Anger was an easier reaction than sorrow and, under the circumstances, it seemed a more useful reaction too.

"I can explain, but you've got to calm down."

"Don't tell me to calm down."

"*Please.* Calm down."

Slowly, he released her and backed away.

"Randy, Death is alive, I promise you."

He opened his mouth to protest again because he didn't believe that. He didn't dare. She leaned into him, reaching up one small hand to cover his mouth.

"No, wait! Just listen to me. When you were kidnapped, the Marines hadn't retrieved his body yet. Do you remember that? It took them three days to secure the area. When they did, and they moved in again, they found him and Corporal Barlow alive."

"How is that even possible? Three days behind enemy lines in a burned-out Humvee?"

"Death got them out before the Humvee got hit and hid them in a cellar. When the Humvee exploded, it collapsed the cellar on top of them, which is probably why they didn't wind up in the hands of the insurgents. Our guys went back looking for them. Semper fi, remember? No man left behind? Death was unconscious by then and nearly dead. It was a British unit that actually found them, and only because Barlow was delirious with fever and singing 'Coal Miner's Daughter' at the top of his lungs."

Randy dropped into the nearest chair and leaned forward, scrubbing his hand over his face. "Death's alive? He's *really* alive?"

"Yes. He's really alive."

He thought about this, wanting to believe it but afraid to.

"But my brother's married. Even if he were alive, he wouldn't have a girlfriend."

"She left him. She'd been sleeping around while he was overseas and she'd gotten pregnant. I don't like Madeline and I don't get along with her at all, but I do kind of understand where she was coming from.

"When all this happened, she was about three months pregnant. She'd been trying to figure out what to say to Death. He'd been having such a hard time of it, with your parents and your grandparents dying, and now she had to give him even more grief. Then she got word that he'd been killed in action. As horrible as that was, it meant she'd never have to disappoint him, or see him sad and angry again. Two days later, you were dead and he was in a coma in a military hospital in Germany. She cut and ran. She cleaned out their bank account and went to Reno for a quickie divorce."

"That is just what she'd do. The bitch."

"Yeah."

"So how'd you supposedly meet him?"

"Last spring, I got involved in a case he was working on." She hurried on, anticipating his next question. "He's not in the Corps anymore. His lungs were damaged and he received a medical discharge. He's a private investigator now and sometimes a bounty hunter. He's got an office and an apartment in my hometown, East Bledsoe Ferry, on the other side of the state. And he's mine now. And Whoreticia isn't getting him back, either."

"So where is he now? Because if my brother were alive and he thought I was in trouble, he'd be here."

"He's out on the river with Alaina and her brother, getting them out of the house so I could sneak in and look for proof that you were you."

"Yeah, good job at that."

"Don't be a smartass."

"But he's alive? You swear to me he's really alive?"

"*Yes!* I swear."

Randy jumped up, restless, and paced away from her, circling the room like a caged beast. "We gotta get out of here. I need to see my brother."

"And he needs to see you. But, in case

you haven't noticed, there's this big, locked door in the way."

He waved a hand at the door and made a rude noise. "It opens out. I'm a fireman. Firemen don't get locked in rooms with doors that open out. The problem is the woman with a gun on the other side. We need to figure out some kind of a weapon."

"Oh, that," Wren said. "I got that covered." She yanked off her necklace and reached into her bra. "I've been just dying to throw rocks at that woman."

Randy's eyes widened as she fastened the sling to its handle and dropped most of the stones in her pocket, keeping three or four in her fist for quick ammo. "A slingshot," he breathed. "I haven't touched one of these since the walnut incident when I was five."

Wren fitted the first stone into the pocket of the sling. "You said you think you can get us out of here?"

He snorted. "Please."

She took up a position just inside the door, sling at the ready.

Randy took a second to brace himself, then reared back, lifted his right leg, and kicked the door, landing his foot right next to the lock. The wood splintered, the knob and lock busted free and the door slammed open. Sling at the ready, Wren ducked under his arm and led the way out into the hall.

TWENTY

Wren rushed into the hall and stopped short. Randy just caught himself from running into her. Maria lay on her back just outside the bedroom, gun loose in her right hand, blinking groggily. "What happened?"

Wren kicked the gun out of the other woman's reach.

"I think you got her with the door. Huh. That's anti-climactic. Dang! I was really looking forward to flinging rocks at somebody."

Randy laughed shortly. "Yeah, you're my brother's girlfriend all right." He went over and retrieved the gun, put the safety on, and stuck it in his pocket. Maria sat up, rubbing her head. "You haven't won, you know."

"Looks like victory to me," Randy said.

Wren grinned. "Is this the part where you tell us all about the diabolical plan that would have worked if it wasn't for us pesky kids?"

"Joke all you want to," Maria said, "but your boyfriend's as good as dead right now."

Wren readied her slingshot again. "What are you talking about?"

"Why do you think they invited him to go boating?"

"Why did they invite him to go boating?" Randy asked, directing his question at Wren.

"Gregory said they wanted to hear about his experiences as a private investigator, but we figured they wanted to pump him for information, to see how much he knows. There was a newspaper story about him investigating your death. They already tried to kill him once, though. He thought it was a coincidence, but I knew it wasn't. Your friend here put on a fake mustache and made it look like he got caught in a convenience store robbery. He disarmed her with a bottle of mustard."

Maria sneered. "Let's see him disarm the Mississippi."

Wren shot Randy a worried glance. "He said they wouldn't be stupid enough to try anything on a busy river in broad daylight."

"All they have to do is get him in the water and wait for him to drown. Gregory's rigged a section of the railing on his boat. Pretty boy leans on it, he'll go right through."

343

"That's a stupid plan," Randy said. "Death swims like a fish."

"Not anymore." Wren looked around, frantic. "Wounded warrior, remember? His lungs are damaged. I need a phone."

"Damn! Right. You had one?"

"It went out the window."

"Oh. Sorry."

"Where's the house phone?"

"I don't know. I've only ever seen people talking on cells that they carry in their pockets." Wren looked at Maria.

"I don't have one. But if you let me go, I'll call and tell them the game is up. That the police know everything and if they kill him they'll go down for murder."

Wren hesitated.

"Think about it," Maria encouraged. "They're the real villains. I'm just a minion. You said it yourself. Let me go and I'll disappear. You'll never see or hear from me again."

"But how will you call them if you don't have a phone?"

"Fine," Maria said. "I have a phone. It was in my hand when you attacked me with the door. It should be around here somewhere. But I'm not going to call anybody without some kind of guarantee."

"If your boss hurts my boyfriend, I'll kick

344

your ass. How's that for a guarantee?"

Wren looked around the hallway, then exclaimed and dived off to the side to retrieve a fancy, new smartphone from under the hall table. She turned it over in her hand as she came back. "Hell."

The screen was intact but the back had busted and the battery and data card were gone.

"This can't be happening! Death doesn't have time for us to play hide-and-seek with electronics."

Randy reached up and stabbed a finger at the ceiling and both women jumped as a frantic, high-pitched beeping filled the house.

"Smoke alarm," he said. "Fancy place like this will have everything hooked to a private security company. The smoke alarm goes off, the company will call the police and the fire department. We should have reinforcements in a couple of minutes."

"Would you like to drive, Lainey?"

"I don't know," she hedged.

"Oh, come on," her brother coaxed. He looked to Death "I'm trying to get her used to taking the helm. She does okay on the quieter parts of the river, but traffic and turbulence tend to fluster her."

345

Reluctantly, the small woman crossed to starboard and took her place in the captain's chair. "Do you want to head back toward the dock now?"

"No," Gregory said. "Let's keep going downriver. I promised Mr. Bogart that we'd show him where his brother's ashes were scattered, remember? That was near the confluence with the Missouri. We're still a couple of miles above there."

"Don't go out of your way on my account," Death said.

"It's no trouble," Gregory assured him. "And I think you should see the place. I think it'll do you good."

When the call came in for Fire Station 41, the address sent a chill up Captain Cairn's spine. Einstadt Avenue. The last time he'd gone on a call to Einstadt Avenue, nearly a year ago now, he'd come home short a firefighter. That had been in the morning, not the evening, but the weather was identical. With a strong sense of déjà vu, he took his place. The engine led the way out of the station and they raced across town.

The address was a big, brick mansion across the street from the abandoned brewery. There were no hysterical occupants in the yard and no sign of smoke coming from

346

the building, so he figured it was most likely a false alarm. They pulled up in front of the place and he saw a large man in the side yard, doing something to a small tree. Cap sent two of his men around the house to look for signs of fire and went to talk to the gardener.

"Is there a fire?"

He had to tap the larger man's arm to get his attention. The man looked up, puzzled. "I said, is there a fire?"

Frowning, the man reached up and fiddled with his ear. He was turning up a hearing aid, Cap realized. "Sorry. I keep it off so I can't hear my boss. What?"

"We've got a fire alarm going off," Cap repeated. "Do you know anything about that?"

"No, I don't. I'm not burning anything. The maid probably is, if she's trying to cook. But don't tell her I said that or I'll never hear the end of it."

Cap started for the house, the gardener trailing behind, but before he reached the door it slammed open and the ghost of his long-lost firefighter barreled out. "Bogie?"

He was thinner than he should have been, his face looked gaunt and pale and his hair was gray, but it was undoubtedly Randy Bogart. Cap heard Rowdy shout and Talia scream and then Bogie grabbed him, frantic and breathless. "Cap, you gotta stop them! They're trying to kill my brother!"

Death's phone rang. He slipped it out of his pocket and lifted it, but before he could answer or see who it was, Gregory stumbled against him. He hit the phone and it flew out of Death's hand and disappeared below the surface of the river.

"Oh, my God! I am so sorry!" the doctor said.

"Damn. Um, can I borrow your phone?" Death asked. He expected the other man to have some excuse as to why he could not. Still, he had to try. The missed call was sending tremors of worry up his spine. He hadn't seen who was calling, but figured it was only important if it was Wren.

"Of course," Gregory said. He took out his own phone but held onto it. "What's the number?"

Death hesitated, then reluctantly repeated Wren's number and watched while the other man punched it in. Gregory put his phone on speaker. "I'll just hold on to it." He held the phone out. "No offense, friend, but you're a little tipsy and I don't want this one going in the drink."

Wren had her phone set to vibrate for the

dangerous foray into enemy territory, but Death knew she'd answer it if she could. As it rang and rang and rang, dread settled like lead in his belly.

"No answer," Cap said, voice grim, keeping his phone to his ear. "Watch your step."

Wren took the hand he offered and let him help guide her off the dock and into the fire boat. She'd ridden here sitting on Randy's lap, crammed into the middle of 41's fire and rescue truck between Rowdy and the kid who'd taken Randy's place. They'd had the siren going and were traveling at a rate of speed that normally would have terrified her. She'd leaned forward the entire way, as if somehow that would help them to go even faster.

Cops were scouring the Grey house, looking for the missing SD card. Gregory's phone wasn't registered in his name and Maria hadn't known the number, nor even the number of the phone she was using. It was one Gregory had provided, with strict instructions that she wasn't to call anyone on it but him. They couldn't even get her number from one of her friends or relatives and use it to trace his phone.

The fire boat had been waiting for them. Randy was already on board and the paramedics followed her, lugging gear they hoped not to use. "Good luck," Cap said. "Go get your brother. You call me the second you know something, you hear? And be careful."

There were two firefighters already on board. As they pulled away, the one who wasn't piloting turned to them.

"The police and water patrol have craft out looking for them, too. According to the registration, Gregory has a 27-foot pontoon called the *Zaca*. Registered to St. Charles."

"That's where Death went to meet them," Wren confirmed.

"St. Charles is between the two rivers," the officer said. "Gregory's yacht club has its main facility on the Missouri and an auxiliary location on the Mississippi. They could be on either river, going upstream or down. The Sheriff's Department has choppers up with searchlights. The problem is, with the sun all the way down now, a lot of the river is in shadow. It'd be awfully easy to miss them, especially if they're somewhere with a lot of trees."

"Is he trying to be helpful?" Wren asked Randy. "Because this doesn't feel helpful."

Randy ran a hand across her back, reassuring her. "Just keep an eye out for pontoon boats. They're pretty popular so there are apt to be a lot of them on the water." He leaned forward and addressed the firefighter who'd been talking before. "You guys got any spare eyes?" The fireman leaned down, fished around in a tool box, and handed back two pair of binoculars, small but powerful.

"Thanks!"

Silently, side by side, Wren and Randy scanned the darkening water.

"I don't understand why he didn't answer his phone," Wren said finally, barely finding the breath for a whisper as despair clutched at her heart. "He should have answered his phone."

Randy's voice came back to her, just as soft and pained. "I know."

This would be poignant, Death thought, if he still believed his brother was dead.

"The ceremony was in the morning," Gregory said. "It was very impressive. They came in a procession of fire trucks, down to the landing below the Arch where the riverboats dock. Your brother's station, I believe, boarded one of the official fire boats, with his ashes carried in a fireman's helmet. A lot of the other firefighters had people waiting to pick them up in private craft, and by the time they were ready to go, most of the other boats out on the water had joined the fleet, whether out of respect or curiosity."

"It sounds impressive," Death agreed. *And ironic, a bastard like Andrew Grey getting a hero's send-off.*

"This is about where they scattered the ashes. A piper played 'Taps' on the bagpipes. I've never been really enamored of the bagpipes, but I have to admit that, in that instance, they sounded lovely. Come up here by the railing and you can get a better look."

Alaina cut the throttle back to idle and let them drift. Death obediently joined James Gregory at the rail. It was a perfect summer evening. The water was wide here, the Big Muddy curving in from the northwest through a vast expanse of wetlands. The sun was down, but the sky was still bright. Venus hung in the west, a silver pendant against the soft, blue-purple twilight. This part of the river was largely empty of watercraft. Only a single speedboat approached, moving fast and leaving a long plume in its wake.

Death was expecting the hand to the small of his back and the push, propelling him up and over. What he wasn't expecting was for the railing he had braced himself against to give way and drop him into the swift, muddy river channel.

It was Randy who spotted the *Zaca*. He pointed it out to them just in time for everyone on the boat to see Gregory give Death a shove and send him flying into the water.

The pilot hit his siren and surged forward, speaking urgently into his radio as he did. He cut his engine when they were close, so as not to imperil the swimmer. Randy kicked off his shoes and hit the water before Wren even realized he was in motion.

On the *Zaca*, Gregory and Alaina were feigning distress, as if they hadn't all seen the doctor pushing Death overboard. Gregory spoke to his sister and she jumped for the helm. A cold, sick feeling settled into Wren's stomach. Death and now Randy were too close to the boat. If Alaina revved the engine, they'd both be sucked in and cut to ribbons. The fire boat captain had seen the danger as well. He had a megaphone out and was commanding Alaina not to touch the throttle. Wren didn't trust the effectiveness of that for a second. She looked around for something to throw and realized she was still clutching her slingshot and a fistful of stones.

The top foot or so of river was as warm as bath water. Death plunged through it quickly and into the cool, murky depth. He'd taken as deep a breath as he was able while he was falling, but that wasn't very deep anymore and he was already out of oxygen before natural buoyancy reasserted itself and he began to rise. Currents swirled around him, tugging at him, and the weight of his shoes tried to drag him down.

Lightheaded and desperate for air, he toed off his sneakers and let them drop into the mud, then concentrated on not breathing before his face broke the water's surface.

His instincts were screaming at him to get the hell away from the *Zaca*. He expected the propellers to come to life at any second. That was why Gregory had put Alaina at the helm. It would be more convincing to the authorities. She was an inexperienced pilot. She panicked. She didn't know what to do and she was only trying to help.

Death was disoriented, though, confused by the water's agitation and his own hypoxia, and he couldn't be certain where the boat was.

He surfaced half a dozen yards from her

starboard side. The current was taking them both downstream, him and the pontoon boat, but the slower stream he had gone through under the surface had left him closer to the back of the boat and the deadly outboard motor. He coughed and spluttered, on the verge of blacking out. Something moved in the water near him. *Jaws,* Death thought. *Damn.*

Then a pair of strong arms came around him and a familiar voice said, "Relax. I got this."

He whipped his head around, trying to see behind himself.

"Randy?"

"No, I'm the Little Mermaid. Stop it! Don't fight me."

Death choked on a sob. "Randy."

"Hush. It's okay. *I got this.*"

"Get the helm," Gregory hissed. "Rev the engine, like I told you. Quickly! Do it!"

Alaina ran for the helm, crying and already hysterical.

All the better to convince the authorities, Gregory thought. In his head he was already rehearsing what he would say to the police. *I was trying to catch him. I'd been concerned about him already, you know. He'd just started a course of antidepressants, and suicide is always a danger. I thought it would help if he could see where his brother was buried. Find some closure. But he was so distraught, and then the railing gave way . . .*

A second official craft was closing in from behind and there were two more coming upriver, heading in their direction. Dark water reflected flashing red and blue emergency lights and sirens reverberated through the river valley. Alaina reached for the throttle. She was almost touching it when she shrieked in pain and staggered away holding her nose. Blood streamed down her face.

The first official craft Gregory saw was a fire boat, not a police boat, coasting up alongside the *Zaca.* A small, redheaded woman stood braced against the railing. She held a slingshot, stone at the ready, and addressed Alaina in a hard voice. "The nice fireman said not to touch the throttle. Keep your hands off the throttle, bitch."

The firefighter who was holding the megaphone dropped it and moved to the side of the boat, swiftly and expertly tethering the two crafts together. By the time he'd finished, a water patrol crew was making their own boat fast on the other side. The first cop to board them spun Gregory around, pushed him up against the bar, and slapped a pair of handcuffs on him. "James Gregory, you're under arrest for kidnapping and attempted murder."

"Kidnapping? Murder? Why, I don't know what you're talking about! He was suicidal. He jumped. I tried to stop him!"

Behind him, a second officer was arresting his sister. He cuffed her hands in back, careful to avoid the blood streaming from her nose, and read her the Miranda warning. Two of the firefighters had also boarded the *Zaca*, carrying equipment and trailed by the anxious redhead.

One of them, a pale, blonde female, grabbed the *Zaca*'s life preserver, stepped on the loose end of the throw rope, and tossed the ring into the river. She was holding the rope in her left hand and she let it play out completely, then took it in both hands and pulled it back in a few feet. "Bogie? The buoy's just behind you. Can you get it?"

Gregory, pushed down into a seat and sandwiched between two burly officers, watched with a sick fascination as the line went taut. The second firefighter joined the first on the line as they reeled it in. Then they were pulling the ex-Marine, dripping and exhausted, from the river onto the pontoon boat's swimming deck. When he was safe, the blonde reached down. A second hand came up to meet hers and Baranduin Bogart climbed aboard after his brother.

He pulled himself to his full height and spared the siblings a brief, withering glare. In that moment, Gregory reflected, he really didn't look like Andrew Grey at all. Alaina, apparently, didn't share that sentiment.

"Andrew? Andrew! Oh my God! Jamie, it's Andrew!"

"It's not Andrew. Shut up!"

"It *is* Andrew. He was in the water! He could have been killed!" She was leaning toward him now, straining against the officer holding her back. The exertion had restarted her nosebleed and she was screaming at him, gory and vengeful. "Did you know he was in the water? You promised me we were only going to kill his brother! *Did you know?*"

The cop to Gregory's left leaned down, clasped his shoulder, and grinned insufferably.

"You do know we already read her the Miranda warning, right?"

With a helping hand from Yering, Death sat up. Talia was leaning over him, stethoscope at the ready. Randy snatched it away from her, put the earpieces in his own ears, and set the scope on Death's back. "Can you take a deep breath for me? Wren said your lungs are damaged. How much of that river did you swallow? Did you breathe in any?"

Death batted the instrument away, grabbed his little brother, and pulled him into a fierce hug. After a few seconds, Randy gave in and returned it. The baby of the family, he always tried extra hard to come off as a tough guy. Death didn't care. He was crying openly and, when he finally spoke, there were tears in Randy's voice too. "You big, dumb, jarhead. I told you to keep your stupid head down. I *told* you!"

It was Randy who finally pulled away, taking up the stethoscope again and putting it back in his ears.

"Seriously, man, you gotta let me check you over. We're gonna take you in for chest X-rays and they'll probably want to keep you overnight. In fact, I'm gonna insist they do —"

"No." Death pushed his brother away and climbed clumsily to his feet. "Hell no. I don't need to go see a doctor. I'm fine."

"You're fine when I say you're fine."

"I'm the big brother. You are not the boss of me."

"That's just stupid."

"Anyway," Death said, "if anyone needs to go to the emergency room, it's you."

"Me? I'm fine!"

"You don't look fine. You're pale and you've lost weight. God only knows what those two have been doing to you."

"Nothing," Randy said. "I'm fine. I'm not going to any ER. I just want to go home, put on my own clothes, and be *me* for awhile."

Wren suddenly gasped in dismay.

"Oh, Randy! I'm sorry. I'm *so* sorry!"

They both turned to look at her. She had one hand to her mouth and her cheeks were as red as her hair. "Sorry?" Randy said. "What have you done to be sorry about?"

She blushed even harder, gave a tiny shrug, and admitted, "I threw away all your underwear."

EPILOGUE

"I even undressed him. I undressed him and I still thought he was you!"

"Well, was he hot? 'Cause if he was a *hot* dead guy, I can understand you thinking that."

Death cuffed his little brother on the back of the head as he dropped down next to him at the picnic table. "Be nice. Sophie helped us save your sorry butt."

"Careful!" Randy rubbed his head. "You could give me brain damage."

"Can't damage what you don't have."

The celebration in Rowdy and Annie Tanner's backyard was joyous though tinged, for the firefighters, with regret. Randy was alive and that was the main thing, but he was also leaving. "Since the last time I saw this moron," he'd said, throwing an arm around Death's shoulders, "he's been ambushed, blown up, buried alive, shot at, kidnapped and threatened at knifepoint, kidnapped again, beaten up, threatened at knifepoint *again,* then *shot at* again, and almost drowned. Clearly he needs to be under the supervision of a responsible adult."

"And where do you come in?" Rowdy shot back.

"He's gonna help me look for a responsible adult," Death grinned.

Randy would have to pass a refresher course to get his paramedic certification restored, but he already had a job lined up as an airborne medic with the Rives County Life Flight service, and he'd been accepted as a member of the East Bledsoe Ferry Volunteer Fire Department. Wren, with her local connections, had helped to smooth his way. They both understood that, while finding Randy alive had helped immensely, Death was still struggling in ways that were not going to be fixed overnight. Together, they would provide him with the support system that he needed so badly and had gone so long without.

"Are you going to sell your house?" Cap asked.

"No, not planning to. Not anytime soon. I'm only moving a few hundred miles away. I will be back to visit from time to time. I'd like to have a place to stay when I do."

Trinka, Talia's girlfriend, bounced out of the house with a pan held in hot pads. "Look! I made cornbread!"

Talia gave her a dubious look. "You? Made cornbread?"

Trinka laughed merrily. "Well, okay, technically Annie made it. But I cut it. That's practically the same thing." She set it on the table.

"Wouldn't you guys love to have seen Leilani's face when she found out Alaina tried to cheat her out of her inheritance?"

"Yeah, that's a funny thing," Death said. He snagged a piece of the hot cornbread and glanced around at his audience with a faint grin. "We talked to the lawyer. Seems that will Andrew showed the wives was just for show."

"It wasn't real?" Annie asked.

"The Einstadt fortune is all tied up in trust funds. Andrew had access to the interest and a percentage of the profits from business holdings while he was alive, but very little wealth that was actually at his disposal after he died. The estate will pass to his children now. There were provisions for supporting a childless widow, but whoever drew up the legal papers — Aram Einstadt probably — was as concerned about the family name as he was the family fortune. The one thing that could get anyone disinherited was being convicted of a felony. Instead of securing her fortune, Alaina's killed the golden goose." They were still laughing about it when a horn drew their attention and everyone turned to find a gold station wagon pulling into the yard.

"Oh, look!" Wren said. "It's the Keystones!"

"All of them?" Death asked.

"Looks like just the twins and their wives." She got up and ran to meet them.

"This is the family Wren works for," Death told Randy. "You're gonna love these people." They stood up to meet them as Wren brought them over. "This is Roy and Sam," Death introduced them. "And their lovely wives, Leona and Doris."

"You're such a charmer," Doris said, kissing his cheek.

Roy and Sam shook hands with Randy.

"I've heard of some weird things running in families," Roy said, "but being mistaken for dead is a new one."

"But we're so glad you're okay and home where you belong now!" Leona gushed. She caught Randy in a fierce hug. "Quick, sweetie, tell me. What's your brother's middle name?"

"Randy," Death growled warningly.

Randy cocked his head and considered. "What's in it for me?"

"Don't you do it!"

"Pie. Homemade pie."

"What kind of pie?"

"Pecan."

"Randy!"

"With whipped topping?"

"I'm warning you."

"With whipped *cream. Real* whipped cream. And homemade ice cream."

"Dúnadan," Randy said swiftly. "What flavor ice cream?"

"Dúnadan! From *Lord of the Rings*!" Wren smiled and clasped her hands together. "That's perfect!"

Leona patted Randy's cheek. "Any flavor you want, sweetie."

"Randy, how could you?" Death asked, betrayed and tragic.

"It's not my fault. She offered me *pie.*"

"You're a slut."

"Yeah. But I'm a slut — with pie."

Rowdy and one of the younger firefighters dragged another bench over so there'd be room for the Keystones at the table. "We apologize for crashing your party," Sam said.

"Not at all," Rowdy told him. "I'm glad you could make it."

"Well, our work got put on hold and we

were all dying to meet Death's brother so we thought we'd take a day trip." He addressed Wren. "You're going to like this job, Wren, when we can get back to it. The old Hadleigh Plantation is going to auction."

"The Haunted Hadleigh House?" she asked, excited. She turned to the others to explain. "It's an old plantation with a lot of weird stories and legends attached."

"Some weirder and more attached than others," Roy said. "The hot topic right now is The Vengeance Trail."

"Sounds spooky!" Annie commented. "What's The Vengeance Trail?"

"It's a trail that runs across the Plantation and a legend from the Civil War," Wren said. "They say a soldier — some versions say Union and some say Confederate — killed an old man and stole his horse. That night, when it was too dark to see and the soldier was ready to stop for the night, the horse suddenly bolted down The Vengeance Trail. He ran under a tree with a low-hanging branch, killing the soldier and avenging his master's death. Now, on nights of the new moon, they say you can still hear the horse's pounding hoofs and the soldier shouting at him to 'whoa!' "

"Creepy," Death agreed. "But why is that a hot topic right now?"

"Because," Roy said, "yesterday morning some hikers found a body on The Vengeance Trail. He was lying under a low-hanging branch and his neck was broken. They haven't identified the body yet, but he was wearing an apparently authentic Confederate Cavalry uniform. The only tracks besides the hikers' footprints were the hoof marks of a running horse."

ABOUT THE AUTHOR

Loretta Ross is a writer and historian who lives and works in rural Missouri. She is an alumna of Cottey College and holds a BA in archaeology from the University of Missouri–Columbia. She has loved mysteries since she first learned to read. *Death and the Redheaded Woman* is her first published novel.